MW01074635

Praise for the Dave Cubiak Door County Mystery series:

DEATH STALKS DOOR COUNTY

"Can a big-city cop solve a series of murders whose only witnesses may be the hemlocks? An atmospheric debut." *Kirkus Reviews*

"A satisfyingly complex plot . . . showcasing one of the main characters, Wisconsin's beautiful Door County. A great match for Nevada Barr fans."
Library Journal

"Murder seems unseemly in Door County, a peninsula covered in forests, lined by beaches, and filled with summer cabins and tourist resorts. That's the hook for murder-thriller *Death Stalks Door County*, the first in a series involving ranger Dave Cubiak, a former Chicago homicide detective."
Milwaukee Shepherd Express

DEATH AT GILLS ROCK

"The latest Dave Cubiak Door County Mystery sees Cubiak investigating the mysterious carbon monoxide deaths of three prominent World War II vets who are about to be honored for their service" *Chicago Tribune*

"Three World War II heroes about to be honored by the Coast Guard are all found dead, apparent victims of carbon monoxide poisoning while playing cards at a cabin. . . . The second installment of this first-rate series provides plenty of challenges for both the detective and the reader." *Kirkus Reviews*

"Skalka captures the gloomy small-town atmosphere vividly, and her intricate plot and well-developed characters will appeal to fans of William Kent Krueger." *Booklist*

DEATH IN COLD WATER

A DAVE CUBIAK
DOOR COUNTY
MYSTERY

PATRICIA SKALKA

THE UNIVERSITY OF WISCONSIN PRESS

The University of Wisconsin Press
1930 Monroe Street, 3rd Floor
Madison, Wisconsin 53711-2059
uwpress.wisc.edu

3 Henrietta Street, Covent Garden
London WCE8LU, United Kingdom
eurospanbookstore.com

Copyright © 2016 by Patricia Skalka

All rights reserved. Except in the case of brief quotations embedded in critical articles and reviews, no part of this publication may be reproduced, stored in a retrieval system, transmitted in any format or by any means—digital, electronic, mechanical, photocopying, recording, or otherwise—or conveyed via the Internet or a website without written permission of the University of Wisconsin Press. Rights inquiries should be directed to rights@uwpress.wisc.edu.

Printed in the United States of America

This book may be available in a digital edition.

Library of Congress Cataloging-in-Publication Data

Names: Skalka, Patricia, author. | Skalka, Patricia. Dave Cubiak Door County mystery.
Title. Death in cold water / Patricia Skalka.
Description: Madison, Wisconsin: The University of Wisconsin Press, [2016] |
Series: A Dave Cubiak Door County mystery
Identifiers: LCCN 2016012946 | ISBN 9780299309206 (cloth: alk. paper)
Subjects: LCSH: Door County (Wis.)—Fiction.
Classification: LCC PS3619.K34 D39 2016 | DDC 813/.6—dc23
LC record available at https://lccn.loc.gov/2016012946

Map by Julia Padvoiskis

Door County is real. While I used the peninsula as the framework for the book, I also altered some details and added others to fit the story. The spirit of this majestic place remains unchanged.

To

Eddie

I will cause the arrogance of the proud to cease, and will lay low the haughtiness of the terrible.

Isaiah 13:11

DEATH IN COLD WATER

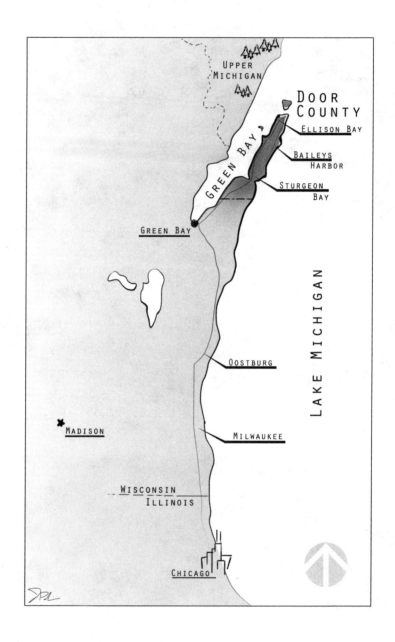

A SECOND SKIN

1

Dave Cubiak cast his line into the gray water and waited. Perched on the rock ledge along the Green Bay shore, he'd waited all afternoon: For the sun to break through the clouds. For a fish to take his hook. For the autumn leaves to be done with their annual display of color. For the tourists to pack their bags and depart. For Cate to come home.

Watching the sun fall toward the horizon, Cubiak checked the time. It was late and he'd missed pretty much all of Sunday's big football game: the Bears versus the Packers or, because this was Wisconsin, the Packers versus the Bears. He'd done so deliberately, even though skipping the match was an unforgivable sin in his adopted Door County. He'd have to pick up the highlights later. A few of the important details would provide fodder for a week's worth of small talk around the department and elsewhere on the peninsula.

The day was cooler than predicted, and Cubiak wished he'd worn gloves and an extra layer. He tugged his collar up to his chin and reeled in his line. For the third time in thirty minutes, the bait was gone. Maybe he should try a lure, he thought, and reached for his dented red tackle box. As Cubiak rummaged through the jumble of jigs and plugs, he heard a rustling in the bushes and looked up to see a white bundle sail over his head toward the bay.

The sack hit the water about fifteen feet from shore.

"What the hell?" he said.

He figured it was a plastic bag filled with trash and wondered if he could snag it with his line.

Then something inside the bag wiggled, and there was a sound. A cry like that of a baby.

Cubiak struggled free of this boots and jacket and jumped in.

The momentum pulled him under, and the sheer cold of the water left him unable to move. After a panicky moment, he began to flail about. Pumping his arms and kicking his legs, he fought his way up and surfaced ten feet from the bag. It was sinking fast. Never much of a swimmer, Cubiak stroked desperately toward it. When he was within an arm's length, the bag went under, trailing the rope that knotted it closed. Cubiak lunged for the cord and snared the end between his numbing fingers.

Not trusting his grip to hold, he snaked the rope around his wrist, drew the bag to his shoulder, and clumsily paddled toward shore, veering past the sheer ledge toward a patch of rocky beach. As he struggled to catch his breath, he clutched the water-soaked bag to his chest and stumbled over the wet, slippery pebbles. When he reached solid ground, he dropped to his knees and lowered the sack to the grass. It was an old pillowcase. Cubiak loosened the rope and began unknotting the top. The cries had ceased. Was he too late?

Cubiak peered inside and then fell back on his heels. He'd braved the icy water to save a litter of newborn kittens. The sheriff would have laughed if his teeth hadn't started chattering. Who else would go out for fish and come back with kittens?

He took a second look and realized that something was not right. The kittens were ensnared by a thin cord that bound their paws and twisted around their necks and bodies. The more they tried to squirm free, the more they became entangled. At first Cubiak didn't understand;

then he realized that something had gone wrong when the kittens were born and that the rope was part of the afterbirth. There were four, maybe five kittens. He couldn't tell. They meowed pitifully and crawled around each other, blind and terrified and probably colder than he was.

Cubiak got the scissors from the first aid kit in the jeep and started cutting through the dried tissue. The kittens squirmed as he pulled the sinew from their scrawny, hairless bodies, but one by one he freed them. When he finished, he swaddled them in a wool blanket and laid the bundle on the passenger seat. With the heat on high, he headed home.

The shortest route took him past groves of yellow and scarlet maples but he didn't notice the trees or their flaming colors. He was too cold and too mad about the kittens. He knew all too well that he could have drowned trying to save them, and he had the uneasy feeling that maybe he didn't really care all that much if he had. Not that day.

Still, it was a cruel thing to do to such helpless creatures. And Cubiak had no tolerance for wanton cruelty. Which is why when he saw a familiar blue pickup outside the Tipsy Too, he swerved into the parking lot and pulled up alongside the truck. Just as he expected, the dented hood was warm. Cubiak left the jeep running with the heat on for the kittens and went inside. The tavern, a favorite with locals, was dimly lit and loud. Smoking had been banned for years but the faint stink of cigarettes still seeped from the woodwork and all those places that never saw a mop or cleaning rag.

Cubiak didn't care that he appeared ridiculous to the crowd in the bar. Ignoring the sniggers and sideways glances from the clientele, he searched through the cluster of regulars until he found the owner of the truck. Leeland Ross, thirty-four, was a serial loser who smelled as nasty as he looked with his grimy clothes and tangle of dirty hair hanging over the collar of his frayed barn coat. Cradling a beer in thick, pawlike hands, he hunkered at the bar and stared up at one of the half-dozen TVs broadcasting the last few minutes of the game. The sheriff slapped the wet pillowcase in front of the burly, bearded man.

"This yours?" he said.

Leeland drained his beer. "Ain't never seen it in my life," he said, his eyes riveted to the screen.

The sheriff had had more run-ins with Leeland than he cared to remember. The most recent was some six months earlier when he'd responded to a neighbor's complaint about possible animal abuse on the farm where Leeland lived with his father, Jon, another ornery sort. Then, as now, Cubiak had no proof.

"I found it full of kittens floating in the bay. Looks like your handiwork," he said.

Leeland swiped at the pool of water dripping from Cubiak's sleeve. "I eat what I kill, Sheriff."

Cubiak grabbed the sack. He was tempted to wring it out over Leeland's worn cowboy boots. There were times he wanted to provoke a man like Leeland. But he'd heard there'd been a death in the family recently and figured this was neither the time nor the place. "Sorry about your uncle," he said.

Leeland grunted and the sheriff spun away.

The rest of the way home, Cubiak talked to the kittens: Assuring them that most people were decent, not sons of bitches like Leeland. Telling them how lucky they were that he'd been fishing the bay that afternoon. Wondering aloud why he'd been fishing at all. It wasn't something he did regularly or often. It was the game. He'd gone to avoid watching the game being played at Soldier Field with the familiar glimpses of the Chicago skyline, reminders of the city where he'd once been a cop and had once had a wife and daughter. He had come to Door County to escape the past and had slowly adjusted his attitudes and lifestyle to the slower, more gentle pace of the peninsula. His new life fit like a second skin that was in need of tailoring. Yes, he told the kittens, he was growing into it, as they would into their own little kitten bodies, but sometimes— sometimes—the old skin prickled beneath and it was on those days that he needed to get away and try to lose himself.

Cubiak had hoped to find that Cate had made it back from her most recent assignment. Maybe she'd even had time to heat up one of the leftovers in the freezer and there'd be a warm supper on the table. But the house was dark and empty. And Cate's mail—addressed to C. L. Wagner—lay unopened on the table. After a hot shower he downed the last two shots of vodka—the most he'd allowed himself in more than a year—and then he tended to the kittens.

The poor little things looked half starved. Cubiak poured warm milk into a baby bottle—the same one he'd used to feed the runt from Butch's first litter—and let each of them take a turn. The dog bounced around nervously. Though unsettled by the kittens, she seemed to instinctively understand that they were to come to no harm. When he'd finished with the feeding, Cubiak put the kittens in a towel-lined box by the stove and left Butch to stand guard over them.

"Don't worry. They'll be gone soon," Cubiak assured the dog while he heated a can of chili.

Hours later, the sheriff pried his eyes open to the neon glare of a digital clock. It was 11:17 p.m. and he was in bed, though he couldn't remember how he got there. Out of habit, he reached to the other side of the mattress. Empty.

"Quiet," he said to Butch, whose barking had wakened him.

The usually obedient dog ignored the command. Still cold and bleary with sleep, Cubiak realized that Butch was trying to get his attention. Had something happened to the kittens? Was Cate in trouble?

Over the dog's yapping, Cubiak heard the pounding at the back door.

"Coming," he said loudly as he swung his feet to the floor and dragged the blanket around his shoulders. Butch followed him down the short hall and into the kitchen. At the stove she took up her post by the kittens, leaving Cubiak to approach the rear porch alone.

"Where the hell is he? Knock louder." A man was shouting. The voice was deep, slurred, and unfamiliar.

"Pipe down." It was sheriff's deputy Mike Rowe, answering back.

The yard was dark. Clouds scuttled across the moon and blanketed most of the stars. The bits of light that got through glanced off the water and cast shadows along a narrow strip of Lake Michigan's rocky shore. Cubiak stepped into the dark porch.

"Chief! You there?"

Cubiak opened the door.

"Sorry to disturb you, Sheriff," Rowe said, but before he could go on the stranger shoved past him. The man was tall and broad chested, and even in the faint moon glow Cubiak caught the arrogant thrust of his chin and the expensive cut of his clothes.

"Sorry, my ass," the interloper said on breath that stank of beer and onions. Then, raising his voice again, he added, "Do you know who I am?"

Cubiak refused to be baited. "It's nearly midnight," he said as he stepped back and allowed the two into the kitchen. "What's going on?" The sheriff directed the question to his deputy.

Butch growled.

"Quiet," Cubiak said and the dog dropped to the floor. The sheriff turned to the stranger. "Sit down," he said. The man hesitated, and then he grabbed a chair from the table and sat.

In the uneasy calm, Rowe explained that he was driving home from a party when he saw the stranger fly by on Highway 57 near Sturgeon Bay. "I clocked him pushing ninety and pulled him over. When he refused to provide his license and then couldn't walk a straight line, I put him in my car and headed toward the jail. He said his lawyer would take care of the problem and kept insisting on seeing you. Claims his father's disappeared and that there'd be hell to pay if you didn't get on it right away."

"Why didn't you call me?"

"I did, but there was no answer at either number."

"Right," Cubiak said, picturing his cell phone on the jeep's dash. "Sorry. Left the cell in the garage." He lifted the receiver from the wall phone. No dial tone. "Damn squirrels must have chewed through the line again."

He turned to the stranger, who'd gotten up and walked over to the box of kittens. "Who's your father?"

The man looked up, his face a combination of disdain and surprise. "My father is Gerald Sneider."

"Holy shit," Rowe said.

Cubiak drew a blank and nodded to his deputy to go on. "Gerald Sneider is a local legend. He made a fortune in lumber in the UP and retired to an estate up near Ellison Bay. For years he was known as Mr. Packer. This guy hasn't missed a game in decades. Every season he buys as many tickets as he can get his hands on and gives them away to kids and local residents who can't afford the price of admission. Any time the team needs money for improvements, he's good for it. Rumor has it that in the lean years, he even provided the bonuses to coaches and players to keep up team morale." Rowe looked at the man he'd stopped for drunk driving.

"You must be his son, Andy."

"Andrew."

Cubiak pointed to the empty chair. "Well, Andrew, why don't you sit down again and tell us what happened."

It started in Chicago. Third quarter they were sitting in the family skybox at Soldier Field when his father got a phone call. "The score is tied. It's fourth down. The Packers are on the ten-yard line, and all of a sudden my dad stands up and announces that he has to leave. This is like against his religion. He never leaves any event until the end. He's never left a game until the last player has walked off the field."

"Did you say anything to him?"

"No. I thought it was pretty odd but I didn't say a word. I'd learned a long time ago not to question or cross my father." Later, when he, Andrew, was driving back, he called his father's cell but there was no answer. "I must have tried ten times."

"Maybe his phone died," Cubiak said.

"No chance of that. My father prides himself on being the kind of person who never runs out of gas, never forgets to pay a bill, and never lets his phone battery lose more than fifty percent of its juice."

Also, Andrew went on, he knew his dad had plans to stop at a

9

friend's house just north of Milwaukee, but when he checked with the friend he hadn't seen him either. "Everything seemed wrong, so naturally I was in a hurry to get back to the house. Then this guy"—he jerked a thumb at Rowe—"stopped me."

"As he should, considering how fast you were driving and the fact you're in no condition to drive at all." Cubiak scrubbed the top of Butch's head. "The game ended seven hours ago. Allow five hours for the drive up with traffic, where were you the other two?"

Andrew stiffened. "I had business to take care of."

"On Sunday?"

"You know what philately is?" he said.

Cubiak nodded, then for Rowe's benefit, he said, "Stamp collecting."

"Well, collectors can be idiosyncratic. This particular man happened to have an item I wanted, and to get it I had to bend my schedule to accommodate his."

"Despite your concerns about your father."

"I didn't get worried until later. Really worried, that is."

"You checked with security at Soldier Field?" The sheriff knew the sprawling complex could easily swallow up a man confused by too much alcohol or in too much of a hurry to pay attention to where he was headed.

"No." Andrew looked guilty. Here was something he should have done. "I didn't want to cause a fuss," he said defiantly.

Which is what you're doing now, Cubiak thought.

"Have you tried calling your father at home?"

"Of course. The house has two landlines, so if he was there and all right, he'd have answered one of them. Something's happened. I just know it."

"Before he left the game, did he say he was meeting someone?"

"No, just that something had come up that he had to attend to."

"Was he upset, anxious?"

Andrew frowned. "Not at all. In fact, he seemed happy and excited. He was whistling when he walked out of the skybox."

"Then why the concern? He probably didn't feel like driving all the way back after his appointment. I assume he'd been drinking at the game and maybe had more later on. If so, he may have not wanted to be on the road. Probably checked into a hotel along the way."

"That's just it, Sheriff. He might not tell me where he was headed or who he was meeting if he was meeting someone, but at some point he'd let me know where he was." Andrew paused. "My father is a cautious man. He knows he has the kind of money that makes him a target."

"For what?"

"Who knows? Whatever? Kidnapping. Extortion. This kind of thing is on the news all the time. And I'm guessing it happens more often than the public is told."

True enough, Cubiak thought.

"He didn't want me to be snatched either. Some time back we agreed, or should I say he insisted, that we keep in touch, let each other know where we are. A call. A text. This is the first I've lost track of him."

"Anyone else you can check with? Your mother?"

"Mother died twenty years ago. And there is no one else. No girlfriends in case you're wondering."

Andrew had touches of gray at the temples and the facial lines of a man well into middle age. "How old is your father?" Cubiak said.

"He's eighty-two, but at his last physical his doctor said he had the body of a man ten years younger, and he's sharp as a tack. No issues with dementia, if that's what you're implying."

"Other health problems?" Rowe said.

"You mean like a bad heart?" Andrew shook his head. "My father was an orphan. He never knew anything about his birth parents, but whoever they were, they had golden genes and they gave them all to him. Never sick a day in his life. He's got a good ticker, low blood pressure, low cholesterol. The whole shebang."

Cubiak pulled a notebook from a kitchen drawer and slid it toward Andrew. "Write down whatever information you can about your father's car. Model, color, year, license number if you know it. Rowe will call the state police and have them issue an APB, see if they can locate it anywhere. Meanwhile, I'll go change and we'll take you up to the house." He dropped the blanket over the back of the chair. "Oh, and now that we know your name, Rowe can write you a ticket and you can pay your fine while I'm getting ready."

Andrew started to protest but Cubiak cut him off.

"You're getting away easy on this. Don't push your luck."

DRIVING NORTH

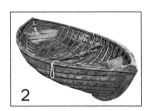

2

A few minutes before midnight the trio climbed into the sheriff's jeep and took off. Navigating the ebony interior of the peninsula on a network of narrow blacktop roads, they drove north to Ellison Bay. The cloud cover had thickened and erased the moon, leaving Door County awash in inky black. An occasional yard light blinked through the darkness and then faded from view as they rolled past sleeping farmsteads and acre after acre of orchards and fields that had given up their fruit and crops to the harvest of human hands and machines.

The sheriff rode shotgun, cradling the thermos of tea Rowe had made for him. Earlier in the kitchen, Cubiak had finally shrugged off the chill from his plunge into the bay but he felt the residue cold creeping back, bone deep. He was grateful for the hot drink, and once again surprised by the deputy's thoughtfulness.

Andrew dozed in the back seat. When they were about halfway, he jerked awake and began to thrash around.

"You sure this is an unmarked car?" he said, leaning forward, his breath more rank than before.

"Yep." Rowe's response was clipped.

"Good." Andrew dropped away again, kicking the back of Cubiak's seat as he crossed his legs and settled in. "Plenty of nosy neighbors, even way up there. Creeping around in the middle of the night. People who notice everything and then start talking. Making things up when they don't know what's going on."

After several minutes of silence, Cubiak turned around.

"I thought small-town folks pretty much kept to themselves."

Andrew snorted. "That's what they want everyone to think. But folks like to be entertained and believe me, they've got their radar out for every juicy tidbit they can pick up."

"Your father ever have trouble with any of his neighbors?"

"Not that I'm aware of. Still, you know, people talk, and sometimes there's resentment against those who are more successful."

Or those who have given people something to talk about or resent, Cubiak thought. And maybe Gerald Sneider was one of that ilk. Or maybe he was losing a good night's sleep on a fool's errand.

They were north of Sister Bay when the fog came up and walled them in from all sides.

"Can't see a fucking thing," Rowe said, slowing to a crawl.

The edges of the road had vanished, forcing the deputy to drive down the middle. They were hostages, functioning at the mercy of this greater force. Cubiak sat up, on alert for deer and unexpected curves. After some four years in Door County, he knew the geography of the peninsula well, yet in the surreal environment of the nighttime fog, he had difficulty following their progress. When the back road they were traveling finally connected with Highway 42, the sheriff was momentarily disoriented.

"Where are we? How much farther?" he said.

"Couple miles. Another five minutes," the deputy said.

It took nearly three times as long for them to reach the high plateau outside Ellison Bay. The rise was on a segment of the limestone palisades that cut down from Canada and extended along the western edge of the peninsula like a gently curving spine. In daylight, the ridge provided a spectacular view of the forested cliffs and blue water that spread out below. But on a fog-shrouded night there was only descent into murky darkness.

Andrew had fallen asleep again, but as the jeep started to roll down the incline toward the village, he jolted awake. "We're there," he said as they crept down the slope.

Ellison Bay had a year-round population of 165 and a smattering of shops in the tiny heart of the town. Half the businesses were shuttered for the season, and the rest had long been closed for the night. Despite what Andrew had said about people skulking around at all hours, there was neither movement nor sound and almost no light in the sleeping community.

"Left past the restaurant," Andrew said as they came up to a building with a faded sign advertising a weekly fish boil.

"How much farther?" Rowe said.

"I'll tell you." Then, after a few minutes, Andrew said, "Up there," pointing to a pair of dim reflectors that blinked through the murk.

The entrance to Gerald Sneider's estate was an unremarkable dirt path cut through dense forest. Then, some fifty feet in, they pulled up to a massive iron gate. Was it a prelude to what lay ahead? Cubiak wondered. The gate was déjà vu for the sheriff. He remembered the first time he'd seen The Wood, the estate Cate's grandfather had built farther north, at the tip of the peninsula. Behind the gate at The Wood, which he'd opened with a massive, iron key, he'd gotten his first look at the kind of old wealth that had long claimed Door County as its own.

"Hold on." Andrew pushed a button on a small black remote and the gates opened.

From there, the road was paved and where the fog occasionally fanned out into a fluttery wisp, the forest appeared neatly trimmed back. After two gentle curves the lane straightened again, and as they approached lights flickered low on either side of the road, illuminating the mist with a ghostly bluish-gray hue and then fading as the jeep rolled past. They were north of town where the peninsula jutted out toward Green Bay, and Cubiak knew instinctively that they were heading to the water.

Suddenly the headlights flashed across the façade of a monstrously large building that loomed up through the veil of fog.

Andrew grabbed the back of Rowe's seat. "Here. Stop."

Rowe hit the brakes and cut the engine.

In the silence, Cubiak heard the familiar bang of waves crashing on a rocky shore. He stepped away from the jeep and looked around, but in the eerie darkness he saw nothing. Had he imagined the gigantic house?

"No lights?" he said.

"Father prefers the dark." Andrew pushed another button on the remote and a row of decorative flower lamps glowed, revealing a wide flight of marble stairs not twenty feet away.

Cubiak and Rowe followed Andrew up the steps to a massive oak door.

Inside, Andrew disarmed the security system and turned on the lights, giving the sheriff and his deputy their first glimpse at Sneider's grand home.

"It's not to everyone's taste," Andrew said apologetically as he waved at the interior.

Standing in the foyer, Rowe gawked at the stream of water bubbling from a wall fountain that hung on a richly veined slab of marble. "No shit," he said and tried to smother his comment with a cough.

Cubiak frowned at his deputy. "We're not here on an architectural tour," he said. Then he asked Andrew, "Where would you normally expect to find your father this time of night?"

"Upstairs in his room."

"Start there, then. Check all the rooms on the second floor. My deputy will come with you." Cubiak gave Rowe another kinder look that said: don't let him out of your sight. "I'll take the downstairs."

A thick, green and russet Oriental runner ran down a hall lined with gilded mirrors. To the right an archway opened to a living room stuffed with ornate Louis XIV furniture that appeared more decorative than functional. Heavy draperies framed the oversize windows, paintings that looked authentic to the sheriff's uninformed eye filled the ecru walls, and a crystal chandelier the size of a newborn elephant hung from the ceiling. In the dining room, Cubiak counted sixteen chairs around a gleaming Queen Anne table over which dangled another sizable chandelier. He was no expert on fine crystal and china but guessed that the two glass-fronted cabinets held Wedgewood and the kind of dinnerware only the upper crust knew by name.

Despite their studied perfection, the two rooms seemed steeped in a sad emptiness. Perhaps once they'd been host to lavish parties and festive celebrations, but the glory days were behind them. Cubiak wondered if the elderly widower even bothered with them now.

Life is unfair, Cubiak's father used to say. It's the one thing he got right, the sheriff thought as he moved through the house. So many had so little and so few had so much.

His mother would have given anything for such a house, but Cubiak was unimpressed—until he stepped into the library. He could have camped out for months in that room, which looked like something lifted from a British manor house. The library had a massive fireplace and floor-to-ceiling bookshelves along three walls. He ran a hand along the spines of the leather-bound books—books on philosophy, religion, and history and all the classics. But no current fiction. No magazines or newspapers. He tapped the glass-topped desk, bare except for an old-fashioned pen stand and black rotary telephone.

The tenor of the house changed when he reached the rear addition. Here he found Sneider's office. The room was small compared to the others but still large enough for a working desk and a conference table with four upright chairs. Next to it was the media room with two cushy sofas, three leather lounge chairs, a flat-screen TV that covered half a wall, and built-in speakers for the sound system. A cranberry wool throw tossed carelessly over the back of a chair indicated that someone, perhaps the owner, had been there before the cleaning woman had a chance to tidy up.

And then there was a family room that could only be called Packer Land. It was a sprawling space filled with nostalgia and memorabilia. Signed footballs and posters. Original jerseys in heavy gold frames. More and more. A trove of treasures worth a small fortune. Here, finally, was a worn leather chair, indicating that this room was special. He'd found Sneider's retreat.

Cubiak had to detour back through the dining room to find the kitchen, which, with its two pantries, occupied its own separate wing. There he saw high-end appliances, ceramic tiles that were probably imported and expensive, cabinets that he guessed were ash or some exotic light wood.

On the far side of the kitchen, a cozy breakfast nook with large uncurtained windows looked out to either the water or the forest. The room was furnished with a simple round oak table and chairs. A row of healthy asparagus ferns lined the deep sills, and a Tiffany-style lamp hung over the table. After the bling of the rest of the mansion, the unadorned room barely warranted a second glance.

Cubiak had started to turn away when he noticed a thick cord dangling from the lamp. The clunky string didn't fit with the delicate fixture. It couldn't be a pull chain, because there was a light switch on the wall. The sheriff turned on the lamp and stepped in for a closer look. The cord was a length of dirty white-and-blue rope, and suspended from the end was a Super Bowl ring. The gaudy piece of jewelry was festooned with glittery white diamonds that rimmed the surface and outlined the raised *G* on the face.

The heavy ring swung slowly back and forth like a pendulum bob. As it moved from left to right and then back again, it passed over a piece of thin cardboard, nearly grazing the surface. In this house of wealth, the cardboard, like the shabby piece of rope, was an aberration. The flimsy piece of corrugated paper looked like the end flap torn from a case of beer. There was a message on it, a note that was half-written and half-printed in bold, red paint.

Pay or he dies.

MISSING

3

Gerald Sneider had been kidnapped.

Or had he?

"Pay or he dies," the message read. If the *he* referred to the owner of the estate, then the note was a demand for ransom.

But what if the *he* referred to someone else, someone like Andrew? Pay up or your son dies. If that was the case, the note was a threat against Andrew that had been directed to Gerald. After all, the message had been left in his kitchen. Did Andrew have large outstanding debts? Cubiak wondered. Was Andrew being targeted by someone with a long-standing grudge against the man who'd become famous for his support of the Packers?

Was it possible that Gerald was testing Andrew? By pretending to disappear, had the father set the stage to see how his son would react? Cubiak had seen more bizarre things happen in families.

The sheriff pinched his eyes shut. He was tired, overtired, and losing his focus. Always start with the obvious, he reminded himself, and in this case that meant that the note referred to Gerald.

Cubiak dabbed at the paint. It was wet. He sniffed and recoiled at the acrid smell. The message was still fresh. It had been written that evening, perhaps within the past hour or two. And it had been left inside the house without the alarm being triggered, perhaps intending that it not be discovered until the next day.

The rumble of voices came from deep inside the house and moved toward the kitchen.

"Over here," the sheriff said as he snapped off the breakfast room light. He intercepted Rowe and Andrew in the kitchen. "Anything upstairs?"

"Just the five bedrooms," Rowe said. Then he mouthed a word Cubiak couldn't make out.

"Nothing's been touched in Father's room," Andrew said, filling a glass at the sink.

Cubiak motioned his deputy toward the far doorway. "Turn on the light when I give the signal," he said quietly and pointed to the breakfast nook.

"Sorry, forgetting my manners. You two want anything?" Andrew said, turning from the sink.

"Nothing, thanks. I'm fine," Cubiak said.

Andrew looked round, puzzled. "Where'd Mike go?"

"Don't worry about Rowe. There's something I want to show you," Cubiak said.

The sheriff took Andrew by the elbow and propelled him toward the darkened room.

"What the hell's going on?" Andrew said.

Cubiak coughed and Rowe hit the light switch. Andrew glanced at the deputy and then over to Cubiak. Somewhere in the background a clock ticked. Seconds passed and then Andrew noticed the dangling ring and the note.

"Oh, God," he said and lunged toward the table.

Cubiak caught his wrist.

"Don't touch anything," the sheriff said.

Andrew resisted. He was pale. A sour aroma of sweat and fear rolled off him. Cubiak tightened his grip, hooked a chair with his foot, and pushed Andrew down.

"They snatched him. I told you something was wrong." Andrew looked like he was about to be sick. He turned on Cubiak. "I knew it. I told you, didn't I?" He was shouting now.

"You did and here we are. Now we take this a step at a time." Cubiak kept his voice low and tone neutral.

"We need to find my father before something happens to him. You should have started earlier, when I told you to. Not now. Look at the time you've lost. But no, not you two"—he looked at them with disgust—"you've done exactly nothing. What a fucking joke." Andrew was flushed and panting.

"There's been nothing to indicate foul play. Even this note, as threatening as it sounds, may not mean anything. It's not going to do your father any good if you get rattled by this. You need to listen to us and keep a level head."

Andrew glared, defiant, and then he slowly folded, took a breath, and steadied himself. "How much do they want?"

"Doesn't say."

Andrew pulled at his neck. He was a big guy, built like a football player. "Jesus, who would do this to an old man?" He started to reach for the note and then pulled back.

"What do I do?" he said as he stood and shoved the chair into the wall. "Jesus. What do I do?" he said again as he paced toward the kitchen.

"Nothing yet." Cubiak pulled a notebook and pen from his pocket. "Who else lives here?"

"The housekeeper and cook have rooms on the third floor. Sometimes they stay overnight but not always."

"They're locals?"

"Two women from town."

"Where are they now?"

"They have the day off when my father goes out of town for a game."

"I'll need their names and phone numbers." He turned to Rowe. "You checked those rooms when you were upstairs?"

"I didn't know there was another floor. You want me to do it now?"

"No, we'll get that later." He said to Andrew, "First thing tomorrow, you contact them and tell them they're not needed for the next couple of days. Don't let on that anything's wrong. Just make a plausible excuse for your father's absence. Tell them he decided to spend a few days with friends or that he's away on business."

Cubiak wanted Andrew closer. He needed to see the man's face as they talked.

"That your father's ring?" he said.

Andrew circled back to the table and studied the ring. "Could be. Looks like it. He had a couple two three."

"Two or three? How'd he get them?" Rowe asked.

"One was a gift from the Packers. Later, he bought one at a charity auction. It had been donated by a linebacker Dad always liked. And there was one, he found on eBay, if you can believe it. He keeps them in a safe back in his little football museum."

"You know the combination?"

Andrew shook his head and then hesitated as he realized the implication of the situation.

"It's not that my father doesn't trust me. I know everything that's going on with his financial and business holdings. He's just, well, used to being in charge and you know how it is when people get older and have to start letting go of things. It's hard. I figured if he needs the satisfaction of having the safe under his control, well, what's the harm?"

Andrew had regained a bit of color and calmed considerably. What he said made a certain amount of sense to Cubiak. "What besides the rings does he keep in it?" he said.

"The deed to the house, car title. The kind of stuff most people keep in a safety deposit box."

"Any cash?"

"Probably but generally not much. I've seen him take a couple hundred out when he needed to. But he pays the staff in cash, so if it's coming up on payday there'd be more, maybe a thousand or so."

Working in an impoverished Chicago neighborhood, Cubiak had seen a man killed for a pair of shoes. He couldn't imagine something like that happening here. But Door County was moving into winter, when the tourist trade dropped off and many of the residents went on welfare. For someone with bills to pay and no income, a thousand dollars—even a couple hundred—could be very tempting. Would Sneider open the safe or give the combination to the kidnappers? he wondered. Probably not, unless he was threatened with physical harm. The sheriff motioned to Rowe. "Go see if the safe's been jimmied open."

Cubiak looked at Andrew. "Do you live here with your father?"

The son huffed, as if insulted by the suggestion. "I have a house on the other side of Green Bay."

"Married? Single?"

"Divorced."

"Where's your ex?"

Andrew laughed. "Exes. Four of them."

"Children?"

"Four. One kid with each. Son, daughter, son, daughter, in that order."

Four ex-wives and four kids could add up to a considerable chunk of alimony and child support over the years.

"What is it you do for a living?" Cubiak said.

"I'm an entrepreneur."

Cubiak waited while Andrew decided how to expand on that nebulous title.

"I've bankrolled a number of start-ups—everything from basic manufacturing to high-tech ventures."

"Sounds iffy."

Andrew puffed out his cheeks. "Some have been more successful than others."

Meaning, Cubiak thought, they'd all been pretty much flops. If Andrew needed money or had another motive for wishing to harm his father, he could be behind the kidnapping scheme. He'd know what it would take to get Gerald to leave the game early and could easily have arranged the mysterious phone call that lured the elderly man away from the skybox. But Andrew couldn't be in two places at one time. He'd need an accomplice. Someone else would have had to waylay his father while he sat through the rest of the game. He couldn't lie about having stayed to the end; there were too many potential witnesses in the skybox for him to leave early without being seen. Cubiak ran through the timeline. Sneider gets the call that prompts him to depart first; Andrew stays until the end and then races to Ellison Bay and leaves the note before circling back and making the manic drive into Sturgeon Bay that gets him stopped for speeding. Even that could have been part of the plan. By demanding to see the sheriff, Andrew is able to bring Cubiak onto the scene without drawing attention to himself.

"When we came in, the security alarm was on, correct?"

Andrew nodded. "It's always on when we're gone. You saw me turn it off."

"Who else knows the code?"

"The housekeeper and the cook. Dad's secretary, certainly. Me. And anyone else he accidentally shared it with." As he talked, Andrew clenched his fists and paced.

"Earlier you said your father worried about the possibility of kidnapping. What you're saying about the security code contradicts that."

Andrew slumped against the wall. "He liked to be precise and was always writing notes to himself. Maybe he jotted down the number and then misplaced it or put it where someone else would see it. I don't know. About the only place he went these past few years was to the games, whenever the team played at home or in Chicago. Usually he'd know the people in the skybox but not always. Anyone could have picked up the information, even one of the waiters." Andrew straightened again and for a moment it looked as if he was going to start pacing again. Instead he sat down.

"What about security cameras?"

Andrew shook his head. "Father thought they were intrusive."

Another contradiction, Cubiak thought.

"We need the names of everyone who was in the skybox Sunday. Any contact info, too, if you have it."

"Why?"

"Someone could have overheard part of the phone call that prompted your father to leave. Or your dad let slip something that might prove helpful. You can pull together the list first thing in the morning. Make sure to include the secretary as well."

"Him? Father hasn't actually needed his services for ages."

"Doesn't matter. I also need a recent photo of your father."

"Tonight?"

"Sooner the better."

Andrew pushed to his feet. "I'm sure there's one in the office."

There were, in fact, dozens of photos—a few taken at charity events and others with the Green Bay Packers.

Cubiak selected two pictures.

"It's late," he said. "You should get some rest. I assume you have a room here?"

"I have a suite in the first guest house." Andrew motioned toward the water.

"You'll need to stay there, at least for the night. Don't let anyone in. If the phone rings, answer it. We'll put a trace on it as soon as possible."

"You're not leaving me here alone! What if there's some crazy out there with a vendetta against the family?"

"Rowe will stay the night and I'll send a relief deputy in the morning. Also the technicians will be here to dust for fingerprints." He studied Andrew, who seemed suddenly overwhelmed. "Life will be very different until this is over. You need to accept that."

"I understand," he said but without conviction.

"Rowe will help you get settled in. If you need anything later, tell him. I don't want you wandering around in the dark." He rested his hand on Andrew's arm. "I know this is difficult, but try not to worry. We'll do our best to find your father."

While Rowe escorted Andrew to his quarters, Cubiak had time to search the grounds for intruders or signs of forced entry. A switch by the patio door lit up several acres of the estate. For someone who preferred darkness, Sneider had installed an impressive battery of floodlights on the property. But perhaps the outdoor lights, like the elaborate furnishings inside, were remnants from a time long gone. In the fog, they did little but cast eerie shadows among the trees and buildings that dotted the grounds.

During those times in his life when he'd had to invent ways to make ends meet, the sheriff had sometimes wondered what people with money did with their wealth. Walking through the mist that blanketed the estate, he saw firsthand how people like Sneider spent their fortunes. They tamed the forest with pruning shears and leveled the unwelcome bumps and contours of the land to accommodate clay tennis courts and an Olympic swimming pool. Beyond that they built a small community of guest houses—each larger than his own modest rental at the other end of the peninsula.

Cubiak was circling back to the main house when Rowe emerged from a swirl of fog.

"Everything okay?" the sheriff asked.

"Yeah, all shipshape and ready to roll, as my father would say. What about out here?"

"No sign of intruders. But difficult to see much, and the ground's too hard and dry for footprints. Where are you staying?"

"In the suite next to Andrew's. He gave me the key and told me I'd find everything I needed inside. Can you believe how some people live?"

"Takes all kinds, Mike. When you're in this business long enough you'll learn that those who live like this aren't necessarily any happier than the rest of us."

Rowe snorted. "Wait until you go upstairs and see what money can buy. Pretty weird. Especially the master bedroom. The old man's got it outfitted like a hunting lodge. There's even taxidermied trophy heads on the walls. I'm used to seeing dead deer but this place gave me the creeps."

Cubiak laughed. "Is that what you were trying to tell me before, in the kitchen?"

"Yeah."

"The world's full of weird shit. I'm only concerned with the stuff that's not legal," the sheriff said as they stepped onto the patio. He looked at his deputy. "Did you notice anything odd about the kidnappers' demands?"

"They didn't specify how much money they wanted."

"That's one thing, but there's more, too. The kidnappers said nothing about not contacting the police. Usually that's one of the first demands: don't bring in the authorities."

"Amateurs? Or someone who wants Sneider to be found? You think maybe Andrew could be behind this whole thing?"

Cubiak smiled, pleased that Rowe had the same suspicion. "It's certainly possible. But he couldn't have pulled it off alone," the sheriff said.

"There's the cook and the housekeeper. The secretary, as well. They can't be ruled out." Rowe looked around. "Think about it. All this fucking money. Might be tough working somewhere like this, surrounded by the kind of stuff you don't have a chance in hell of ever owning yourself." The deputy hesitated. "You think someone's really grabbed him? That they might harm him?"

"I don't know," Cubiak said. "You go in and bag up all that stuff with the ransom note."

While he waited, Cubiak made two phone calls, the first to the Wisconsin crime lab requesting a priority for the tech wagon Monday morning and the second to the Illinois State Police asking for video from the two toll booths between Chicago and the Illinois–Wisconsin state line starting at 4 p.m. Sunday afternoon.

He was still on the line when the yard lights went dark. Rowe must have switched them off, leaving only the perimeter lamps on the patio to shimmer in the fog. A door sprang shut and Rowe stepped up with the evidence bag.

"If you want, I'll get the word out to the department," he said as he handed the material to Cubiak.

"Good. Tell them to be in by eight, everyone except you. At this stage, you know as much as I do about the situation and I need you here to get the evidence technicians started as soon as they arrive. Once I've briefed the staff, I'll send up your relief."

Cubiak glanced at his deputy. "It's a good thing you got that vacation in when you did. What'd you end up doing down there in Mexico?"

"Mostly water stuff. A little snorkeling. Some scuba diving. Even swam into a shark cave." Rowe thrust his hand down toward a patch of light. "Look at that, I've been back barely a week and my tan's nearly gone already."

THE INCIDENT ROOM

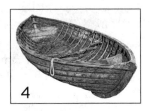

4

Cubiak woke to the smell of coffee and the sound of music, classical guitar, floating in from the hall. He was groggy and lay still, imagining himself somewhere far from his little house on the Lake Michigan shore. Mexico, perhaps. Or Belize, even. He'd never been to either but after listening to Rowe's chatter about his vacation the sheriff couldn't help but fantasize about palm trees and water sports, the kind that didn't include swimming into shark caves.

Maybe last night's business with Andrew Sneider had been a dream, and in reality he and Cate had flown to the tropics as they'd so often planned. Or they were starting another morning at home in Door County with Cate in the kitchen fixing breakfast. When he'd returned from Ellison Bay, Cubiak had expected to find her sound asleep, with Butch curled up at the foot of the bed. But at a quarter past three, when he finally got in, the house was empty. Had Cate come in later or had she spent the night at her condo? He ran a hand over her side of the bed. The sheet was smooth and cool.

In the shower, Cubiak faced up to the real truth about why he'd been fishing the day before. Yesterday was the day his daughter should have turned eleven. He'd spent the afternoon away from home to avoid seeing reminders of Chicago flashed on the TV screen during the game and being reminded of Alexis's birthday, but sitting on the rock ledge, all he could think of was the cake lit with candles, the party, and her gleeful delight as she ripped the wrappings off her gifts. This was the nature of grief and its litany of perpetual reminders.

He was still learning what it meant to forfeit one reality, to lose those he loved, and still trying to understand what it meant to try to create a different and separate existence. How to be faithful to what had been, while being true to what was now. His friend Evelyn Bathard had found a way forward following the death of his wife. Could Cubiak do the same? And how did Cate fit in?

Like him, she was carving out a new life on the peninsula. Cate had spent her childhood summers in Door County with her aunt Ruby and uncle Dutch, but after witnessing her aunt's tragic death, she'd fled and gone back to Milwaukee. Cubiak differed from Cate in many ways and had been surprised to slowly find himself attracted to her that first summer they met. When she left, he resigned himself to never seeing her again. Since her return two years ago, they'd grown closer: To the point where they were more or less living together and more or less a couple. More than less, really. To the point where Cubiak had started imagining a future for them. Was it even possible, he wondered, considering what had happened with Ruby? Cate said she didn't blame him. But Cate didn't know her aunt's whole story, and Cubiak did.

He'd kept quiet about Ruby's secret for four years, but he knew that eventually he'd have to tell Cate everything. He'd have to take the chance that the truth wouldn't jeopardize their relationship.

Cubiak was toweling off when his phone dinged. A text from Rowe gave the names and numbers of Sneider's cook and housekeeper. So the nightmare was real. Andrew's father was missing, possibly kidnapped. He had work to do and once again his personal life had to be put on hold.

The sheriff dressed quickly and called Rowe. The deputy reported a quiet night at Sneider's homestead. No calls, e-mails, or visitors. The staff had been given the day off, as the sheriff had directed, and Andrew was on his fourth cup of coffee.

"You get any sleep?" the sheriff asked.

"Enough."

Cate had the coffee poured and the bacon on when Cubiak reached the kitchen.

Despite lingering fatigue, he was cheered by the sight of Cate—a woman born to money and privilege—standing in his kitchen like a short-order cook with a cast iron skillet in one hand and a spatula in the other. Seeing her, Cubiak felt his heart lurch. In the morning light she was beautiful. To him, Cate was always beautiful: tall and streamlined, with long brown hair so naturally dark it looked black.

"I got into town late and didn't want to disturb you, so I went to my place to sleep," she said.

For Cate, at least temporarily, home was a rented condo at a nearby lakefront development. For the time being, at least, she chose to avoid both her grandfather's estate and the homestead she'd inherited from her aunt and uncle.

"But I see you've been busy." She glanced at the kittens. "Did they follow you home?"

Oh gawd, he'd forgotten the kittens. "Fished them out of the bay yesterday."

Cate's smile vanished. "Someone threw them in?"

"Yeah. Good chance it was Leeland Ross."

She grimaced.

"You know him?"

"Only by reputation. You went in, didn't you?"

"There wasn't much choice."

She laughed. "They are cute, and, anyway, I found the little bottle you'd left on the counter, so I filled it and fed them this morning."

He kissed her cheek. "Thanks."

Cubiak ate quickly and between bites told her about Sneider.

"That's a name from the past. I saw him once, I'm sure, at Ruby's. I was just a kid and he came by after grandfather died to offer his condolences to the family. They'd been good friends when they were younger, but by the time I started spending my summers up here my grandfather hadn't spoken to him in years. I remember Ruby being upset by the visit and Dutch having to calm her down."

"Ruby didn't like him?"

Cate stirred milk into her coffee. "They'd had a falling out but I don't know over what. Funny, though, I remember not liking him either. It wasn't just because of Ruby's reaction. I guess some adults are scary to kids. Bushy eyebrows or whatever."

"Did you know his son, Andrew?"

Cate cradled her mug in her hands. "Until this morning I didn't even know Gerald had a son."

While Cubiak laced up his boots, she talked through her schedule for the day: She was starting the next phase of her photo assignment on Wisconsin historic sites for a special Midwest edition of the *National Geographic* and planned to shoot The Ridges Sanctuary later that morning. "Weather's going to start turning and I need to get the outdoor shots in while I can. I was hoping you could join me for lunch."

Cubiak was printing a sign about free kittens when his laptop dinged, announcing an e-mail. It was a message from the state crime lab informing him that the evidence team was on its way to Ellison Bay.

"Sorry, but I can't. It's going to be a busy day," he said to Cate.

The lineup of staff vehicles in the parking lot for the Door County Justice Center told Cubiak that Rowe had rallied the force. Even his very pregnant assistant, Lisa, was at her desk.

"What are you doing here? You should be at home, resting," Cubiak said. He'd watched Lisa move through the stages of pregnancy—the early excitement and anxiety, the exhaustion, the calm energy. He remembered when Lauren was pregnant with Alexis and was still remorseful over how much of that he'd missed because of work.

Lisa gave him a tolerant smile. "I'm fine and I want to be doing something. May as well wait here as at home. It's only five minutes to the hospital. I'll be okay." She glanced at the hand-scrawled poster he held. "Free kittens?"

Cubiak shrugged. "If you get a minute, maybe you could make a few copies and put them up around the station, okay? But don't exert yourself."

She laughed and pushed to her feet, heading to the copier.

In his office there was a message from the state police following up on the APB Rowe had submitted the night before: no sign yet of Sneider's car.

Earlier that year, Lisa had cataloged Door County's arrest history for the previous five decades. Cubiak skimmed the summary: Drunk driving. Domestic violence. Drug possession. Child abuse. Murder. Assault and Battery. Robbery. Arson. But not a single abduction in the previous fifty years.

Nearly half the people who worked for the department were reserve deputies, telecommunications specialists, or personnel connected with the jail and courts. Other officers handled drugs and road traffic. One deputy dealt with juvenile offenders. The sheriff was left with a handful of investigators and deputies to take on the Sneider case.

These men and women had just come through a busier than usual summer with a flurry of break-ins at a couple of the larger resorts. But the perps had been caught, and he knew his team was anticipating some downtime as the tourist season abated. For their sake, he hoped they'd clear up the Sneider situation quickly.

At 8 a.m., Cubiak met with his team in the incident room. Coffee and doughnuts in hand, they looked at him with open curiosity. What was going on? Why had they been called in?

Cubiak stuck the photo of the missing man to the evidence board.

"Gerald Sneider," he said.

A sound like a gasp went up and the room snapped to attention.

They know him, Cubiak realized. They know his reputation in the county and his history with the Packers.

He started all over with the specifics on Sneider's age and description: Caucasian, six foot three, 210 pounds. No known physical scars. Missing. Possible abduction.

Cubiak took them through the sequence of events from the previous night. "We don't know if the note found in the kitchen referred to Sneider, but if it does and state lines were crossed, this may be a job for the feds. For now, it's in our hands. I realize this is not the type of situation we ordinarily come up against, but there's basic investigative work to be done and that's where we start."

Cubiak handed out assignments. A senior deputy was charged with gathering information on Sneider's history with the Packers. "Not just the PR stuff but the backroom deals. Anything that may have left someone with a bad taste in the mouth."

A team of two investigators was to canvas the town of Ellison Bay and the area around the estate. "See if anyone noticed anything out of the ordinary. Check to see if Sneider had any run-ins or longstanding feuds with his neighbors—someone unhappy about property line disputes, or zoning issues. A man with that much money to toss around can step on a lot of toes without even trying. Keep it low key. At this stage, the man is missing. No more. We're not trying to rattle anyone, yet."

Another deputy was to start checking on Andrew's alibis from the time the game ended to the time he was stopped for speeding, while another was to look into his affairs. "Andrew presents himself as the loyal son, concerned about his father's welfare, but we need to know the true nature of their relationship and whether Andrew is solvent or in debt up to his ears. More often than not, the perp is found close to home.

"Deputy Rowe will question the secretary and I'll talk to the cook and housekeeper. In all instances, we're looking for means and motive."

Cubiak was about to ask for questions when there was a knock on the door and Lisa popped her head in. Her eyes were wide and her expression somber. "Sir, Sheriff, sorry but there's an urgent call for you," she said. She held up a piece of paper.

What now? Cubiak thought. Had Andrew disappeared as well? He looked at the note. *FBI*, it said, written in red.

"Wait here," Cubiak told his staff. He followed Lisa as far as his office and waited for her to put the call through.

The voice on the line was brisk. "This is Special Agent Quigley Moore from the Green Bay satellite office of the Federal Bureau of Investigation calling to inform you that we have a situation that we need to discuss."

"The disappearance and possible kidnapping of Gerald Sneider," Cubiak said.

Moore hesitated. "How'd you know?"

"I could ask you the same."

"There was a message delivered to the Green Bay Packers office."

"And one here at Sneider's home."

"I'll be there in an hour. We'll talk more then," Moore said and hung up.

In the conference room, Cubiak reported back to his team. "Under normal protocol, the feds don't come in unless and until we request their assistance. So something's up. Until we're told anything different, we continue doing our jobs. Anything at all, get back to me with it."

A little more than an hour after the call, Lisa buzzed the sheriff. "Visitors, sir, in the lobby."

Cubiak had expected Moore to arrive alone. But when he reached the lobby he found a man and a woman standing side by side in front of one of the Free Kittens notices that Lisa had taped to the wall.

The visitors were a matched set, both tall and with the kind of posture that made Cubiak's shoulders hurt.

As they turned toward the sheriff, the man erased the bemused look from his face and held out his hand. "Sheriff, Special Agent Quigley Moore and my assistant agent Gwen Harrison."

Moore had steady green eyes and the kind of chiseled features long associated with Hollywood icons. Harrison was what the guys in Cubiak's old neighborhood would call a stunner, but he suspected that for a woman to get that far in the agency meant that behind the looks there were brains to match.

The federal agents were a no-nonsense pair. Moore's close-cropped hair was brushed back; his trousers were dark and neatly creased and the cuffs broke on the laces of spit-polished wingtips. Harrison's hair was blonde and slicked into a bun. Her suit jacket was the same dark color as his; her pencil skirt barely covered the knees. And her shoes had that hard shine that comes from good leather with heels low enough to be sensible and high enough to be sexy. Looking at the two, Cubiak wondered if he shouldn't have worn something other than jeans and his faded navy blue sweater that day.

The two held up their credentials but the sheriff didn't need to see their ID to know they were from the FBI; the perfume of calm confidence that they exuded marked them as federal agents.

"We're here to assist in the search for Gerald Sneider," Harrison said, giving him a firm handshake.

Cubiak liked women with a good grip, but that morning he was too focused on the notion of two federal agents on his turf to appreciate it. What makes you think I need your help? the sheriff wanted to say. Instead, he kept them waiting a minute more than necessary before he turned and led them to his office, where he snapped the door shut, pointed them to the chairs facing his desk, and took his place behind it.

"Aren't you supposed to wait for me to call you?" he said once they were settled in.

Watching Moore survey his messy desk with disapproval, Cubiak resisted the urge to sweep the clutter and empty coffee cups into the trash.

"Under usual circumstances, yes, but this case is a bit different," Moore said in a tone that managed to be both collegial and condescending. "In fact we've been waiting for something like this to happen.

You may be aware that over the past several months, there've been threats made against both the Packers and Lambeau Field, all part of a larger pattern focused on the NFL, specifically several Midwest teams. The threats target players, management, and high-profile supporters. People like Gerald Sneider. Homeland Security has been tracking this for months."

As if a secret signal had been sent to her, Harrison took up the story. "Late last evening, Packers headquarters received a message that could be construed as a ransom note. 'Pay or he dies.' Since Gerald Sneider's name was on the note, the general manager called the Green Bay police chief, who immediately contacted our local office."

Cubiak interrupted. "Was the note addressed to Sneider?"

"To be precise, it's a matter of semantics," Moore said. He gave Cubiak a copy of the message. *Gerald Sneider, Pay or he dies.*

"This could be a message addressed to Sneider."

"Yes."

"Meaning pay up or some unknown person dies."

"Unlikely, but yes."

Cubiak smiled. "I like to be precise as well," he said, straightening a stack of reports. "A similar note was left at Sneider's home in Ellison Bay, although without his name on it." He filled the agents in on the events of the previous evening.

"You left this deputy Rowe with Andrew?" Moore said.

Cubiak nodded. "There's another deputy on his way up now to relieve him."

"Good." Moore fiddled with his phone and then looked up. "You understand that while officially Gerald Sneider is considered missing, we are operating on the plausible assumption that he has been kidnapped."

"Fair enough, but that still doesn't explain your presence here. We don't know if he's been taken over state lines. I'm waiting for confirmation," Cubiak stated.

Harrison pulled an envelope from her brief case. "This photo taken at 5:12 p.m. yesterday afternoon at the last toll booth in Illinois shows Gerald in his car sitting in the front passenger seat." She laid a black-and-white print on his desk, proof not only about Sneider's whereabouts but that the FBI had more muscle than a county sheriff. "We can't make out who's driving but it's clear that Sneider's not alone."

"That doesn't mean he's been abducted or taken across state lines. There's still another exit in Illinois."

"If this is a terrorist operation, it doesn't matter where he's being held."

"And you think it is?"

Moore gestured to his assistant and let her pick up from there.

"Most likely," Harrison said. "Either domestic or foreign, we don't know yet. Point is, we don't want to alarm the public. Word will get out about Sneider being missing soon enough, but we need to keep it at that for now."

"How much does Andrew know?"

"About the possible terror threat? Hopefully nothing."

Harrison looked at her watch. "Perhaps you can fill us in on the situation at this end." The impatience in her voice was hard to miss.

Cubiak ran through the previous night's events and the morning's briefing.

"Plenty left to do, then," Moore said and smiled at the sheriff, letting Cubiak know he hadn't missed a beat.

Moore looked about his age, Cubiak thought, but had no gray in his ebony hair. Just that morning the sheriff had noticed that the white strands on his head seemed to be multiplying rapidly.

Agent Moore stood. "Let's cooperate, pool resources. We'll start by setting up phone lines. You have an incident room we can use." It wasn't a question.

"Of course." Cubiak rose to his feet as well. "Just so we're clear, who's in charge?"

"You, of course."

"Of course."

"We'll need to meet with your team." Moore went on as if the previous question hadn't been asked.

"I told you I've already briefed them."

"Well, we need to do it again to make sure we're all on the same page. I assume you don't mind."

Cubiak did mind. If the terrorist threats against the league were coincidental, then the FBI was basing the investigation on the wrong premise and valuable time would be wasted. But with nothing in hand to counter their argument, he had no choice but to keep his peace.

"I've got the state boys up there now checking for prints," he said.

Moore frowned. "And I bet they came in with their nice bright state police van! You think it's a good idea to let the public know something's going on?"

"The note that was left in Sneider's kitchen said nothing about not notifying the authorities. If need be, we could always say there'd been a burglary at the house."

Moore shrugged. "I doubt they'll find anything worthwhile anyway," he said.

By late morning, the federal agents had taken over the conference room. Moore and Harrison had set up work stations at the far end of the table, and while the two conferred in a quiet back-and-forth exchange of questions and ideas, a team of technicians worked around them installing secure communication lines and computer hookups.

Cubiak was almost at the door when he caught himself. Feeling a bit like a schoolboy who'd been instructed to check in with his teacher at every step, he backtracked through the center to let the feds know he was on his way to Ellison Bay. Moore was on his cell, listening intently, his brow furrowed. He nodded as much to the sheriff as to the phone. Harrison barely looked up from her laptop. Neither of them seemed to care. And neither told Cubiak what they were up to.

Moore looked like the type that played by the rules. He probably had to be to get anywhere in the department, which had to be a bureaucratic nightmare. But there were sticklers and there were sticklers, and he suspected that Moore was at the pain-in-the-ass end of the spectrum. He wondered how Harrison dealt with her superior, and how his predominantly male team of deputies would respond to her. A man could be too handsome and a woman too good looking, Cubiak thought.

In the lobby, the sheriff pulled down the Free Kittens sign and tossed it on Lisa's desk. "I think we can do with a few less of these," he said, sounding harsher than he wanted to.

AN INVASION
OF PRIVACY 5

In the bright light of day, Cubiak got his first clear look at Gerald Sneider's sprawling mansion. Four stories high and built of massive brown stones, it had the heft of a fortress and the feel of a castle, with a corner turret and gargoyles jutting from the roofline. What a strange, ugly house to build in the middle of the woods, Cubiak thought.

The sheriff turned his attention to the van that was parked at the bottom of the stairs. The field response team from the Wisconsin crime lab went where needed, and more often than not the Door County sheriff had to wait his turn along with law officials from several other jurisdictions. Not so when a situation involved someone with the stature of Gerald Sneider. That morning his request had leapfrogged to the top of the assignment list.

The sheriff recognized the senior investigator, a man he knew only as Jenkins. "Any luck?" Cubiak asked as the team loaded the last of its equipment into the van.

Jenkins tossed the dregs of his coffee into a bush and shook the sheriff's hand. "We got four sets of prints, each of them found pretty consistently throughout the house. We got a match for Andrew and another from the master bedroom that we figure is the father's. We'll need elimination prints for the cook and the housekeeper to wrap up."

"What about the breakfast nook?"

"Wiped clean."

Cubiak told Jenkins about the ransom note. "I didn't want to leave it here overnight. It's waiting for you in Sturgeon Bay. I'll need the usual rundown: paper, paint, and so on." He hesitated. "As of this morning, the feds are in on this; they may have already taken it."

The investigator took a long pull on his cigarette.

"Those things'll kill you," Cubiak said, aware of the half-empty pack on his dash and his only partially successful attempts to quit.

"Yeah, I know." Jenkins ground the butt under his boot and then dropped the crumpled filter into his pocket. "Place is weird, don't you think? The upstairs, I mean," he said, glancing back at the house.

Cubiak hadn't seen the second floor yet, but he remembered that Rowe had used the same word to describe it.

"Then there's the locked room on the third floor. The son, Andrew, said it hadn't been used in years and claimed he didn't know where to find the key. I didn't think it was worth breaking down the door to see what's inside, at least not yet, and figured you'd want to sort that out with him. At any rate, we're heading to Algoma from here, so we won't be that far away if you need us back any time soon."

"Right," Cubiak replied, but he was wondering about the locked room.

He called his deputy and told him what Jenkins had said. He also told him about Agents Moore and Harrison. "They'll need to talk to you about last night. When you're done with them, I want you to help verify Andrew's movements starting with Sunday morning and going through the day until you stopped him for speeding. Pay special attention to the time he says he spent with the stamp collector."

The tech team had left the main door ajar. When Cubiak pulled it shut he felt the unnatural, heavy silence of the house close in. Even the soft murmur of the fountain seemed to fade. His crepe soles squeaked on the floor of the grand foyer. Cubiak stopped at the foot of the double staircase and looked up. All families had their secrets. What tales were hidden behind the walls of the private quarters on the second floor?

The sheriff took a thick Oriental runner up one side of the staircase. From the top landing he could see straight through a row of arched windows to the bay beyond. A long hallway extended out in each direction. There were two doors to the right and three to the left. Five rooms, just as Rowe had said the night before. Cubiak started with the east wing.

An engraved gold plaque hung on the door of each room. Cubiak opened the one marked Lawrence of Arabia. No kidding, he thought, as he took in the sand-colored floor, the bed camouflaged as a Bedouin tent, and the silhouettes of camels parading the walls. *Weird* indeed, Cubiak thought. Next door was the tropical green Easter Island room with its replicas of the iconic statues and a four-poster bed made to look like a thatched hut. In Venice, a gondola bed rode atop a floor painted in a wet, rippled effect. The concepts were tacky but executed with an eye on detail and no concern for expense.

As he moved from one bedroom to the next, Cubiak thought of the barren, white-walled room of his youth with its narrow bed and tall, painted dresser, the bookcase filled first with plastic cowboys and model airplanes and then piled with books as he outgrew childish playthings. Growing up, he'd always wished for something bigger and more elaborate but now he wasn't sure.

The first door in the west wing opened to the tapestried and mirrored Versailles boudoir with its gold bidet and collection of porcelain pitchers. Finally, Cubiak came to Kilimanjaro, the master bedroom that had disturbed Rowe. Sneider's enclave was easily twice the size of the others and even more bizarre than the deputy had described. A zebra skin rug spread out in front of the massive fireplace. Ancient tribal weapons filled one wall. Exotic carved masks hung alongside several trophy heads of leopards and lions. On a platform two steps up from the floor, animal skins covered the sprawling bed.

Why were the rooms decorated that way? the sheriff wondered. Were they reminders of places Sneider had visited or fantasy visions of places on his travel bucket list? Or was there some other bizarre meaning behind the elaborate themes? Cubiak couldn't imagine Sneider's wife sleeping in the hunter's paradise. Perhaps Venice had been hers. In which room had Andrew spent his childhood?

The aroma of fresh brewed coffee drew Cubiak downstairs, where he found Andrew and the relief deputy.

"Okay for me to be here? I ran out of beans at my place," Andrew said as he reached for a third mug. He was dressed in baggy green sweatpants and shirt and looked more like the estate gardener than the heir.

Cubiak sent the deputy outside and then, to be polite, accepted the drink.

"What gives with the upstairs decor? Was your father a world traveler?" he asked.

"Both my parents liked to travel. The themed rooms were my mother's idea. They're reminders of the favorite places they visited together."

"Did you go with them?"

Andrew gave a sad smile. "No, Sheriff, I did not." He looked away. "My parents adored each other. Theirs was a classic case of love at first sight and lifelong devotion. They were inseparable, as the saying goes. Naturally, they were eager to have a baby, but after I was born, they realized that children needed more time and attention than they cared to give. I was much loved but an inconvenience, a problem they solved with nannies and then boarding school. Very British, you know." He assumed the accent and almost choked on the word.

A clock ticked and Andrew went on. "So, no, we weren't close. After Mother died, my father sold the houses in Green Bay and Miami and came to live here, with the rooms and the memories."

"What about the locked room?"

"Oh, that." He hesitated. "I couldn't have that whole crew of men tromping through there this morning but, of course, you'll want to see it."

Andrew got the key from a carved ivory box in the library and led the way up. He was stooped and slow, whether tired from the previous day or burdened by worry, Cubiak couldn't decide.

The stairs to the third floor were in a separate passageway at the back of the house. Easy to miss, Cubiak thought.

In the hallway at the top of the stairs, Andrew pointed to two narrow doors on one side. "Staff quarters," he said.

He waited for the sheriff to inspect the rooms and then he moved to the double-wide door on the other side. "Father had a wall removed and two rooms converted into one. Ready?" he said almost jauntily as he inserted the key.

Whatever Cubiak expected to find behind the locked door, it wasn't a hospital bed surrounded by the paraphernalia of a quixotic private medical clinic.

"You ever hear of Creutzfeldt-Jakob disease, Sheriff?" Andrew stepped aside and let Cubiak enter. "It's a rare and fatal degenerative brain disorder, affecting one person in a million. Most patients die within a year or two. My mother was diagnosed shortly after her fifty-fourth birthday. But my father refused to accept the fact that there was no cure. He believed that if you tried hard enough, you could overcome any shortcoming or fault in the human system—mental, emotional, or physical."

Andrew pulled the curtain at the window. The sun was out and light flowed in above the treetops, exaggerating the paleness of his parchment complexion and the harsh sterility of the room's antiseptic white walls and surfaces.

He went on in a monotone. "When the doctors at the Mayo Clinic couldn't give him what he wanted, he dragged my mother around the world to every self-professed healer he could find. He was convinced that if he just tried hard enough, he'd find the person who could make her well, and she put her faith in him, like she always did. I protested, of course, but my objections were ignored. When Mother couldn't walk anymore and was too weak to stand, he brought her back and set up a personalized hospital room with round-the-clock, private-duty nurses and a revolving door of gurus, doctors of questionable repute, and even shamans that he put up in the guest houses."

As Andrew talked, Cubiak inspected the room more closely. In his determined efforts to keep his wife alive, Sneider had allowed her to be treated with a boggling array of purported remedies. Opaque green and blue bottles of various sizes and shapes filled a glass-front cabinet marked Potions. Dozens of dried herbs in sealed plastic bags hung in another, while the shelves of a third were piled with metal pill boxes. Cubiak stopped in front of a tall chest of drawers labeled Fungi. He didn't dare open the drawers.

There were gadgets as well. A Jacuzzi tub filled one corner. A white curtain hid an array of oxygen and exercise equipment and multiple IV trees. Electrical appliances, including wrist and ankle straps and a domed cap with wires, lined two shelves on a back wall.

What one can do with money, Cubiak thought. "And how long did this go on?"

"Four or five months. Six at the most. After she died, Father closed up the room. As far as I know no one's been in here until today."

Andrew waited for Cubiak to step back into the hall. "For my father, my mother's death represented the ultimate failure. I don't know if he ever accepted the fact that his egomaniacal ideals had prolonged her suffering, but he was never the same afterward," he said, pulling the door shut behind them.

Downstairs, Andrew headed to the front hall. "Okay if I take a walk? I could use the air," he said.

Cubiak stood on the porch and watched him go, the deputy not far behind. When the two men disappeared into the woods, he retraced his way through the first floor. The evidence technicians had opened the drapes, but even bathed in sunlight the opulent rooms retained their gloom, as if all life and hope had been banished. Passing from one to another, the sheriff felt as if he was walking through a well-maintained museum. Once there had been life within these walls, but no longer.

Cubiak poured a fresh cup of coffee in the kitchen and made his way to Sneider's office. Moore hadn't prescribed any boundaries, so he decided to have a look around. He rolled the great chair away from the desk and was about to sit down when the front door banged open and heavy footsteps thundered across the foyer.

"Sheriff!" The cry was croaked and rigid with fear.

It was Andrew.

"In here, the office," Cubiak replied.

The thick hall rug muted Andrew's steps, but moments later he charged into the room, followed by the relief deputy. Andrew was short-winded and his barrel chest heaved with the effort of breathing. Burrs stuck to his legs and arms, and a dark shadow played across the lower part of his face. Struggling to steady his trembling hand, Andrew thrust out his cell phone, holding it like a miniature bomb.

"Four hundred grand," he said, his eyes huge in his pale face. "They want four hundred thousand dollars."

"They called?"

Andrew shook his head. "No. A text. Here." Again he jabbed the phone toward Cubiak.

The sheriff took the device as Andrew collapsed onto the couch. "What else?"

"Nothing."

"No instructions?" the sheriff said as he laid the phone on the glass-topped desk.

"Just what's there."

Andrew reared up and glared at the phone as if he expected it to explode. "Jesus, I don't have that kind of money," he said, grabbing at his hair. "What am I going to do?"

"Nothing."

Andrew struggled to his feet, sputtering in protest.

"There's nothing you can do, yet. For one thing, they haven't given any instruction. And besides, it's out of your hands."

Andrew sat down again. "What do you mean?"

"Whoever's behind this left a message at Packers headquarters as well as here. The governing board called in the police and the FBI, and this morning two federal agents showed up at my office to help with the investigation. I'll tell them about the text. They'll know what to do." At least Cubiak hoped they would. He assumed Moore and Harrison had experience dealing with kidnappers.

"I see," Andrew said, but his response was drugged with doubt.

"I finished the coffee. Do you want a glass of water? Some tea?" Cubiak offered.

Andrew rubbed his neck. "Water," he said as he leaned back and closed his eyes.

Andrew had been gone less than five minutes when he got the text. Had he been expecting the message? Cubiak wondered. The sheriff motioned the relief deputy into the hall. "What was Andrew doing when he got the text?"

"He was walking by the cliff."

"Were his hands in his pockets or by his side?"

The deputy frowned. "By his sides. He was swinging them along as he walked."

"You saw both hands the entire time?"

"Yeah, for sure. When he pulled out the cell, he held it in both hands to keep it steady while he read the message."

In the kitchen the sheriff filled a glass with ice and then called Moore while he ran the tap.

Moore seemed nonplussed. "We'll trace the text but it's probably from a prepaid phone that's at the bottom of the lake by now. Proves one thing though. If Andrew's behind the scheme, he's not alone. Unless he had another cell in his other pocket with a preprogrammed message that he sent himself."

"Not likely. The relief deputy was with him and said both Andrew's hands were visible the entire time."

Moore grunted.

"What about the ransom demand?" the sheriff asked.

"With no instructions, it means little. A message to keep us guessing and let us know the game's still on."

The game? Cubiak thought. A man's life might be at stake. "Doesn't it seem like an odd amount? Four hundred thousand instead of an even half a million?"

He could almost see Moore shrug over the phone. "Four hundred, five hundred grand, whatever. If the perp is a disgruntled employee or a neighbor, someone with a personal grudge, it might seem a little high. But if we're dealing with terrorists or professionals, it's another matter. Worldwide, kidnappings bring in about two billion a year. It's big business out there. In fact, I've seen cases where the ransom demand has been five times what Andrew's been asked for. If anything—assuming we're dealing with a terror threat here—I'm surprised they didn't ask for more. These people need major funding for their operations."

"Andrew claims he doesn't have access to that kind of money."

Again, Cubiak sensed the shrug. "Tell him not to worry. When it comes to the actual arrangements, we'll take care of things."

"You'll pay up?"

"We'll play it out, see how far it goes. The final decisions are made up the ladder."

At the other end of the line, a door opened and Cubiak heard Moore in a muffled conversation with someone else. "Yeah, good. Okay. Sure, now's fine." When he got back to the sheriff, Cubiak asked what the agents in Green Bay had learned.

"Nothing new from the team office but a couple of my men talked to Sneider's secretary. He says he's basically retired and hasn't been to the estate in five years. In the past two years, he says he's met Sneider twice at the Packers office and then it was only to follow through on business correspondence concerning Sneider's logging interests."

"He's from Green Bay?"

"No. Nashville, but he's lived up here for thirty years or so. A bit of a loner, according to my agent. Big house, five cats, expensive tastes.

Follows chess not football. Hard to see how he connected with Sneider. I've got a man tracing his movements for the past six months, see if there's any red flags in where he's been and who he's been in contact with. If this is an inside job, he'd be a good candidate."

Moore was interrupted again. Cubiak was about to hang up when the agent was back on the line. "Have you started going through Sneider's files and personal papers yet?"

"No."

"Don't bother with them then. Agent Harrison is on her way there now. She'll take it from here."

So much for being in charge, Cubiak thought.

Andrew was on the couch with his eyes closed when the sheriff got back to the office with the glass of water.

"One of the federal agents, a Gwen Harrison, is on her way here now," Cubiak said.

Andrew slumped into the sofa. "I've got to talk to the FBI?"

"It's routine. They'll be talking to all kinds of people. Nothing to worry about."

Andrew cast a nervous glance around the office. "Yeah," he said.

Cubiak opened a tall casement window to let in the cool air.

"Your father didn't have a computer?" he asked, taking in the old-fashioned furnishings.

Andrew laughed. "He didn't trust computers. Also didn't know how to use one."

"No laptop, notebook?"

Andrew shook his head. "Didn't even have a typewriter. My father liked to talk things through, settle deals with a handshake. Anything in writing, his secretary handled."

Cubiak considered the wall of custom-made, built-in wood file cabinets. Gerald Sneider had been a powerhouse for decades. There were drawers full of business correspondence that could harbor secret agreements or point to potential enemies. After talking with Moore,

Cubiak knew that leaving Andrew alone with his father's papers could jeopardize the investigation. He had no choice but to wait there with him for Harrison.

The sheriff surveyed the dozens of photos and certificates that hung on the walls. The pictures and documents, all richly matted and framed in gold, created an impressive profile of Sneider as an upstanding citizen. There he was standing alongside a series of Green Bay mayors and Wisconsin governors and U.S. senators. Plaques honored him as Businessman of the Year, Citizen of the Decade, and even State Philanthropist of the Century. There were accolades from the Lions, the Kiwanis, the Rotary, the Boy Scouts, more than a half-dozen civic organizations.

Just as impressive were the photos that traced the missing man's long history with the Packers, first in black and white and then in vivid color: a picture of Sneider with every quarterback and coach since Vince Lombardi, and then one of him with each of the Packers' five Super Bowl teams and five of its NFL championship teams. Big shoes to fill, Cubiak thought, looking at Andrew sprawled on the couch.

"Your father has quite a legacy, especially with the Packers."

Andrew made a sound like a laugh. "To some people, the Packers wouldn't be what they are without him. They're the only franchise team in the league that's publicly owned. He bought his first share of stock for twenty five dollars in 1950 when he was seventeen. That gave him his first vote in the organization. After that, every time there was a stock drive, he anted up. So far, there've been five million shares issued and my dad ended up with six hundred thousand of them, the maximum of two hundred thousand for himself, my mother, and me. That's all very public, but what most people don't know about is the private support, the many times he kept other owners afloat when they ran into financial trouble or pumped money in when the team's economic woes were kept quiet."

"Backroom deals?"

"There were always rumors. You know how it is."

"What did he get in return?"

"You tell me. He loved the sense of power that went with the money, but there were other businessmen involved and who knows what kind of agreements and deals they came up with behind closed doors. He never really talked about it, at least not to me."

Cubiak let the thought settle: First, the child Andrew, loved but ignored by his parents. Later, as an adult, shut out of his father's business dealings. "There were no previous threats against your father, which you know of?" he said after a moment.

"No. Never anything like that. The past year or so, there was some concern that terrorists would try to disrupt one of the big games, but nothing ever came of it."

"How'd you know about that?" Cubiak asked.

"I overheard talk about it early on at a preseason dinner. One of the coaches gets chatty when he's had a few too many. Besides it's been on the news, too. I heard it mentioned on one of those radio talk shows."

"Your dad had no personal enemies in the organization?"

"He was strictly backroom. Didn't keep his opinions to himself, which didn't make him the most popular guy. But enemies? No."

Cubiak circled back to the photos. "The early players didn't make a lot. There could be resentment about the salaries being paid today," he said.

"Those guys are probably all gone now."

"They have family, descendants." Cubiak let the thought hang in the air. "What about some of the later players who might be struggling with injuries or concussion issues?"

"There've been a couple of guys who threatened lawsuits against the league, but not the team, not as far as I know. Anyway there's no way anyone could hold my father responsible in those situations."

"People with grievances, whether perceived or real, don't always think logically."

Andrew pressed his hands to his knees and leaned back into the soft cushions of the sofa. "I guess not. But it's all different now, you know. It's big business. It wasn't always like that. At the start, the guys were in it for the love of the game. Many of them had full-time jobs and played for the thrill of it. There wasn't much money and there was very little fame. Sometimes they'd pass the hat to cover expenses. Of course, that changed over time. But even after my father got seriously involved, there was still a sense of family, and for some of the younger players my father was a parental figure. Anyone on the squad facing difficult circumstances could rely on my dad for help. He knew from his own experience what kind of odds some of them were up against."

Andrew heaved himself to his feet and lifted a framed photo from the desk. "I told you he was an orphan. Grew up at the Child Care Center in Sparta. He didn't have an easy time of it, a bit of a troublemaker, he admits. But when he turned twelve he was apprenticed out, luckily to a good family that ran a big nursery. The parents were older and pretty strict. They kept him in line but they taught him a lot about growing trees and running a business, skills that he put to good use later on. He was grateful for that opportunity and always felt he had a debt to pay to society." Andrew showed the picture to Cubiak.

"That's him," he said, pointing to a tall, well-muscled man with close-cropped hair and a smooth, unlined face. The young Gerald Sneider squinted into the sun. He was hatless and unsmiling, his sleeves rolled up to the elbows and his hands resting on the shoulders of two gangly boys who were part of a larger group of ten or so ranging in age from around six to midteens, as near as Cubiak could gauge. They crowded around a large, neatly hand-painted sign that read, "The Door County Forest Home for Orphaned and Needy Boys—Fresh Air, Clean Water, A New Start."

"Most people don't know it, but my father's generosity went well beyond the Packers. Not only did he start the camp, but he pretty much paid for it out of his own pocket."

I'd be one of those needy kids, Cubiak thought, staring at the photo and the somber, well-scrubbed boys with the haunted look of kids who knew what it was to be hungry. "A place like that takes a lot of money," he said.

54

"Which my father had plenty of. Got rich in logging, but he supplemented the budget during the summer by taking in sons of the wealthy. For four months of the year, the home was run like a summer camp with the full-time residents helping out as needed."

"Who runs it now?"

"Oh, the place is long gone, burned down about forty years ago."

"He didn't rebuild?"

Andrew shook his head. "Times had changed. By then there were more social services and opportunities for kids in need."

"Where was the camp, up around here somewhere?"

There was a sharp knock on the door and before Andrew had a chance to answer the sheriff's question, Gwen Harrison entered the room.

If Harrison was impressed by the plush surroundings, she didn't let on. The agent strode in with the confidence of one who owns whatever space she happens to be in at the moment. In one quick glance, she seemed to take in everything, and Cubiak wondered if, like he, she had the kind of mind that retained visual cues and images.

"Sheriff." She dipped her head at Cubiak, her manner aloof but not unfriendly. Then with hand outstretched she approached Sneider's son. "You must be Andrew."

"Indeed." He tossed the photo to the desk and sucked in his paunch. "And whom do I have the pleasure of addressing?" he said just as she flashed her ID. "Oh. I see."

Cubiak tried not to smile at the man's knee-jerk reaction to Agent Harrison. Were all men so transparent? Had he reacted similarly? he wondered, chagrined to realize that probably he had. At some basic biological level men were wired to stand tall and to puff out their chests in the presence of feminine beauty, no different than male butterflies or gnus.

"Nothing's been touched?" she said to the sheriff, echoing Moore as she looked around the room again, this time more deliberately.

"Just waiting for you," Cubiak replied.

Andrew scowled and sagged, forgetting or forsaking the urge to impress. "I have to show the feds my father's private files?"

"That's why Agent Harrison is here."

"Seems like an invasion of privacy."

Ignoring the men, Harrison walked to the windows and took out her phone. Then she started texting, a signal to Cubiak that she expected him to handle the uncooperative local. The sheriff looked at Andrew. "Your father is missing and may be the victim of a crime. His files and personal papers may contain clues that will help us get to the bottom of this."

Andrew frowned. "I doubt it."

"At any rate, you don't have a choice. In a situation like this your father's life is an open book where the authorities are concerned. Yours, too, for that matter. If you want to be helpful, which is to your benefit, I suggest you can start by giving Agent Harrison your father's appointment calendar and the keys to any locked drawers in this room."

ON THE BEACH

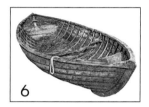

6

Road construction detoured Cubiak off Highway 42 and onto 57. The alternate route back ran near The Ridges, where Cate was shooting. It was still lunchtime and, hoping that they could have a quick bite together, Cubiak called to see if she'd eaten. She hadn't, and so he stopped in town for sandwiches. When he arrived, he found that Cate had walked to the small beach north of the village and that she'd brought Butch with her.

"The poor thing seemed restless. I think the kittens are stressing her a bit and I figured she could stand a break," Cate said as the dog scampered away. They ate sitting on a log that had come ashore in a recent storm and watched Butch trundle back and forth across the sand.

Cubiak reached for Cate's hand. "I'm glad you're back," he said.

She smiled. "Me, too."

"I missed you." Cubiak wanted to say more but Butch was barking, demanding attention. She'd wandered into the rolling mounds of soft dunes along the road and raced back toward them. Almost smiling, she bounded down the sand with a small branch in her mouth. When she reached Cubiak, she dropped the stick at his feet and waited patiently while he stripped off the leaves. He hurled the twig into the water, and the dog leapt into the waves. For several minutes the game went on.

Overhead, tiers of cloud pillows floated against a backdrop of brilliant blue.

"It's a Georgia O'Keeffe sky," Cate said as she looked across the bay. "You've seen the painting at the Art Institute."

Was it a question or a statement? Cubiak wasn't sure. He hadn't been to the Art Institute since he was a kid on a school field trip but was embarrassed to admit as much to Cate. True, he had seen pictures of the famous painting but he wasn't sure if that counted.

"I . . . ," he said and stopped. The beach was suddenly empty. The dog had disappeared. "Where's Butch?" he said.

"There," Cate said. She pointed to the far end of the sand where Butch had emerged from a patch of tall grass bearing another treasure.

The new stick was long and slender. As the dog ran toward them it shimmered pearly white in the sun. Delighted with her performance, Butch deposited the stick at their feet and sat panting.

"Good girl," Cubiak said.

He stroked the top of Butch's head as Cate bent over for a closer look.

"Oh, God," she said, pulling back. "I think it's a bone."

They were both silent a moment. Then Cate spoke again. "Do you think it's human?"

Cubiak went down on one knee and picked it up. "It might be," he said.

"How'd it get here?"

"Probably washed ashore from somewhere out there."

Wordlessly they looked toward the water. From the beach, the shoreline followed a spit of land that extended out toward the lake and then curled down into a long tail that ran parallel to the beach before it tapered off in a pile of rocks and scrub trees. The sheltered bay lay inside the curving sweep of terrain, but on the far side, the vast expanse of Lake Michigan stretched to the horizon.

"So many shipwrecks, and with the currents . . ." Cate's voice trailed off.

"It could be from anywhere," the sheriff said, completing her thought. Holding the bone seemed an oddly intimate act. Cubiak loosened his grip. The piece was solid and surprisingly heavy. It was narrower at one end and slightly bowed where it grew wider at the other end. The surface was gouged and pitted, worn by repeated contact with underwater rocks and stones on the beach. There were two nicks in the middle. Teeth marks, Cubiak thought as he touched them gently. They were too worn down to have been made by Butch and probably were the work of other dogs or carnivores on the prowl. "It's pretty worn, probably bleached by the sun, too," he said.

Cate knelt beside him. "In Paris there are a couple hundred miles of underground tunnels filled with millions of human bones."

Cubiak stared at her.

"In the 1800s, the cemeteries were poisoning the water supply and had to be emptied. At night processions of carts moved through the city, bringing the remains to the tunnels where the priests used them to build altars and shrines. It's eerie but also very beautiful."

"Sounds macabre."

"Their way of laughing at death."

Again they both looked down at the bone that lay across Cubiak's calloused palm.

"Maybe it's not human. Maybe it's from a large animal," he said, but he spoke without conviction.

"Should we bury it?"

"No." Cubiak stood, brushing sand from his knee. He didn't know why but the bone seemed important, not something to be ignored. If it was from an animal, he'd discard it later, but if it was from a human, it deserved to be treated with respect.

"I want you to photograph it here on the beach. I'll look around the dunes in case there's more. Then I'll take it to Emma Pardy to see what she has to say."

The medical examiner was at her desk, frowning at her computer monitor. Pardy wore her uniform of the day: jeans and a cotton sweater, the sleeves pushed up to her elbows. Her Harvard diploma shared the wall with her children's finger paintings and a family photo taken out west where there were mountains.

"What's going on?" she said when he walked in. "I was at the court this morning and there seemed to be an unusual amount of activity on your side of the building."

"Big case. A missing person," Cubiak said as he slipped into the visitor's chair Pardy pointed him to.

"Must be someone important."

"Gerald Sneider."

"Never heard of him."

"That's because you're not from around here," Cubiak responded. Then he ran through the highlights of Sneider's pedigree and a condensed version of the situation.

When he finished, Pardy gave him a quizzical look. "FBI? And how's that going?"

"So far, so good. They're smart."

"You aren't just being polite?"

Cubiak shrugged. "The feds have instant access to information it would take weeks for me to get my hands on, as well as other classified data that's off limits to me. They're also very high tech. Not exactly my style but I appreciate what it can do."

"But you're not here to tell me about the feds."

The sheriff put the towel-wrapped bundle on the medical examiner's desk. "Something my dog found on the beach near Baileys Harbor," he said as he undid the cloth.

Pardy's face hardened. She picked up the bone. "When?"

"Today, maybe an hour ago."

"You think it has something to do with the case?"

"No, but I couldn't leave it there, and I wanted you to have a look," he explained.

The physician studied the bone from a number of angles and then put it back down. "It's definitely human and one of the long bones that make up the limbs. This one, the radius," she said as she held up her arm and ran a finger along the inside from wrist to elbow. "The narrower end connects at the elbow and the wider end here at the wrist."

"Any way to determine gender?"

"Not really. Could be male or female. No way to know the exact age either, though I could make a reasonable guess."

Pardy carried the bone to the skeleton model suspended from a black metal frame in the corner. "This is an average adult male, and look how much longer and thicker the radius is than the one you found," she said, holding up the bone from the beach alongside the arm of the model. "Depending on how long it's been exposed to the elements, erosion could account for some shrinkage, but this doesn't look like it's from the skeleton of an adult, unless it's from a very slight man or a petite woman."

Cubiak winced. "You mean it could be from a child?"

The medical examiner nodded. "Sadly, yes, or perhaps an adolescent." Then she added, "But I hope not."

They avoided eye contact, Cubiak thinking of his daughter and suspecting that Pardy's thoughts had gone to her two children.

"You think it was washed ashore?" she said after a moment.

"Pretty likely, yeah."

"Do you spend much time on the water?"

"A bit." Two years earlier, Cubiak had helped Evelyn Bathard, the retired coroner, refit an old wooden sailboat. The project took months and when they finished, Bathard had taught the sheriff to sail in return for his efforts.

"It can get pretty rough out there," Pardy said.

"I know." Cubiak had never been caught in a storm but he'd heard harrowing stories from those who had. Nature's immense power was impossible to ignore when sailing, and he knew an angry sea wouldn't distinguish between gender or age. Cubiak found it difficult to imagine a child in that kind of danger, but of course it was possible. Children as well as adults were passengers on ships that went down. Before child labor laws were passed, countless young boys worked under harsh conditions aboard ships that regularly traversed the inland water system.

Children drowned, too. Swimming accidents in summer. Falling through thin ice in late fall and early spring.

Cubiak wondered how much of this the doctor was thinking as she set the bone back on her desk and slid into her chair. She was tall and sat erect, prompting Cubiak to straighten his shoulders.

"You ever been to a body farm?" she asked.

He shook his head.

"Very bizarre when you think about it, yet vital to helping researchers study the decomposition of human skeletons under various conditions. Most of the work focuses on bodies that are left to deteriorate in the open or those buried in different kinds of ground. But there's some work that's been done with bones in water."

Pardy rubbed the rough edge at the narrow end of the shaft. "Human bone is very durable but not impervious. Anything in the environment will affect it. In acidic water, the inorganic compounds, mostly calcium and phosphate salts, will leach out more quickly. Microflora, mineral content, and even the speed at which the water moves will affect the condition of submerged bones. A lot also depends on the rate of tissue deterioration, which is accelerated in water. Then there's the corrosive effect of abrasion against rocks and gravel and such, which we can pretty much see."

The medical examiner looked at Cubiak. "There are tests I can run to determine how long it's been in water but I won't be able to give you anything very exact, more like a range. And it will take time." She paused. "The FBI could do a better job faster."

"No doubt. But they won't be interested in this."

That afternoon, Gerald Sneider was the lead story on the TV news broadcast by the three Green Bay stations that served the region. Earlier the Green Bay Packers had announced that the team was offering a ten thousand dollar reward for information about the emeritus director, who, it was reported, had disappeared Sunday afternoon while driving from the game in Chicago to his home in Ellison Bay. In his office, Cubiak flipped through the channels. On one, a talking head breathlessly suggested that Sneider might have fallen ill along the way or become disoriented and gotten lost.

As a reporter related Sneider's life story and extolled the virtues of the missing man, the department phones started ringing. The sheriff went into the incident room and confronted Moore. "You know about the reward?" he asked.

"We approved it."

"I see," Cubiak said. So much for being kept in the loop, he thought. "Now the deluge starts. The media demanding answers, and calls from people claiming they know where he is."

Moore shrugged. "For now, it's 'no comment' to all media inquiries. As to the leads, we already heard from a man who claims he saw Sneider being lifted aboard an alien spaceship. But seriously, this could be helpful. Anything out of the area will be handled by our Green Bay office, but I'm depending on your team to follow up on all the local leads."

"Of course."

Later that evening, Cubiak sat in his kitchen and nursed a beer while he fed droplets of goat milk to the kittens. He'd hoped to have dinner with Cate, but she'd left a note saying she was working and would be home late. The sheriff heated a bowl of leftover stew in the microwave and forced down a couple of bites. After lunch on the beach with Cate, he didn't feel like eating alone. He gave the rest of the food to Butch and opened another beer for himself.

WORD GETS OUT

7

As he turned up the drive to the justice center, Cubiak swore under his breath. The multimillion-dollar complex occupied once vacant pastureland a couple miles from downtown Sturgeon Bay and was usually quiet this early. But that Tuesday morning, cars and SUVs littered the parking lot and three remote broadcasting trucks from Green Bay's TV stations were lined up along the curb, their roofs sporting a sophisticated array of satellite dishes and antennas. A throng of men and women swarmed the main entrance.

The center housed the sheriff's department, the jail, and the courthouse, and Cubiak figured the media mob was heading toward his side of the building. The news people were hot on the trail of the Sneider story.

Bypassing his reserved spot, the sheriff parked in the farthest corner of the lot and loped around the west end of the building, intending to sneak in through the side entrance. After yesterday's news, he figured a couple of reporters would show up looking for local color on Sneider, and he was fine with that. Cubiak generally got along well with individual reporters. He found them entertaining, hardworking, and founts of knowledge about obscure topics. It was reporters as media that made him uncomfortable.

The media wanted black and white, and he was usually mucking around in the gray. Media didn't like gray and grew impatient with him when that was what he insisted on providing.

On the Sneider situation, he didn't even have that much. He had nothing. As far as he knew, the feds had nothing either.

Cubiak's phone vibrated with a text from Moore: *Press conference 30 min.* The sheriff swore again. The FBI had pledged cooperation but it already looked as if the agents were holding out on him. What did they know that he didn't?

The sheriff pulled his tie and sports coat off the hanger on the back of the door and headed to the lobby.

Moore and Harrison were waiting. The two were dressed and polished to a hard shine, a match for the anchors who were buffed and suited up in equal measure. The rest of the media were mostly a motley crew—up since dawn, buzzed on caffeine, and dressed in tired jeans and flannel shirts. They spent their time off camera, waiting endlessly for news to break, and were determined to be comfortable on the job.

Cubiak glanced at the bank of microphones less than ten feet from Lisa's desk.

"A press conference?" he said quietly to the feds. "Nice if someone had given me a heads-up."

Harrison avoided eye contact.

Moore arched an eyebrow. "Sometimes these things just happen," he explained.

Cubiak straightened his tie and gestured toward the mics. "Your show, then," he said.

When Special Agent Quigley Moore stepped up to the front, every take-charge instinct he'd displayed expanded exponentially.

"I am here to give you an official statement concerning local philanthropist Gerald Sneider of Ellison Bay. Mr. Sneider was last seen at approximately 4 p.m. Sunday afternoon at Soldier Field in Chicago, when he left his skybox near the end of the game. He was unaccompanied and is presumed to be missing, which, as you all know, is why the Packers home office has issued a reward seeking information as to his whereabouts. At this time, this is all I can tell you."

Moore turned away from the microphones as if to leave.

"Has Gerald Sneider been kidnapped?" The question came from the back of the room.

Agent Moore spun around. "As I said already, we consider Mr. Sneider to be missing, nothing more."

"Do you suspect foul play?"

"No."

"Is there any chance Sneider merely wandered off? Is he suffering from dementia?"

"Mr. Sneider is reportedly in excellent health."

"Is it possible his disappearance is linked to the terrorist threats that have been made against the Packers and other NFL teams?"

"There is nothing to indicate a connection between the two."

Standing before the press mob, Moore performed like a man born to the task. Cubiak had to hand it to him, the guy was a natural. Smooth. Evasive. Just distant enough to avoid being overly familiar but not so aloof that he seemed unapproachable.

A husky cameramen slipped forward and knelt in front of the microphones. His powerful lens moved from Moore to Harrison, lingered on her, and then quickly skipped past Cubiak. Another hand shot into the air.

"Why is the FBI involved?"

Moore smiled. A photo op. "We just happened to be here as part of a routine field activity."

"Doing what?"

"It's routine. No comment beyond that at this time."

"You mean you're not looking for Sneider?" The reporter could not hide her skepticism.

"The Door County Sheriff's Department is gathering information on the possible whereabouts of Mr. Sneider. Since Agent Harrison and I are here, we're happy to assist in any way possible."

"If you're just helping out, why isn't the sheriff taking the questions?" The call came from across the room, and Cubiak recognized the voice of Justin St. James, a local reporter for the *Door County Herald*.

Moore either didn't hear the question or ignored it.

"Do you have any evidence of domestic terrorists in Door County?" This from came one of the Green Bay anchors.

"No."

"What about the rest of the state? Madison especially?"

"We are always on the alert for disenfranchised individuals."

The questions continued to pick up tempo. Had there been threats made against the shipyards? Was the coast guard tracking arms smugglers? Had officials discovered a cache of bombs on the peninsula?

No to each.

A dozen hands shot in the air.

Moore glanced at his watch. "Time's up, ladies and gentlemen. Thank you and good day."

Cameras clicked in a mad flurry, and then slowly the media circus spun to a close. There'd been plenty of B-roll shot but no news reported.

St. James waved, trying to get the sheriff's attention. The reporter was stuck across the room, blocked by the crowd of men and women heading for the door. Cubiak turned down the hall before the young journalist could get through. The sheriff knew that for the *Herald*, the mere presence of federal officials was news and that St. James, who too often had nothing more to report on than upcoming festivals and unexpected bridge closings, would want to make as much of it as he could.

Cubiak was hanging up his jacket when he heard the steady, harsh slap of Moore's wingtips march down the tiled hall and stop by his door. The agent was not smiling when he stepped inside and glared at the sheriff.

"The press must have gotten wind that we were here and figured that meant news. That's what they're all after, the big lead, the byline that will make their reputation. Now, how'd they find out the FBI was in Sturgeon Bay?" he said.

Cubiak wasn't smiling either. "No idea."

Moore inhaled sharply and pinched the bridge of his nose. Bags were starting to form under his eyes. There were jobs that aged a person, and Cubiak suspected that working for the FBI came with its own set of pressures. How quickly was Moore expected to produce results? the sheriff wondered. When they'd first met, Cubiak had assumed that the agent was in the hinterland working his way up, but maybe it was the other way around. Maybe Moore had messed up in one of the larger arenas and was on his way down. Botch this assignment and he'd find himself even lower on the food chain.

After a moment Moore held up a hand in apology. "Sorry, but it's always frustrating when this happens. Doesn't bode well for the investigation when you don't know whom to trust. But who else is there? The son doesn't have anything to gain by attracting the press."

"No, but the Packers do. Plenty of free publicity for the team, if nothing else. If I had to guess, I'd say the story was leaked by someone in their office and not here."

Uninvited, the agent took a seat. "Maybe. Sneider's going missing is a big enough story on its own to garner attention but toss us in and . . ." Moore threw up his hands. "At this point it doesn't matter, but if it happens again, we may have a real problem. For now, the media's not going anywhere soon, you can bet on that. They'll camp out and wait for something to happen."

Moore swallowed a yawn and came back all business. "So what have you got? Anything?"

"Our preliminary investigations haven't uncovered any ongoing problems or anything illegal or unusual in Sneider's past."

"Agent Harrison hasn't finished combing through his papers but she hasn't found anything remarkable yet either. So, so far a dead end.

But of course she's still looking, and she's checking into Andrew as well. Looking for possible bad debts, questionable business associates, a rift in the family fabric. All the usual."

Moore stared past Cubiak to the window and the pasture across the road. When Cubiak arrived that morning, there'd been a herd of Holsteins grazing on the grass. He wondered if they were still there.

"My family raised beef cattle, a bit different from dairy," Moore said.

"You, on a farm?" Cubiak said, unable to imagine Moore slinging a hay bale or mucking out a barn.

"Actually it was a ranch. I grew up in northern Wyoming and couldn't wait to get away. I thought life in the big city was the answer to every question I had. Now, I'm not so sure. What about you? This is a pretty tranquil environment you find yourself in. You like it?" Moore asked with a rueful smile.

"I do, though it's not always as tranquil as you think."

"Oh, yeah, I remember hearing about a string of murders. When was that, three or four years ago?"

"Four." The start of my career here, Cubiak thought.

"And you're the guy who nailed it."

Cubiak glanced out the window. The cows had moved on. Moore was waiting for him to say something about the investigation that had led to his election as sheriff. But it wasn't a case he wanted to think about.

"There's a pattern to life here that pretty much repeats day after day. But there are surprises as well. The unexpected is really as much a part of the norm as the usual. There's just not as much of it as in the city," he explained.

To illustrate his point Cubiak mentioned the bone Butch found on the beach. "Now that's not something I'd expect to come across, not here. It's probably human so I gave it to the medical examiner to see what she can come up with."

Moore got to his feet, suddenly impatient again. "I'm sure there's a sad story there, but it's nothing to do with us," he said. "You want something useful to do, follow up on this call that came in this morning." He held out a slip of paper. "Maybe it'll lead to something."

An hour later, Cubiak followed a rutted lane through a meadow of tall, dried grasses. The sun was warm on his shoulders as he walked toward the string of low buildings silhouetted against the cloudless sky. He was at the Hopewell Resort, following up on the anonymous phone tip Moore had given him from a caller who claimed he had seen Sneider wandering around the grounds.

"You know this place?" Cubiak had asked earlier, showing the note to Rowe.

"The old hopes-gone-sour resort? Sure, it's been deserted for years. Door County's version of a ghost town. I used to hang out there in high school and drink beer with my friends. You want me to go?"

"That's okay. I'm heading that way to see Sneider's cook and house-keeper. Easy enough for me to check it out," the sheriff said.

Halfway up the peninsula, Cubiak left highway 42 for the county road that ran along the bay shoreline. He passed a half-dozen houses and several plowed fields but little else. Cubiak was about to turn back and retrace his path when he saw a weather-beaten sign half hidden in the brush. The sign had been carefully painted by hand, but its luster was deeply faded and it stood forlorn and forgotten, a piece of the past that time had left to the insects that buzzed in the grass and the hawk that circled overhead.

Cubiak counted ten buildings in all. They were lined up as if in formation. From a distance they looked well tended, but as he got closer he saw that they were in various states of collapse. Doors hung off hinges. Windows were shattered. A roof caved in. The resort was in ruins, the victim of neglect, weather, mice, and drunk teenagers.

Everywhere he looked, Cubiak found evidence of former glory. Gigantic fireplaces, beamed ceilings, masonry walls of gleaming white fieldstone, and remnants of the kind of heavy oak table he associated with old European monasteries left to rot and decay or sit amid growing mounds of trash and beer cans.

There's no one here, he thought, and then he saw the man standing on the flagstone patio that overlooked Green Bay. The man wore corduroy pants and a forest green canvas jacket. He was stooped and gray and seemed consumed in his own world. Could Andrew have been wrong about his father? Was this Gerald Sneider, wandering around in some vestige of his past?

"Mr. Sneider?" Cubiak called out.

He had to repeat himself twice.

Finally the man turned around. "Excuse me?" he said, suddenly alarmed.

Whoever the man was, he was not Gerald Sneider. Cubiak held up his badge and identified himself.

The stranger relaxed. He was from Omaha, he told the sheriff. He'd stayed at the resort several years running when it first opened. Now he came back for nostalgia's sake whenever he was in Door County.

Cubiak showed him Sneider's photo and asked if he'd seen him.

"I don't really go anywhere except to walk around here, and there's never anyone else that I see. No one has any reason to come here anymore. Except the kids. It seems to have turned into a gathering spot for them," the man said sadly.

Cubiak took in the crumbling ruins. "What happened?"

"Eric Hopewell ran out of money. Anyway that's the story. He died without a will and his descendants have been fighting over the land ever since."

"I see. Same old story." There was a sadness to the air and a heaviness to the silence that made the sheriff feel like an interloper in the remnants of another's broken dreams. There was nothing for him here.

"I'll leave you then," he said to the man from Nebraska.

TWO LADIES

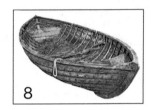

8

After stopping for gas in Ellison Bay, Cubiak turned right at the village's lone intersection and headed inland. Sneider lived on the water; his staff did not.

Eva Carlson, the cook, was the closest to town. Cubiak followed a zigzag path down several county roads to her brick ranch. The well-kept house was small and set back in a grove of trees that shimmered in a patchwork quilt of autumn colors. He rang the bell and waited several minutes before he heard noise from inside. Eva opened the wooden inside door leaning on a cane and clutching a heavy, moth-eaten, green sweater tight around a cotton housedress.

"Sheriff Cubiak?" she said, squinting into the bright morning from behind the glass storm door.

He held up his ID and was happy to see her inspect the badge before she undid the lock. Inside, he explained that he was checking into the whereabouts of Gerald Sneider, who'd not been seen since leaving the Sunday afternoon football game in Chicago.

"Well, he sure enough ain't here," Eva said, making a pretense of looking about her austere living room. Then she frowned. "Figured something was up when Andrew called and said not to come in for a few days. Thought maybe the old geezer croaked."

"I need to ask a few questions," Cubiak said.

"And I need to sit a spell." Dragging one foot behind the other, the pace painfully slow, Eva led the sheriff to the kitchen.

"I know what you're thinking: some cook. Right?" she said as she gingerly lowered herself into a chair and hooked the cane on the table.

Cubiak sat facing her. "It does look hard to get around."

Eva chortled. She had a long face and loose teeth that clicked when she talked. "Old man never ate much. Oh, he did once, when the wife was alive. Exotic food from around the world, I'm told." Her nostrils flared at the word *exotic*, and she pronounced it as if it represented something sinful. Perhaps to her it was, Cubiak thought, taking in the Early American samplers on the wall and the tchotchkes that lined the two windowsills.

"He had a real chef then," she went on. "Now it's just me and gruel."

"Gruel?"

"Chicken soup, too, once in a while. But mostly mush that he likes sprinkled with coconut flakes, almonds, and dried cherries. All organic." Again, a hint of disapproval in her voice.

"Was he ill?"

"Naw. He had some crazy idea that he'd live longer eating like this. His wife had been, how shall I say this, very plump. From what I hear, she'd order up fancy meals three times a day from the cook, and they'd eat in that big dining room with lit candles and all. After she died, Gerald fired the chef and hired me. Said he wanted simple food. There was fish, at first, and a lot of brown rice. Once in a while he'd ask for eggs for breakfast." Eva lifted her chin and flashed a pair of bright blue eyes at Cubiak. "Of course, I got around better then, too. Lucky for me I guess that by the time I had my stroke, he was down to gruel."

Cubiak gave a sympathetic nod. "What about when Andrew visited?" he said after a moment.

73

Eva huffed. "Andy never visited but when he needed money, and he never ate my cooking. Said he'd rather starve than eat that . . . well, you can imagine what he called it. When it came to food, he'd go out or maybe toss something in the microwave over at the guest house."

"He didn't stay in the main house?"

Eva reached for her cane. "Not that I ever seen. Cup of coffee, Sheriff?"

That was his cue to act: the coffee maker was on the counter by the stove, the green light on. Cubiak didn't want to think for how long the coffee had been steeping but knew it would be rude to refuse. "Thank you, I'll get it," he said, pushing to his feet.

Eva smiled. "Two sugars, please. And milk for me."

Cubiak took two cups from the drainer. They were stained but otherwise clean. The milk was just a day or so from curdling, and he was glad he took his black.

"There's cookies, too, up there." Eva pointed to the cabinet above the sink.

The sheriff took his time getting the snack to the table. She's stalling, he thought, wondering how much more to tell me.

"Did you cook for Gerald's guests?" he said when he sat back down.

Eva dunked a cookie. "Oh, there weren't any guests. He was in his office on the phone often enough talking business, but no one except Andrew ever came to the house. Gerald mostly just sat in that fancy media room, watching TV and videos of old games and talking about how important he was. That man was always telling me and Babbs, she's the housekeeper, all the grand things he'd done."

"Sounds pretty sad."

Eva tightened her mouth. "Would be if he wasn't so pompous. Lots of people in this world do good things, Sheriff, not just Gerald Sneider. But to hear him go on, he was God's gift to the Packers, to his poor wife and son, and to all the charities he ran."

Cubiak sat up. This was new. "What do you know about those, the charities?"

"Nothing, really. Before my time on the peninsula." Eva bit into another cookie. "Gerald was generous with his money when he wanted to be, I'll give him that, but I just got sick and tired of listening to him boasting about it all the time and didn't really pay much attention."

"Was he generous with his son?"

"Well now, Sheriff, you'd have to decide that for yourself. As far as I could tell, Andrew didn't ever do a day's lick of work but he always dressed nice and drove expensive cars. He lives in Green Bay and has one of those condominiums in Chicago, too. I've been with Gerald maybe fifteen years now, and when I first started his son didn't come around much, but the last couple of years he's up at least once a month. The talk is all behind closed doors but sometimes you can hear what's being said and seems to me it's always about Andy needing money."

Cubiak was at the door when he thought to ask Eva how she got to work every day.

"Oh, Babbs picks me up and we go together. She lives just up the road, you want to talk to her, too," Eva said, pointing further inland.

"I called and left a message but didn't hear back."

"That's Babbs," Eva said with a laugh. "But you just go on ahead, she's always home."

Babbs Shadowski was Eva minus twenty years. *Feisty* was the word that came to mind when Cubiak found her splitting firewood behind her double wide.

As soon as he displayed his badge she started to protest. "Now, look here, Marshal or Sheriff or whatever you are, they've got no right to be sending you after me."

"Who?"

"My goddamn nosy neighbors who claim it's illegal to heat a mobile home with a woodstove. Well, it ain't, and I've got proof." Babbs slammed the axe into a log and scooped her jacket off the pile.

"I'm not here about your stove. Gerald Sneider appears to be missing . . ."

"And I'm a suspect. You think I've done something nefarious to the old coot, don't you?" Babbs said. "Well, hot damn, then, sir, come right in."

For a housekeeper, Babbs kept her own surroundings in disarray: laundry piled on the couch, dirty dishes in the sink, yellowing plants on the floor and in the windows.

"Make yourself comfortable," she said, sweeping a stack of magazines off a chair for Cubiak. "Drink?"

"No, thanks. I'm on duty, but you go right ahead."

Babbs opened a beer and took a swig. "I'm not really a suspect, am I?" she said as she made space for herself at the tiny table.

"Well, since we don't know that anything's actually happened to him, no, not at all. But you sound disappointed. Why would you think you were?"

Babbs laughed. "No reason, just something to talk about," she replied and took another pull at her drink. "Rich man goes missing, there must be all kinds of theories."

"Besides being rich, what kind of man is Mister Sneider?"

Babbs hesitated. "Between you and me, after all, this is my boss we're talking about, an odd duck I'd have to say. On the one hand a loner and on the other a man who likes a little noise in the house and wants people about. That's why me and Eva—you know about Eva Carlson the cook?"—she waited until Cubiak nodded—"that's what we're there for. That's my theory, anyway. Eva cooks for a man who only eats mush, and I clean house for a man whose house never gets dirty because there's never anybody in it. Day after day, Gerald sits in that football room from morning until night, reliving the past. And there I am running around with the vacuum five days a week, and then sitting in the kitchen an hour or two a day talking with Eva. Making noise, like I said."

"His son visits."

Babbs made a disparaging sound. "If you want to call it that. You ask me, Andrew's just there for the money, but then who can blame him. It seems there's plenty of it, and no love lost between the two of them."

"They argue?"

"Not so much argue as not talk. Huge silences when the two of them are together." She drew her calloused hands apart, illustrating the enormous distance between father and son.

"You clean the bedrooms, too?"

Babbs's face clouded. "I do them twice a week, hate it up there. Just goes to show what you can do with money." The housekeeper glanced around her stingy quarters.

She's imagining what she could do with a little of Sneider's fortune, Cubiak thought.

"What about the locked room?"

Babbs raised both eyebrows. "Ah, the mysterious locked room. You know, in fifteen years, I've never so much as had a peek inside," she said.

Something in the way she spoke told Cubiak that she was telling the truth. No visitors other than Andrew, no known enemies or disputes with neighbors, occasional phone calls from business associates. The housekeeper confirmed what little information Cubiak had gleaned from the cook. Either both were telling the truth or both were involved in what to this point appeared to be a very amateurish attempt at kidnapping and had synchronized their stories.

"You're from around here?" Cubiak asked as he took his leave.

"Not originally. I was born and raised in Manitowoc. Came here for the job at Gerald Sneider's place."

Was it a coincidence that no one on Gerald Sneider's staff was from the area? His secretary had lived in Nashville before relocating to Green Bay thirty years ago. Both the cook and the housekeeper had been on the peninsula for less than two decades, a blink of an eye compared to the generations by which many long-term residents measured their heritage, as Cubiak knew all too well. The sheriff had lived in Door

County for four years but was still pegged as an interloper by the genuine old guard.

Cubiak doubted that Eva and Babbs were more qualified than most local women to do the work on the estate. So what did it matter that they had come from elsewhere to work on the estate? By the time they moved to Door County, Sneider was already an old man with few needs. By then, his wife had died, his son had grown and moved away, and he'd started to embrace a more solitary existence.

It was Sneider's early years that were writ large on the peninsula and that had become the stuff of both fact and rumor. If he hired Eva and Babbs because he wanted to be surrounded by people who knew little or nothing of this part of his past, the question was *why*?

TROUBLE AT THE ESTATE

9

Cubiak was hungry. At the bar and grill in Ellison Bay, he was contemplating the specials scrawled on the blackboard when Rowe texted him saying that Andrew's story about the stamp collector checked out. Just as Cubiak was about to place his lunch order, another message came through.

Com hurri. The muddled text was from Andrew. The sheriff called. No answer.

Heading out the door, he called the duty deputy. "What's going on?"

"Nothing. Why?"

"Where the hell are you?" Cubiak said.

"Gills Rock. Andrew wanted smoked fish."

"Jesus. Get down here now. He just texted me. Something's happened."

A few minutes after two, Cubiak pulled up to the estate gate. He nodded to the half-dozen reporters who swarmed the jeep but ignored the recorders they thrust at the closed window and the notepads in their outstretched hands. A newly hired security guard let the sheriff pass. He was taking the first curve when Andrew emerged from the trees.

Cubiak braked, and Andrew grabbed the door.

"I can't stay here," he said, hauling himself into the passenger seat. His face was ashen and slick with sweat.

"What happened?"

Andrew pointed down the drive. "There. You'll see," he said.

When they reached the mansion, Andrew jumped out and hurried toward the lawn. He wore the same baggy clothes he'd had on the day before, and the loose clothes flapped as he moved. When he reached the grass, he shifted his gait into something that was half between a hop and a skip. One foot planted on the lawn, then the other up and over to the side in a crazy zigzag pattern. Back and forth he went, head down as if he were trying to avoid stepping on something.

Bathed in full sunlight, the grounds took on a majestic air. In the distance, a lone sailboat tacked back and forth on the glistening bay. Was it Bathard out enjoying a last hurrah? the sheriff wondered.

By the time Cubiak caught up with him, Andrew had reached the deck along the edge of the cliff. Built-in benches framed three sides of the wooden platform; the fourth opened to a flight of stairs that ran down the face of the palisade. Andrew dropped to a bench and waved Cubiak toward the steps.

"Down there," he said, motioning with his head.

The steps led to a short dock. Three large letters had been painted on the pier in black: *SOS*. The international distress signal.

What the fuck? Cubiak thought. Gerald Sneider was the one in distress who needed to be rescued. He couldn't have left the message, could he? If the kidnappers had done it on his behalf, why take the chance of being seen so near the estate? Unless they were trying to force Andrew's hand. Or, maybe this was a prank, the workings of a sick mind or some lame-brained teenagers.

Cubiak started down the stairs. He was nearly to the bottom when he realized the reason for Andrew's panic.

The SOS hadn't been printed with paint. The letters were formed from snakes. Brown reptiles, the kind he knew as pine snakes. In all, there were six of the long, slender reptiles. Two for each letter. They'd been laid end to end and pinned to the wood with U-clamps.

Cubiak grabbed one of the oars that was leaning against the cliff and walked out on the deck. He tapped the pier but the snakes didn't react. He prodded one. Then another. The reptiles remained inert. They were dead.

Someone's gone to an awful lot of trouble but to what end? Cubiak wondered.

By the time the sheriff climbed back up, Andrew had retreated to the front steps of the mansion.

Cubiak sat beside him. "When did you see it?"

Andrew had his elbows on his knees. He stared at the ground. "Right before I texted you. I wanted some sun, so I went over to the deck to sit down."

"Where were you before that?"

"Inside, watching a movie."

"Did you hear anything? See anyone?"

Andrew shook his head.

"Why'd you send the deputy to the store?"

"I was hungry."

"He could have gone to the little shop in town. Why all the way to Gills Rock?"

"I had a taste for smoked whitefish," Andrew said. He spoke like a spoiled, petulant child who was used to getting his way.

"From now on, the deputy stays put unless I say otherwise. You got that?"

"Yeah." It was more a mumble than a word.

Andrew exhaled. "There's more," he said and heaved to his feet. "I don't know what made me look here," he continued as he headed toward the gazebo on the other side of the lawn.

Overhead two hawks rode the currents back and forth. Silent hunters in the sky.

The gazebo was built of the same brownstone as the house. The mansion was large enough to accommodate the bulk of the large stones, but the gazebo seemed overwhelmed, as if the great weight of the material was dragging it into the earth. When he reached the base of the entrance, Andrew hesitated and stepped off the path. Cubiak moved past him and climbed the three steps. The gazebo was empty except for a white wooden crate that sat in the middle beneath the vaulted ceiling. The box was covered with a large piece of cardboard with a note taped to it. *You know what this means*, it read.

Cubiak pushed the cardboard aside with his foot, revealing the wire screen that had been nailed over the top of the box. Inside, there were dozens more snakes. Cubiak felt his stomach clench. Like the hawks that rode the wind, signaling their menace by their mere presence, the heap of slithering snakes hinted at unseen danger. There were brown snakes and garters in the mix but others, too, that he didn't recognize. Unexpectedly, a snake tail emerged from the quivering morass and rattled. The sheriff jumped away. Jesus, no wonder Andrew is freaked, he thought. Cubiak could tolerate one or two snakes at a time and even the truncated alphabet on the dock didn't bother him, but there was something about this tangle of cold-blooded reptiles with their hooded eyes and sinuous movement that left him cold.

"God, I hate snakes. Give you the creeps, don't they," Andrew said, still standing at the base of the stairs.

If it were up to Cubiak, he'd shoot the snakes on the spot, but the feds needed to see the spectacle, and the crate had to be checked for prints.

"Probably harmless," the sheriff said, hoping Andrew hadn't seen him shudder.

Inside the guest house, Cubiak fixed a small pot of tea. Andrew was still so shaken, it took him three tries to get the cup to his mouth.

Cubiak waited for him to drink it half down. "You tell Moore about this?" he asked finally.

Andrew shook his head. "I know I have to, but not yet."

"Why not?"

"After talking to that woman agent yesterday, I know her boss as much suspects me as anyone," Andrew said, playing with the sugar bowl.

"Why would he do that?"

Andrew grimaced and gave a nervous laugh. "The usual, you know. Gambling debts. I'm pretty much a regular at the casinos in Green Bay and Milwaukee."

Cubiak knew the type. "A regular loser."

Andrew laughed again, but it was a sound of bitterness, not mirth. "Yeah, something like that, I guess. Anyway, I owe enough that I guess it wouldn't be hard for the feds to imagine me staging this to get the money. That woman Harrison kept giving me a look."

"You couldn't have borrowed against your inheritance or your allowance or just asked your father to help you out?"

Andrew colored. "I've already used up those options."

"And you're here?"

"Huh? Yeah, I'm here, so what?"

"You have easy access to the dock."

Andrew sniggered. "Not with your deputy around. He's like my shadow. I get up in the middle of the night to pee and he's standing in the hall waiting for me to flush."

"You got rid of him today."

"First time, and it wasn't easy," Andrew said. He tossed down the dregs of the cold tea and looked at Cubiak. "Here's what I'd like to know: How the hell did those fuckers do it without being seen?"

They'd row up quietly just before dawn, Cubiak thought. "What about the note?"

Andrew groaned. "The note! They want more money! That's got to be it, right?"

"Not necessarily. The note says, 'You know what this means.'"

"Yeah, it means they want more money." Andrew glared at the sheriff as if he were a simpleton.

To Cubiak, the scrim of arrogant sarcasm was an intentional distraction. He's hiding something, the sheriff thought.

"Well, that could be," he said, playing along. "On the other hand, there may be more to it than that, don't you think?"

Under the sheriff's gaze, Andrew shifted and blinked. "Naw," he said.

He's lying, Cubiak thought as he watched Andrew push back his chair and then cross the room to the small white TV on the counter. It was four and the Sneider story was on every channel, even CNN. Each report was accompanied by the same scene: B-roll of the heavy black gate at the entrance to the estate while one or another of the look-alike anchors breathlessly talked into a mic, updating the story of the missing businessman and implying that sinister forces might be responsible. Each report featured a litany of Sneider's credentials, including his link to the venerated Green Bay Packers. Andrew was invariably mentioned as an afterthought, as was the sheriff. This was a story about a self-made midwestern legend, the FBI, and speculation about a possible kidnapping by homegrown terrorists.

Cubiak waited for the deputy to return, and then he left. Heading south, he called Moore and told him about the snakes and the note. "Andrew claims not to know what it means. He thinks you suspect him because of his gambling debts," the sheriff said.

"We consider all possibilities."

There was an uncomfortable silence before the federal agent went on. "What do you think?" It was the first time Moore had asked for Cubiak's input.

"I consider all possibilities as well," the sheriff replied.

A door opened and someone started talking to Moore. "Later," the agent said into the phone and hung up.

THE NATURE OF EVIL

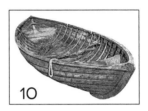

10

Late afternoon shadows fell across the landing outside Bathard's back door where Cubiak stood listening to the quick clip-clop of footsteps advancing along the inside hallway. From the sound, he knew that Sonja was coming to greet him. At home, Bathard favored soft-soled slippers, but Sonja wore Swedish clogs. "Good for your posture. You should try them," she'd said more than once. The thought of maneuvering around in wooden shoes always amused Cubiak, so he was looking cheerful when the door opened to a wave of warm air and the aroma of fresh baked bread.

"Ah, David, just in time for supper," Sonja said. Her face was flushed, her grayish-blonde hair brushed back, and her hands dusted with flour.

Cubiak colored as he straightened his shoulders. In the two years since Bathard had married the widowed schoolteacher, the sheriff had enjoyed many meals with them. Had he unconsciously timed his visit to coincide with dinner? He started to protest but she leaned forward and bussed his cheek. "You'll join us, of course. I'll set an extra place."

Sonja took Cubiak's jacket and laid her hand on his wrist, the fingers starting to crook with age. "I'm glad you stopped by," she said. "You're good for Evelyn. When summer's over, he gets restless but you keep him sharp. He's in the library now, with his books." She smiled knowingly and left the sheriff to make his own way.

Cubiak knew several Door County residents who boasted of larger personal libraries, but he was sure that unlike the other bibliophiles, the retired coroner had read everything on his shelves, probably more than once. The sheriff found his friend in his favorite high-back chair, his feet on an upholstered ottoman and an oversized, illustrated book in his lap. He seemed to be dozing. But as Cubiak settled into the facing chair, Bathard opened his eyes. "*Paradise Lost.* Ever read it?" he asked, lifting the heavy tome an inch or two.

"I tried."

Bathard laughed. "With the aid of Cliff's Notes, no doubt. You really should delve into it, and now may be as good a time as ever. There's a lot to learn here, applicable even in our day." He shifted the book onto a side table. "Something about recent events made me start thinking about people and the nature of evil."

"So, you've heard?" Cubiak asked.

Bathard harrumphed. "Everyone's heard. A nip of sherry, perhaps?"

Cubiak raised his hand, the index finger close to the thumb. "Hopefully we still know more than the general public."

Bathard handed him a small drink and arched an eyebrow, a gesture that Cubiak had learned to interpret as a question.

"Official word is still that Sneider is missing. No confirmation yet that he's been kidnapped despite something that appears to be a ransom demand and a possible terrorist connection."

"Really? In Wisconsin?"

"That's what brought the FBI here, though they won't admit it publicly."

"I know that there've been threats against the Packers and other teams but thought that was just hyperbole to keep funding up for Homeland Security," the coroner said.

"The feds think there could be a connection with a Madison group trying to ingratiate itself with one of the international organizations."

"Sad to say but in today's world, this could be reality." Bathard looked at the sheriff. "But you don't sound convinced."

"Not entirely. I've never had to deal with a kidnapping case but there's something about this situation that feels wrong to me." After a sip of sherry, Cubiak told Bathard about the snakes and the second note.

"I can see why Andrew was upset. Although it may well be that the note is more telling than the drama with the reptiles."

"Right, but considering the effort and time it took to set up the scene on the dock, I don't think it sounds like something that terrorists, domestic or otherwise, would bother with."

"And the ransom demand?"

"Moore says it's not out of line."

"You trust what he says?"

Cubiak shrugged. "I have no reason not to." Despite the overly polished shoes, he thought.

Bathard pushed aside the ottoman. "What else? I can tell from your tone that something's bothering you."

Cubiak showed the coroner the photo of the bone that Butch found on the beach the previous day. "Why there? Why now?" he asked.

"Coincidence?"

"I don't like coincidences."

Bathard smiled. "Neither do I, but they happen." He looked at the photo again. "There's no question, it's an old bone. One that could have washed up years ago and been buried on the beach until Butch dug it up. I've heard similar stories before. In fact, a few years ago, a parent chaperoning a school field trip to The Ridges came across a fragment of a patella not far from where you found this. She brought it to me and I passed it along to the authorities, but nothing ever came of it. I presume you gave this one to Emma?"

"She confirms that it's human. Based on the size, she thinks it's from a woman or a very small man—perhaps a young teenager, even. Maybe someone who drowned in a shipwreck. There's nothing to connect it to the Sneider case, but I can't shake the feeling that it's important."

"Emma's right. There have been numerous vessels that have gone down in these waters. I don't know of any in that area that involved loss of life, but given the way the lake shifts, an object could travel a considerable distance before washing up on shore." He was quiet a moment. Then he continued, "The historic collection at the library has several boxes filled with old documents and clippings, probably some of which haven't been looked at in decades, if ever. I can check into things the next time I'm on duty there."

This time Cubiak raised an eyebrow.

Bathard chuckled. "I started volunteering two days a week as a way to keep myself occupied and out of the house. It was Sonja's idea."

When they'd finished the dinner of roasted chicken and lentil soup, Bathard walked the sheriff out. In the cool, dark evening, the men were drawn across the yard to the boat barn where they'd worked together on the *Parlando.* The boat was still in Egg Harbor where it had been moored all season, but when they walked in the old barn Cubiak still half expected to find the vessel looming overhead in its wooden cradle.

"What now?" he said, looking up into the empty space.

"I'll dry-dock it here for the winter, again. That will give me the opportunity to clean the hull and make any necessary repairs."

"More work?"

"Endless. You know the old saying: the two happiest days in a sailor's life are when he buys a boat and when he sells it."

Cubiak laughed but as he slowly moved along the barn wall full of myriad tools and equipment, he grew thoughtful. "The day Sneider went missing, I found a note laying on a table in his house, and above it a Super Bowl ring hanging from a piece of white rope. The rope had a blue stripe in it, like this." The sheriff fingered one of the nautical lines looped overhead. "At the time, I thought it was ordinary rope but maybe it was a piece of boat line."

"Well, that's not going to help narrow things much. There's probably a hundred miles of rope or line like that around, used for one thing or another," Bathard said.

They were back outside and near the jeep when Cubiak remembered the coroner's earlier comments about the nature of evil. "You never told me what Milton had to say about it."

"Ah, Milton. For one, the great bard considered evil as something very real. We tend to dismiss the notion that malevolency is an actual force in the world, but Milton saw things quite differently. In his view, God represents good and Satan represents sin. And just as goodness or virtue exists as a tangible entity, so too, does its opposite."

"And you, do you agree?"

Bathard looked up to where moonlit clouds skittered above the trees. "I've lived long enough to appreciate that the world is a place of balance and contrasts. If there's one, why not the other? Certainly, if evil exists, it's a lot like nautical lines in Door County. Plenty of it around."

The parking lot behind the Rusty Scupper was full that evening when Cubiak drove into Sturgeon Bay. A late cocktail hour, he thought. Of course at the vintage tavern, which was a favorite with local shipyard workers, a cocktail ran more to a shot and a beer, or in winter, a glass of blackberry brandy, than to any concoction that was shaken or stirred. Whatever primed the pump, gossip ran freely when drinks were involved. "Everyone knows," Bathard had said earlier in reference to the Sneider case, and Cubiak wondered both what the tavern patrons knew and what they thought they knew about the missing man.

When Cubiak walked in, the group of regulars hunkered near the door turned as one, but seeing who it was—nobody new and therefore nobody requiring closer scrutiny—they refocused on their drinks. Drifting past, the sheriff caught snatches of their conversation. The men were talking about work, not Sneider, happy about the overtime they'd been putting in refurbishing a luxury yacht and worried about shortened shifts when the boat left the hangar the next day and the building went dark.

A second cluster of people was gathered midway down the bar. There were six altogether. The four men and two women were dressed in a casual but decidedly upscale urban style that included designer jeans and, depending on gender, either well-cut sports coats or clingy sweaters. Cubiak recognized them as the reporters who'd been at the station that morning. They'd littered the bar with cash and were leaning over their glasses of draft beers and wine with that loose manner of people who'd been imbibing since lunch.

Hank the loquacious bartender was regaling them with one of his theories. He had several: one about the lost island of Moo, which he claimed predated Atlantis; another about black matter being the source of disease; and, Hank's favorite, the reason brandy was the unofficial drink of Wisconsin. Something about European heritage and the liquor being easy and cheap to produce from just about any fruit or vegetable—including plums and potatoes. Cubiak had heard that particular spiel before.

The sheriff wanted to ask the media crowd how they'd learned the FBI was in Door County but he knew they'd clam up if he approached them as a whole. His best chance of getting inside information was to talk to Justin St. James, who wasn't there tonight.

Cubiak was turning away when the surly face of Leeland Ross came into focus farther down the bar.

Leeland was thumping a thick index finger against the shiny wood surface and carrying on a one-way, spitfire conversation with a man in a houndstooth sports coat, not Leeland's usual style of companion. The stranger had his back to the door and one arm bent at the elbow, giving Cubiak a good look at his elbow patches. The sheriff was sure he'd seen the coat before. Curious, he stepped around the media posse and waved a couple of singles at Hank, signaling a call for a beer. The bartender served him without breaking his raconteur stride, making it difficult for the sheriff to catch more than a growling hiss from Leeland's animated discourse and leaving him no choice but to make a clumsy turn that brought his arm in contact with the hunched shoulders of the man in the black-and-white jacket.

"Sorry," the sheriff said as the man spun toward him.

"No problem." The man had long straight black hair and a wan complexion, like someone sprung from a sunless world.

Cubiak recognized him from the press conference as well. "You're a reporter, aren't you?" he asked.

"Fucking *New York Times*," Leeland said.

His companion shot him a look.

"Well, pardon me," Leeland said as he started twirling one of the half-dozen bottles they had emptied.

"Searching for a little local color for your story?" Cubiak said.

The stranger hesitated, then gave an aha smile and extended his hand. "Not hardly. I grew up here. Name's Steve Ross, Leeland's cousin."

Leeland smirked. "Kissing cousins, even. Uncle Freddie was Stevie's daddy."

"My sympathies on your father's passing."

Steve nodded.

"You've been here for a while then, since the funeral last week," Cubiak said.

"I was scheduled to leave the morning the Sneider story broke. This is not my usual beat, but since I was already here my editor asked me to stick around and see what I could come up with."

"But there's been nothing in the *Times*. I've been reading it online," Cubiak added by way of explanation.

Steve made a what-can-you-say gesture. "The editors want something longer, more in depth."

"They're willing to wait and see how this plays out?"

"Something like that."

Suddenly, Leeland shoved the empties aside and slid from the stool.

"I'm outta here. You coming?" he said, striding past the sheriff and calling over his shoulder to his cousin.

And like that they were gone, but Cubiak barely noticed their absence because when Leeland vacated his spot at the bar, the view to the back of the room opened and the sheriff saw Cate sitting at a corner table. Cate, who disliked noisy places, especially noisy bars, was in an intimate conversation with a man Cubiak didn't recognize. More media? he wondered. A photographer, perhaps. Maybe one of her colleagues. Whoever he was, he had chiseled good looks and the body of someone who worked out hard and regularly.

Cate was the kind of woman men paid attention to. Traveling the world as she did on assignment, Cubiak knew there were advances made and suggestions dropped, but he succeeded in not thinking about any of these when she was gone. He preferred to picture her working on the assigned shoot. He thought he'd finally weaned himself from jealousy and couldn't understand the tug of suspicion he felt seeing her now with this man.

Cubiak was several feet away when the man with Cate reached for her hand. She let him take it, just as she had let Cubiak take her hand the day before at The Ridges. Sitting on the beach with her, Cubiak had sensed a strong bond between them. Now he felt betrayed.

He watched as the stranger leaned toward Cate, his head close to hers. The man said something. She shuddered. Cubiak knew he should turn and walk away, but his anger propelled him forward.

As he approached the table, Cate looked up. Her eyes were red. Her cheeks wet. She pulled her hands free and swiped both across her face.

"Dave."

"Anything wrong?" He looked at her, ignoring her companion.

Cate shook her head. "Dave, this is Garth Nickels." She hesitated. "My ex-husband. He's with *USA Today*."

Another of the bothersome reporters. Cate had once called Nickels an opportunist and said he'd only married her for her money, but she'd also said that her ex had published two books and written a script that had been optioned for a TV movie.

Nickels set cold blue eyes on the sheriff and made no move to stand or offer a hand. He was a man full of himself. For his part, Cubiak wanted to slug the itinerant journalist—payback for whatever he had said that day to hurt Cate and for all the past injuries and slights he'd flung at her.

The men exchanged indifferent nods.

"Everything okay?" Cubiak asked, mentally kicking himself for the inanity of the question.

"We're good," Cate replied.

She smiled but she did not ask Cubiak to join them, and during that split second of waiting for an invitation that he knew would not be forthcoming, the sheriff felt a bitter wave of resentment toward the two of them. Cate and her former husband shared a history that did not include him, and the sense of his exclusion made him feel even more isolated and separate than the badge and gun. He mumbled something about needing to get back and clumsily retreated. At the bar, Hank had moved on to another of his theories, and the reporters were sucking down another round of drinks, but Cubiak moved past in a blur, paying as little attention to them as they did to him.

On the way home, Cubiak stopped and bought a fifth of vodka. He hadn't intended to replace the bottle he'd finished earlier that week, but he rationalized that it was okay this one time, that it was just a little something to help him keep his mind off Cate.

Alone in his kitchen, he sat and drank. He tried to stay focused on the Sneider case but kept detouring to Cate. After she'd returned to Door County they'd spent months dancing around each other. At first just friends, then occasional lovers. Gradually, bits and pieces of her wardrobe started showing up in his closet. Initially, he'd been unsettled and unsure of how much commitment he was prepared to make. By the time she had claimed her own shelf and half the hangers, he'd grown comfortable with the idea of spending more and more time together. For the past eight months, Cate had basically been living with him, absent only when she was on assignment or the few times she'd stayed at her condo working against deadline. Now here she was cozying up to her ex-husband, who'd ridden into town chasing the Sneider story. Had she been with him the night before as well? Is that why she hadn't come home?

Home. Half in his cups, Cubiak said the word out loud. "Home. Who am I kidding?" he asked Butch, who lay on the floor, her head on her paws and her worried eyes fixed on him. Cate would never want a permanent home with him. She was cut from a different cloth. She deserved better. Not Nickels, either. Someone better than both of them.

It was past midnight when the phone rang and Cate's cell number popped up on caller ID. Cubiak stared at his mobile and then pushed away from the table. Hurt and angry and shamed by what he knew would be his slurred voice, he stumbled into the cold, still yard. The crunch of his boots on the gravel muffled the ringing phone. Cubiak walked to the rocky shore and looked up at the bright night sky, waiting for the house to fall silent again.

BLACK DOTS

11

Cubiak crawled up from the dark depths into the bright light of Wednesday morning. Everything hurt. His eyes, his stomach, his mouth, his head. Mostly his head. He thought he'd transcended the wretched ordeal of the hangover, had vowed he'd never endure such misery again, not since the last time, which really had been a long time ago. Flat on his back, he gingerly pushed away the covers and stretched his hand to the other side of the bed, conflicted by the cool emptiness beneath his fingertips. Cate had not come back. On the one hand, the realization saddened him. But she had not seen him like this, and for that small gift he was grateful.

He should have called her last night. He should have asked why she'd been crying. He groped the nightstand and pulled the phone onto the mattress. Maybe it wasn't too late. He dialed three digits of her number and hung up, defeated. Cate had spent the night with the bastard ex-husband, Cubiak was sure of that.

"Fine," he said. If that was the kind of miserable man she wanted to waste her time on, she was welcome to him.

Sitting up, Cubiak caught his blurred image in the dresser mirror. No prize here, either, he thought. Butch hovered in the doorway. Uncertain. Deferential. Confused. Put off by the stink of liquor or tired of trying to rouse him? He called the dog in and rubbed her head. Then he plodded to the bathroom and rinsed his mouth. Hungry for the taste of coffee, he made his way to the kitchen, stripping off his clothes and dropping them on the floor as he went. Too disoriented the night before even to undress himself. Or to toss the empties into the trash. Had he really drunk all that beer along with half the vodka? This was not the man he wanted to be.

Ignoring the mess, he filled the coffee maker and fed the kittens. Bolstered by caffeine he called Lisa and made his excuses for coming in late. "They're all in with Agent Moore," she said. He cringed. Well, what did he expect? Rather than embarrass himself by showing up in the middle of the session, he went for a jog instead. It would clear his head and loosen his stiff joints.

Thirty minutes later a much revived Cubiak was dropping empties into a black plastic trash bag when Emma Pardy knocked on the back door.

"Rough night?" she said, walking into the kitchen.

He grunted and tossed the bag into the corner.

"Fresh scones," she said, pulling a small white bakery box from the oversized canvas tote draped over her shoulder. "And the latest news," she added, dumping a half-dozen newspapers on the table. "I haven't had my morning caffeine yet. Do you mind?" she said, indicating the coffee pot.

Cubiak shook his head. He'd already sat down and started flipping through the papers. The Sneider case was front-page headline news in the Green Bay, Milwaukee, and Madison papers. Nickels's piece was in *USA Today*, but only in the sports section, not news, Cubiak noted with small satisfaction. Again, there was nothing in the *New York Times*. Cubiak scoured the paper twice to make sure he hadn't missed anything. Even with Steve Ross working on an in-depth report, the sheriff thought it odd that the paper didn't bother with a mention of the case.

A frosted cherry pastry appeared on a plate before him. Beside it, a mug of fresh coffee. Whether it was because of the fresh air or the morning exercise, he was suddenly hungry. "Thanks."

"I've got more for you on that bone, too," Pardy said as she slipped into a chair opposite the sheriff. She laid a red folder on the table and from it pulled a single sheet of paper. "Not much, sorry. But I can tell you that as we both suspected it's not recent. Looks like it's been submerged for years, decades even."

Cubiak skimmed the report and when he looked up, Emma was cuddling one of the kittens.

"Has Cate claimed one yet?"

"No." His answer was harsh.

"Oh." She seemed surprised. "Can I have one when they're ready?"

"You can have them all."

Pardy tucked the kitten back into the nest. "You know, Dave, it seems you have plenty on your plate at the moment. And my daughter's Brownie troop is having an adopt-a-pet campaign. I can take the whole litter with me and then the girls will help find good homes for them. If it's okay with you, that is."

"Really? You'd do that?"

Pardy laughed. "Why not? We already have a house full of animals — gerbils, fish, two dogs, even pet rats. What's a few more kittens temporarily added to the mix?"

Something about the carefree manner in which the medical examiner spoke of children and pets threatened to open a door Cubiak didn't want to go near. "Sure. That would be fine. Good to be rid of them."

Pardy was about to say something when the phone rang.

"Chief." It was Rowe shouting over the sound of a man yelling in the background. "Quiet," the deputy trumpeted. Then back into the phone, he said, "Chief, are you at your computer?"

Cubiak pulled his laptop off the counter. "I am now."

"Look at your e-mail. You gotta see this."

Cubiak logged into his e-mail. Rowe had sent a video attachment. The sheriff stared at the screen.

"Holy Jesus," he said, motioning Pardy over.

On the monitor, a naked Gerald Sneider knelt on a bed of white pebbles, hands tied behind his back. The captive's face was ruddy and wet with tears, and his terror-filled eyes were trained on the camera as he pled with his tormenters: "No, no, please." Again and again he begged, voice cracking and choking. A sign reading $4 Million hung from his neck.

Sneider was a big man, with the flab of age evident in his arms and chest. His flaccid skin, pale like the stones on the floor, was speckled with black dots.

Pardy gripped Cubiak's shoulder. "Dave, the dots are moving."

"Enlarge it," Rowe said.

Cubiak hit a button and the image of Sneider blew up across the screen. Pardy gasped and sank into the chair alongside the sheriff.

"You see?" Rowe said.

The specks of deranged confetti sprinkled on Sneider's bare skin were spiders.

"Yes, I see," Cubiak replied.

In Ellison Bay, the deputy was still battling to be heard. "You better get up here," he said, his voice hoarse. "Andrew is going out of his head."

There were more reporters outside the estate this time. The sheriff flashed a phony smile but he didn't slow down as he steered toward the gate. Inside, Rowe waited in front of Andrew's bungalow.

"How is he?" Cubiak said.

"I've got him calmed down a bit, but he's still in a state."

"Tell me how this all came about."

"We were in the kitchen having coffee and talking football when Andrew's cell rang. I tried to answer but he got to it first. The call only lasted a second or two. After he hung up, he ran to his laptop. 'What was it?' I asked him but he didn't answer. 'It's here,' he said and opened his e-mail. We both saw the video at the same time. Andrew went white and spit up his coffee. I thought he was going to pass out or have a heart attack. I tried to get the laptop from him but he kept shoving me away."

"Where is he now?"

"He's still in there, probably still watching it. He won't stop," Rowe said, motioning toward the door.

Cubiak hadn't been in the guest cottage before. It was really a house, larger and better furnished than his—Crate and Barrel versus vintage—and more of a mess than the sheriff would have imagined possible after only two days.

"I tried to clean up," Rowe said as they waded through the discarded papers and food wrappers that covered the floor.

"Don't bother. It's his problem," Cubiak said.

Andrew Sneider sat at the island, facing the doorway. His chin was covered with gristle, his hair a greasy mop on his head, and his eyes red and sunken. Food stains dribbled down the front of his sweatshirt.

"Andrew?" Cubiak said.

Andrew stared at the monitor. Had he even heard the sheriff?

Cubiak stepped up and pulled the laptop away.

"No!" Andrew lunged for the computer.

Cubiak snapped the lid shut. "We'll look at it later if we need to. For now we have to talk."

Andrew glared at him. "They're killing him," he said and wiped a line of spittle from his jaw.

"Your father is obviously distressed. But he doesn't appear to be in danger of dying."

Andrew jumped to his feet and leaned over the marble counter. "They're killing him! Can't you see?"

The sheriff sat on a stool, hoping Andrew would follow his lead. "Why don't you tell me what this is all about."

Andrew stalked to the window and faced the glass for several minutes. Finally, he turned back into the room, straightened his shoulders, and breathed noisily, the air rattling to the surface as if it had been trapped deep inside. When he was firmly in control again, he spoke. "As much as it is possible to be terrified of something, my father is terrified of spiders. Even one in a room is enough to force him out the door. Two or three and he goes into a panic. This . . ."—Andrew motioned toward the counter where the laptop sat like a compact bomb—"this is enough to kill him."

"They won't let it go that far. Whoever snatched your father wants him alive," Cubiak said.

"You believe that?"

"Yes."

At the sink, Andrew guzzled a glass of water. His cheeks had gained some of their normal color and his breath had quieted. "The damn thing is, my father can face down just about anything. Spiders are his only phobia."

Andrew dropped onto the seat opposite Cubiak. "I told you how he believed in individual will power. All the business with my mother, how he thought she could heal herself if she was just strong enough, and if she couldn't, then he'd do it for her. That's all I heard growing up. You can do whatever you will yourself to do. He used the same logic to overcome fear. He always preached to me about how we had to face our fears. And he tried, too, I'll give him that. Sometimes at home, he'd make me catch spiders for him, the bigger the better. He kept them in jars and then would take them out one by one and let them crawl over his hand. He'd sit there, sweating like a pig, and watch. Made me and my mother watch with him. We both hated it but he insisted. 'This is how you get strong, son. You face up to the things that make you afraid.' He really believed that."

Andrew glanced at the laptop. "But this. This is different."

"Did your father hate snakes as well?"

"What do you mean?" Andrew got up so quickly, he knocked the stool into the wall.

"The message that came yesterday: 'You know what this is about.'"

Andrew looked away. "I told you, that was about money. Besides, snakes don't bother my father a bit."

"What about you?"

"What do you mean?"

"Are you afraid of snakes?"

Andrew hesitated. "Not any more than most."

Cubiak wasn't so sure about that.

The sheriff went outside and called Moore, but the agent didn't pick up. Same for Harrison. Cubiak phoned the station and Lisa answered.

"You shouldn't be there," he said.

"I'm fine."

The feds had all left, she told him. Moore, Harrison, and the rest of the entourage.

"If they get back before I do, tell them I called. Then go home," he said and hung up.

Cubiak inspected the gazebo and the dock but they were both empty, all trace of the snakes erased. From the deck he watched a freighter glide down the shipping lanes. It rode low in the water, probably carrying crates of rivets and sheets of iron and metal to the shipyards. He was about to walk back to the house when he noticed a spider spinning a web under the railing. First snakes and then spiders. What was going on?

When the relief deputy arrived, Cubiak and Rowe left. Southbound traffic was still being detoured. Coming into Baileys Harbor, Cubiak once again found himself making the turn toward the beach at the north edge of town.

The sheriff was unsure why that stretch of sand beckoned him back. Even if he found more human bones in the dunes, what did that prove? Was he acting out of petty spite? Resentful of Moore muscling in on the headline-grabbing Gerald Sneider case and looking to attract a little attention by shedding light on a local mystery that nobody cared about?

Rowe had followed his boss. As they walked the shore, Cubiak told him about the bone Butch had found.

"I checked around but didn't find anything," he said.

"We're here now, so we may as well take another look. I'll start up there," Rowe said. He pointed toward a cluster of spindly trees and took off before Cubiak could say anything.

Within twenty minutes, Rowe came back carrying two additional bones. They were considerably smaller than the one Butch had first uncovered but the deputy had found them in the same general area.

Cubiak looked out to the water. The cove and lake beyond were calm but the winds had been up the day before, blowing from the east.

"You ever do any diving around here?" the sheriff asked.

"Some. There are a couple of old wrecks there in the lake, but the water around here isn't always clear. Still, if you want me to take another shot at it, I'm game. And I've got a friend who dives. He'd be willing to go down with me."

"It's not too cold?"

"Not yet. And it's only going to get colder."

"Let me think about it some more," Cubiak said.

Emma Pardy was on the phone when Cubiak arrived. "Yes, yes, good. Love you, too," she said into the receiver. "Kids! Another party! Oh, Lordy." Her easy smile vanished when he laid the two bones on her desk.

Pardy studied them carefully before she spoke. "These are metatarsal, two of the long bones in the foot. You're going to tell me you found them in the same spot as the first, aren't you?"

He nodded. "Any chance they're from the same victim?"

"Could be, but it's hard to know for sure. DNA testing might tell us, but size and circumstances of recovery both indicate a possible match."

From outside a bell clanged and Pardy swiveled her chair toward the small window at the far end of the room. Her office faced the old bascule bridge and together they watched as the twin spans of the structure were raised and two sailboats motored through.

"They're probably heading to dry dock. It's that time of year again," she said.

On the other side of the harbor, three large tankers and a gaudy, golden yacht were moored to the shipyard docks. The tankers were the first of the big ships coming in for seasonal repairs. But Cubiak didn't remember seeing the yacht before and figured it was probably the one he'd overheard the shipyard workers talking about the previous evening.

When the double leafs of the steel bridge dropped back into place, Pardy looked at the bones again. "If a ship did go down it seems unlikely there was only one person aboard, doesn't it?"

"So there might be more remains out there somewhere."

"Oh, I'm sure you can count on that, Dave. So much water surrounding us. We sail on it, swim in it, ship lumber and Christmas trees over it, but can only guess at the horrors that lie at the bottom under the waves."

By midafternoon every available surface in the conference room was lined with FBI phones and computers or covered with files and stacks of reports, and the whole lot was interposed with empty coffee cups.

On the incident board, Gerald Sneider's photo formed the center of a web of red, green, and blue lines that radiated out like spokes and led to circles and squares of scribbled codes and blurred photos of unidentified men that Cubiak didn't recognize.

"What's all this?" Cubiak asked, pointing to the mishmash of leads.

"Sorry. Classified information. But here's something you need to see," Moore said as he opened his laptop and the image of a naked, kneeling Sneider filled the screen.

"This is the video that was sent to Andrew. And this"—Moore hit another key—"is the one sent to the Packers."

Cubiak watched as two men in black hoods and clothing shoved the handcuffed Sneider to his knees on the stones and then dangled spiders in front of his face. As much as he could, Sneider lurched and ducked but the men took turns pushing him upward, laughing over his screams and protests as they dropped more and more spiders onto his skin.

"It goes on for about five minutes before they have him sufficiently covered for their purposes and get to the point where they edited the episode for the son." Moore spoke dryly but Cubiak heard the hard edge to his voice.

"Andrew says his father hates spiders."

"We already heard the same from the Packers office manager. Seems the office had to be fumigated on Sneider's orders during the time when he was a regular at the meetings."

"How would the kidnappers know about Sneider's spider phobia?"

Moore didn't blink. "They wouldn't, unless someone at the Packers let it slip. Or Andrew is in on it. Or the exterminator picked up on it and blabbed the news around town, which could easily have happened. I have an agent looking into that. But even without that, it's not a bad guess. Arachnophobia is one of the most common fears in Western civilization. In fact, it may top the list. I don't suspect either of us would take kindly to being covered with spiders."

Cubiak turned back to the monitor. Threatening figures of men dressed in black were becoming all too commonplace. How difficult would it be to set up a camera and mimic that kind of antagonistic behavior?

"You think it could be two guys pretending to be terrorists to throw you off their trail?"

"Anything's possible, but it's really pretty unlikely. We're going on the assumption that these are the real deal. What we don't know is whether they're linked to an international organization or some kind of homegrown variety." Moore pointed to a tall stack of computer printouts. "These are the phone records of suspicious calls made in the U.S. during the past *week*. Most can be traced to foreign sites but there are all kinds of people with wacko agendas walking around. Wisconsin, unfortunately, is not immune to nutcases.

"We've got one team of computer nerds analyzing the phone data and another working on the video. The crime lab passed along the ransom note as well. And our tech team is on that. Plus we're continuing to comb through Andrew's bank records."

"And you think somewhere in that haystack of data, you're going to find the compass needle that points you to Sneider."

"It's how we do things, Sheriff. Data analysis and good police work following down the leads. Science puts us ahead of the game. We've got technology working for us and that's where I put my faith."

Cubiak started to protest. Then he recovered. He had heard that kind of testimonial before, when he worked for the Chicago police, from officers who insisted that hard facts alone solved crimes: everything was black and white.

The sheriff considered telling Moore about the two bones that Rowe had found on the beach earlier that day but decided not to say anything yet. The bones belonged to the sphere of gray that he valued. And there was no room for gray in Moore's world.

Later, Cubiak called Cate. Listening to the phone ring, he grew increasingly impatient. Wouldn't she get in touch with him if she wanted to talk? Was calling a sign of strength or of weakness? When she didn't answer, he felt relieved. Then just as he was about to disconnect, he blurted out a message: "Can we talk?" Ball in your court, he thought, and was immediately appalled by his juvenile smugness.

A few minutes later, the sheriff's phone buzzed. After five rings, he picked up. He expected the call was from Cate but it was Bathard on the other end of the line.

"I've managed, rather unofficially, to borrow several files from the library's historical collection. Plus I've done some of my own research. I was hoping you could come by," the doctor said.

Bathard had coffee ready and he listened intently as Cubiak told him about the spiders.

"It does seem oddly personal, doesn't it?" the doctor said.

"The feds don't seem to think so."

Bathard shrugged. "Eventually you'll find out, of course."

He led the sheriff to the study, where he'd organized several stacks of material and opened a well-worn map of the county on the table.

"If I were to ask you to guess how many ships have been lost in these waters, what would you say?" Bathard pointed to the vast stretches of Green Bay and Lake Michigan that surrounded the peninsula.

"Fifty? Maybe seventy-five?" Cubiak replied, though he thought that was too high.

"Two hundred and nineteen, according to one source. Another puts it at two hundred and forty."

"Jesus."

"Here's a list." The coroner handed Cubiak a printout that was several pages long. Most of the boats documented on the list had been recovered and most hadn't involved loss of life. But there were still boats that had disappeared without a trace.

"There's no question that people drowned in these waters," Bathard said. "Many of the wrecks were in Death's Door. In fact, in a couple of articles, experts are quoted as saying that the strait had more shipwrecks than any body of fresh water in the world. But there were vessels lost here." His finger moved down the bay side of the peninsula, pausing along the rocky shoals near Peninsula State Park and then nearer the entrance to Sturgeon Bay. "And plenty on the lake side as well. Four near Baileys Harbor."

"But all these ships have been identified. Somewhere there'd be a record of survivors or a list of those who drowned," the sheriff said.

"That's true, but what about the ships that went unnoticed for one reason or another? A small boat could have gone down without anyone knowing about it. During Prohibition, barrels of whiskey were routinely smuggled across the border from Canada. Some of the stuff came overland across the UP, but there were plenty of vessels of all sizes hauling kegs of Canadian booze and locally brewed beer over the water heading toward Milwaukee and Chicago. If a fishing boat filled with contraband sank, who was going to sound the alarm? Any losses, whether of human life or goods, would be considered part of the cost of doing business." He paused. "All told, more than enough work for the men at the three coast guard stations."

"Three? I thought there were just the two."

"Now, yes, there's the Sturgeon Bay station and, in summer, the one on Washington Island. But back then there was a station at Baileys Harbor as well." Bathard handed Cubiak a faded photograph. "It closed in 1948 and the land was eventually sold to the Baileys Harbor Yacht Club. Here it is." He pointed to the location on the map. "Not far from where Sneider had his camp."

"I thought the Forest Home was in Ellison Bay, near the estate," the sheriff said. As soon as he spoke, he realized his mistake. When he'd asked Andrew about the camp's location, they'd been interrupted before Andrew had a chance to reply.

"No, it was on the lake side. Actually, there were a couple of camps right in that area. But Sneider's was different from all of them," Bathard said. He picked up a brochure from the table. "Another treasure from the archives. Have a look."

The brochure opened with a collage of photos that showed young men of means at play on the water and in the woods. The inside panels were filled with pictures of the cabins, dining room, and campfire scenes. On the back panel, in smaller print, a brief paragraph praised Sneider's altruistic generosity in providing a respite for underprivileged boys by offering them food, shelter, and purpose "in tandem with the others."

"The Forest Home was Sneider's first big philanthropic enterprise on the peninsula. A refuge for needy boys set up under the umbrella of a camp for the well-to-do," Bathard said.

"Andrew told me about it. But if you ask me, it sounds more like a camp for rich kids run largely on the backs of the poor," Cubiak said.

"Perhaps to the benefit of both."

The sheriff looked doubtful. "If you believe that, you have more faith in humanity than I do."

Bathard emptied an envelope of photos onto the table. "One thing is sure, Sneider wasn't shy about documenting his work. I found these at the bottom of a box that was sitting on a back shelf."

Most were pictures of the summer kids, the sons and nephews of midwestern gentry: hearty lads in white cotton shirts and khaki shorts being molded into the leaders of the next generation, easy smiles and casual arrogance evident as they took on the archery range and ball field, sailed the fleet of small skiffs, hoisted bolt-action .22 rifles to their shoulders for target practice, and rode tall in the saddle on sleek black steeds. Cubiak felt a twinge of envy. These were the kinds of summer activities he'd never even dreamed of while growing up.

From the jumble, one picture caught the sheriff's attention. It was snapshot size and had ragged edges, but it was the same picture he'd seen in Sneider's office.

"Sneider had this same photo enlarged and framed. Andrew showed it to me. It's on his father's desk." There they were, frozen in time, the proud rich Gerald Sneider and his wards. These were the skinny boys with chipped teeth and forced smiles, the kids with averted eyes, the ones whose hold on the world was tentative and who knew that the future was far from rosy.

Cubiak peered more closely. "What's that on their shirts?" he asked.

Bathard handed the sheriff a magnifying glass.

"Name tags. He must have had them air-brushed out of the picture that he keeps at the house," Cubiak said.

He ran the lens over the photo again. Almost hidden in the shadows were two grim adolescents with shorn heads. One was tall and gangly; the other, short and thin as a twig. "Ross and Ross," Cubiak said.

"Must be Jon and Fred."

"Jon Ross, Leeland's father?" Cubiak asked.

"Indeed, it would have to be. And Fred, his uncle. Didn't he die recently?" Bathard shook his head. "How about that for a small world?

Either I'd forgotten or I'd never known that they'd lived at the camp. But it makes sense. They were from here originally, fraternal twins. Their parents perished in a fire, trying to save the barn on the little farm they owned. I treated Fred once and remember that he had a nasty scar on his back. He said he got it when he was a kid. When I asked him how, he said he couldn't remember."

"I've got plenty of scars from when I was a kid and I know the story of how I got each one."

"Most of us do," Bathard said.

Cubiak looked at the picture again. Fred Ross was dead, but Jon was very much alive and the only link, other than Andrew, that the sheriff had to the camp and to Sneider. "Can you make me a couple copies of this?" Cubiak said, handing the snapshot back to Bathard.

The two men were drinking sherry in front of the fire when Sonja came in from her knitting circle.

"Join us," Bathard said, but she declined, saying she felt a cold coming on.

"Maybe next time," she said and blew them both kisses from the doorway.

"You're a lucky man." Cubiak made the comment when they were alone again.

"Indeed, I am." Bathard looked at him and then put down his glass and got up to stoke the fire. "I'm a man with more blessings than I deserve," he said as he prodded the burning logs. "In truth, I don't understand how any of this came about. How is it possible to be profoundly happy in one life and then be happy again in another? Cornelia and I were young together and we grew old together. When she died, there was nothing left but pain and emptiness. The pain is still there but now the emptiness is gone. I will always love Cornelia but I love Sonja, too, and it makes no sense how this can be unless the heart is capable of far more love than ever imagined. Maybe that's something we simply have to accept."

Cubiak said nothing.

Bathard poked the fire again and then retook his chair. After a moment, he brought up Cate. "I haven't seen her around recently," he said.

"Neither have I. She's busy with her ex-husband." The response was harsher than Cubiak wanted.

"He's here, on the peninsula?"

"He's a reporter with one of the national papers, chasing the Sneider story."

"Ah, I see. And she's spending time with him, is that it? You can't blame her, you know. Cate's past is part and parcel of who she is. She can't walk away from what's happened to her any more than you can." Bathard paused and let the crackle of the burning logs fill the silence as he freshened their drinks.

"None of us are getting any younger, Dave. Sometimes the best we can do is make peace with the past. I wouldn't worry, if I were you. Cate's a smart woman; she'll do the right thing."

A VISIT
TO THE YELLOW HOUSE

12

In the deepening twilight, Cubiak drove the back roads of Door County and sorted through his thoughts. The visit with Bathard had left him unsettled on more than one count.

Cubiak knew why the coroner had asked about Cate. Several times already Bathard had made it clear he hoped they'd find a way forward, as he and Sonja had. It was a tempting idea but Cubiak had resisted. The situation between him and Cate was complicated. There was the long shadow of Ruby hanging over them, and his own fear that, unlike Bathard, he didn't deserve to be happy. How could he expect Cate to commit to a relationship when he felt so tentative? Would she even bother with him now that Garth Nickels was around?

The situation with Cate wasn't the only issue troubling Cubiak. The archival photos that Bathard had found gave him the uneasy feeling that the distant past was linked to the current situation involving the missing man. There was no room for error or misjudgment in the case, yet he'd allowed himself to make an assumption about the location of Sneider's camp. And he'd been wrong.

Alongside an abandoned orchard, the sheriff pulled onto the shoulder and cut the engine. In the calming silence, he stared at the long rows of wizened trees. The trunks had thickened with age, and the bare twisted limbs had gone wild with neglect. In several spots the branches had bridged the gaps between the rows and ensnared one tree with another in their predatory grasps. Cubiak pulled out the photo that showed a young Gerald Sneider gripping the shoulders of his wards. In the picture Sneider was smiling, but there was something ominous in the way he held on to the boys and something fearful in their faces. Cubiak studied the picture. Although the name tags were illegible, two remained clear in his memory: Ross and Ross.

The sheriff was sure he'd overlooked something important. But what?

Sitting on the quiet roadside, Cubiak went back to square one, replaying his first encounter with Andrew Sneider, the drive to Ellison Bay, the walk through the house. Once again, he saw the gaudy rooms, the kitchen, the breakfast nook.

The sheriff scrambled from the jeep. Of course, it was what he'd found there, hanging above the table. If he was right, he'd been driving around since Sunday with what might prove to be an important clue to Gerald Sneider's disappearance.

Cubiak rummaged through the jeep's cargo area. Shoving aside the recycling box, he found the strand of rope he'd pulled off the pillowcase after rescuing the kittens from the bay. The rope was dirty white, with a blue streak running down the middle, and it looked just like the piece of rope that had dangled from the Tiffany lamp in Sneider's breakfast nook the night he went missing.

Cubiak was convinced that it was Leeland Ross who'd thrown the kittens into the water. Could he be involved in the disappearance of Sneider as well?

The sheriff took a deep breath. Ropes or lines like the one he was holding could be found throughout Door County. They hung on the docks and boats and in barns and warehouses, probably loops of them in attics and garages. There was a possibility that forensic testing could determine if the rope from the pillowcase and the one in Sneider's breakfast room were from the same source, but he knew that more than likely the results would be inconclusive.

Four men named Ross were associated with the peninsula. Three of them were still alive: Jon, who'd spent part of his youth as one of Sneider's needy boys; Leeland, his unruly son; and Steve, the *New York Times* reporter who'd come back home for the funeral of his father, Fred.

With the rope in hand, Cubiak decided that it was time to talk to the Rosses. He'd begin with a visit to Fred, because as the sheriff knew, sometimes even the dead can tell stories.

Fred Ross and his wife had made their home in the southern part of the county, close to the city of Sturgeon Bay but far from the glamour that was generally associated with the county. This was the nontourist part of the peninsula, an area dotted with small farms and unpretentious single-family homes. Real estate development was creeping along the rugged rim of Green Bay where small frame houses were being razed and replaced by showplaces. Several farms had been sold to builders who divided the land into one-acre parcels, hoping to attract people from the city of Green Bay who were willing to trade a forty-minute commute for a country home with a Door County address. But most of the land remained largely unchanged and was handed down from one generation to the next with only modest improvements to chart the passage of time.

In the deepening twilight, Cubiak followed a worn stretch of blacktop that crisscrossed a meandering creek and finally brought him to a tan mailbox marked Ross. Slowing, he turned up the driveway to the house where the recently widowed Marilyn Ross lived. Cubiak hadn't known Fred's wife's given name and had called Rowe. "What's this about?" his deputy had said. Cubiak heard the curiosity in his voice but knew he wouldn't ask for more than the sheriff was willing to give. Which amounted to pretty much nothing because even Cubiak was not quite sure why he wanted to talk to her, other than it was a place to start.

Marilyn Ross lived in a yellow frame ranch house that was set back in a thick grove of cedars. The trees were tall and full and added a stately air to what, drawing closer, he realized was a modest but tidy homestead. Beside the house, which was remarkably small, there were two other buildings: a matching yellow garage and a garden shed. The narrow lawn was neatly trimmed, fence posts aligned and straight, flower bed weeded, walkway swept clean. Cubiak followed the white-rock-lined driveway to a small turnoff that faced a kitchen garden littered with plant stubble, the only visible sign of disorder on the property. Closing the jeep door, Cubiak caught a hint of movement at one of the curtains. Was Fred Ross's widow home? Was she watching from behind one of the green-shuttered windows? he wondered.

A shroud of silence encompassed the house and yard. There was no wind through the surrounding ring of gnarled oaks, no birds tweeting or insects chirping. In the heavy, funereal quiet, his boots crunched on the gravel path that ran past a flower bed of red and gold mums and then up to the front door.

The bell was unyielding, so he knocked. After a few moments, he heard the slow shuffle of feet approaching the door, a sound that reminded him of Eva Carlson.

A short, heavy-set woman blinked into the glare from the entryway light. She emitted a stale odor of unwashed clothes and talcum powder. A tuft of unruly white hair stuck up on the right side of her head, a match for the red imprint on her cheek.

"Marilyn Ross?" Cubiak said and introduced himself.

She nodded.

"I've disturbed your nap, Mrs. Ross. I apologize."

"It's Marilyn, and I need disturbing." She tugged her checkered housedress into place and then she stepped back and waved him into the dim, overly warm living room, directing him to the threadbare blue-plaid recliner in the corner by the picture window.

"Can't sit in it myself. Too hard to get up. Afraid I'd be trapped forever." Marilyn added a weak smile to a pretend laugh as she eased into a worn rocker. Besides a sagging sofa, a small corner table, and a console television, the room was unfurnished.

Just as suddenly, she frowned. "This ain't about my Stevie, is it? He ain't got in no trouble with that no-good cousin of his, has he?"

"No. Nothing like that," Cubiak replied.

"Leeland's two years older and always been a bad influence on my boy, though we did our best to keep the two apart."

The sheriff looked around, trying to picture the young New York reporter as a boy in this isolated, pinched house. Where were the books and magazines he might have read as a kid? The music? Cubiak guessed that the house had two bedrooms, and he tried to envision the one that had been Steve's, tried to imagine it crammed with the messy, noisy stuff of youth.

"I'm here to talk about Fred," Cubiak said and offered his condolences.

"Fred!" The widow's mouth quivered. "Why him, Sheriff? He never did a wrong thing in his life. Not like that lousy brother of his," she said, twisting a handkerchief she'd picked up from the arm of the rocker.

"Tell me about your husband," Cubiak said.

"Fred was a good man, Sheriff. He worked hard, always did his best for us. A good husband and father and a regular church-goer, too. But like so many, the poor man drank himself to death. Fred was a big man. Weighed over three hundred pounds, and he had everything wrong that a man that size could have wrong: diabetes, weak heart, gout. When you add the whiskey, well . . ."

Like my old man, Cubiak thought, only he'd been skin and bones. All the drink he'd poured down his throat had gone to produce liver toxins rather than fat.

"I am sorry," Cubiak said.

Marilyn had gotten up and was shoving a picture at him: a younger Fred Ross, hefty and well on his way to being obese.

The sheriff was surprised. "He was such a skinny kid in the photo I saw," he said.

"Skinny! Well, maybe way back when. That must have been a pretty old picture."

Cubiak showed her a copy of the photo from Bathard. "That's Fred and Jon in the back," he explained.

"Oh my word. Look at that. May I?" Tears formed in her eyes as she reached for the picture. For a moment, she stared at the photo as if lost in thought and then, clutching the snapshot and the framed photo to her sagging bosom, she tottered back to the rocking chair.

"I never seen a picture of Fred so young. What a sweet boy. But that terrible place!"

"The Forest Home? I've only heard good things about it. Your husband lived there for a while, didn't he, with his brother Jon?"

Marilyn gave him a scornful look. "'Lived' is a pretty generous term for what those boys endured. Nine worst years of his life."

"What do you mean?"

She shrugged. "I don't know exactly. Fred didn't talk about it much but I knew he hated it."

"Did he ever say why?"

"Not really. I guessed it was maybe his pride. It's not hard to understand how he'd resent having nothing when those other boys had so much. Family. Education. All the material comforts and advantages you could want. Probably more than someone like us could even imagine. For those boys, the lucky ones, the camp must have been a glorious place. For Fred and the other charity cases, it was a miserable sinkhole." Marilyn smoothed her faded skirt. "Those are my words, Sheriff, not my husband's."

"Did Jon hate it, too?"

Marilyn snorted. "Jon hated everything, still does, so probably he did. Couple of times I overheard Fred trying to get him to talk about what things were like when they were kids, but Jon would just cut him off. 'Forget that shit,' he'd say. 'What's past is past.' I think they both wanted to forget, and maybe Jon was able to. But Fred couldn't."

She looked up suddenly. "Tea, Sheriff?"

With a shy coyness, Mrs. Ross offered Cubiak her arm and allowed him to walk her into the kitchen. She carried the camp photo in her free hand and once there she laid it on the table. She let Cubiak fill the kettle and set it on the stove before insisting that he sit. Then she got up and measured out several pinches of loose leaves into a small ceramic pot and arranged a platter of butter cookies.

"Nobody comes by much anymore. I have to keep in practice or I'll forget my manners," she said.

Cubiak warmed to the lonely woman and regretted his earlier harsh assessment of the kind of childhood he'd envisioned for her son. "It must be nice to have Steve home."

"It would be if he were ever here." She sighed and set the platter on the table. "But you know how these young folks are. Always something to do."

The cookies were bland but the tea surprisingly strong. Sitting across from him, Marilyn wrapped her gnarled hands around her mug and stared at the photo. "I almost married Jon, you know. Had both brothers courting me back then." She pursed her mouth and then laughed, for real this time.

"And you chose Fred?"

"Yes, the quiet one. I figured I'd have a better life with him than with that bull-headed brother of his."

Cubiak smiled, encouraging her to go on.

"And I guess that in many ways, I did. Oh, listen to me! I'm starting to sound like one of those women who complain about everything." She batted her hands at the air. "Of course, I did. Like I said, Fred was a good man who did his best. Not that there weren't problems—there are always problems. Life brings them and drops them at your doorstep whether you want them or not. Truth is, Sheriff, they were both damaged men. Both of them hard drinkers. The difference was that with Jon, the alcohol primed the pump. That man never had any trouble letting out his anger. For Fred, it was different. He kept his feelings locked inside, and all that the beer and whiskey did was give him something to try and drown himself in." She looked at him straight and hard. "You tell me, which is worse?"

Cubiak shook his head. "I don't know." I've only known the one, he wanted to say, but he stopped himself. "I'm sorry. Life can be hard. But there are those who make it harder."

Marilyn tapped the photo. "That's Gerald Sneider, ain't it, the one who owned the camp?"

Cubiak nodded.

"Fred didn't like Sneider, but who could blame him. The man was praised to high heaven for all the good he did, but he really took advantage of those boys, the needy ones. To hear Fred tell it, things were pretty peachy when the rich summer boys were around needing to be fed and all, but come winter, the other boys were practically starved. They never had enough wood for the stove neither, and they had to work hard all the time. They did their own repairs. They even had to dig new latrines for the summer kids. That's all what he said about the camp, and, truth be told, there were times I got tired of listening. Most of us had a hard life growing up. I was the youngest of ten kids. Believe me, there was never enough food on the table for any of us."

She closed her eyes and was quiet a moment, as if reliving the hardships of her own youth. Then she blinked.

"But I always knew there was more. Fred had a nervous tic that would start up and not stop for the longest time. Sometimes he had bad dreams, too. The kind that rattle you awake and leave you lying there in cold sweats. He'd never admit it to me, but I always thought something bad was eating at him from the inside."

"And you think it had to do with the Forest Home?"

She gave the question due consideration before she answered. "I don't know for certain, but you live with someone for that many years and you get a pretty good notion how they got to be the way they are. There could be other things, of course, and I'm not saying there ain't, but my gut tells me it went way back to when they were youngsters living at that place. Neither of those boys were ever angels, and probably half the kids there were hellions. I'm sure they got in a pack of trouble. Whatever happened, it troubled Fred to the end. Times I think whatever it was, it may have even helped kill him."

"Did you ever ask Jon about it after your husband died?"

"Bah! That stubborn old goat hasn't talked civil to me in years. He's never forgiven me for marrying his brother instead of him."

Marilyn pulled the picture closer. "Can I keep this?" she asked.

"Of course." He waited a moment. "You've heard that Sneider's gone missing."

She gasped and looked up.

"The story's been on the news all week."

"I don't listen to the news. It's too depressing," she said.

"Steve hasn't said anything to you?"

"No, why would he?" There was fear in her voice.

"I don't know, something to talk about," he said.

"I told you. I hardly see my son. He keeps himself busy doing whatever."

When Cubiak left, Marilyn Ross was sitting at the table with her tea and her memories, wondering if she'd told him more than she should have.

Jon Ross lived just two miles from his late brother's place. His small, unworked farm sat on a parallel road that might as well have been in a separate universe. Instead of stately pines, he was surrounded by soggy marshland. Instead of a tidy ranch house, he lived in a ramshackle shotgun house from which time and weather had stripped all color. Instead of a faithful wife, he had only the memory of a skittish woman in his bed. His partner was long gone, run off at some distant time past, either lured by a sweeter man or desperate to escape her good-for-nothing common-law husband.

Cubiak had heard the stories whispered late at night with a sneer or shake of the head over the last call for whiskey or beer at one or other of the local bars, and he knew the sad rundown homestead all too well.

More than once he'd been called out to break up fights between Jon and his son or one of his unsavory running buddies. There'd been other visits as well and none of them pleasant.

Leeland's blue pickup was in the yard. Next to it was a red car with New York plates. A large, mangy dog barked and pulled at the chain that kept it tied to a tree. The air reeked, probably from creek water that had overrun the banks and then pooled in a low gully. Voices and banging erupted from the machine shed, and he saw a flicker of bright light. Two men were working and arguing.

The sheriff mounted the sagging steps and knocked on the door. A moment passed and the door swung open just far enough for Jon Ross to slip out. He slammed the door shut before the sheriff could see inside.

Ross yelled at the dog to shut up. Then he crossed his arms over his chest and glared at the sheriff. He was a big man, like his brother, with a scowl etched deep into his wide, round face. "Yeah?" he said.

"That your nephew's car?" Cubiak indicated the vehicle with the out-of-state plates.

"Maybe."

"He here?"

"What if he is? Ain't against the law."

"No. Just asking. I guess besides helping Leeland in the shed, he's keeping you apprised about things down at the department. Maybe even letting you read what he's got to say about it."

Ross said nothing.

"I was in the area and wanted to stop by and tell you that I am truly sorry about your brother," Cubiak said.

Ross started to dip his head in acknowledgment but caught himself and snickered instead. "My brother passed some weeks ago. You're a bit late extending your regards."

"I am, and I apologize for that," Cubiak replied. He waited. "You going to ask me in?"

"You know I'm not." The man stepped forward, forcing the sheriff onto the top step.

"Then we'll talk out here." Cubiak looked past Ross at the peeling orange paint on the front of the neglected house. Finally he pulled the old camp photo from his inside pocket and held it up, positioning it just far enough away that Ross had to tip forward for a good view.

"Which one are you?" Cubiak asked, pointing to the twin boys.

Ross jerked back as if slapped. His mouth tightened. "Don't matter, does it."

"Probably not. But that's you and Fred in the photo, isn't it?" Cubiak said as he tucked the picture into his pocket. "You and your brother lived at the Forest Home for nine years. In fact, you were pretty much raised there. From what I've heard, it doesn't sound like a pleasant experience for the charity boys. The summer kids were pampered, but the rest of you were treated like indentured servants, I'm told."

"We got by."

"But not an easy life."

"Like I said, we got by."

"Never enough to eat. Cold in the winter. Even had to . . ."

Ross interrupted. "I ain't got time to go rehashing the past."

"What's done is done."

"Something like that."

"You have much to do with Gerald Sneider?"

Ross turned but not before Cubiak saw the twitch in his eye.

"You know he's missing," the sheriff went on.

"Asshole could fall off the earth for all I care," Ross said and spat over the rail.

"You don't like him."

With a smirk, the surviving brother swiped his sleeve across his mouth. "Don't like people like him."

"Because he's rich?"

"Because he's a mean son of a bitch. Deserves whatever comes to him."

Like you on both counts, Cubiak thought. He let the comment hang in the air for a moment before he continued. "Your sister-in-law says Fred was obsessed by memories of the camp."

A smear of pink spread beneath the gristle on Ross's jowls. "My sister-in-law doesn't know what the fuck she's talking about."

"She thinks that something that happened there worked on him enough that eventually it helped kill him."

Ross sneered. "Now there's a silly woman who should keep her foolish notions to herself. Did she tell you she reads tea leaves, too, and that she believes in the nonsense she sees there? She's just mad that Fred died and I'm still here. My brother and I were twins, but I got all the good stuff, not him. He's the one who grew up fat and sick and died before his time."

The so-called lucky twin groped for the doorknob. "That it, Sheriff? I got things to do," Jon said as he yanked the door open and vanished back into the dim interior.

Cubiak's refrigerator door held a menagerie of animal magnets—deer, fox, raccoon, squirrel, skunk, and beaver. The magnets stood about two inches high and were arranged in a row near the top of the door. They'd been in place when he moved in, and over time he'd pretty much forgotten them.

Driving back from Jon Ross's farm, the sheriff found himself thinking about the magnets. After he let the dog out, he pulled the fox magnet off the refrigerator and used it to pin Sneider's camp snapshot to the door. He wrote the names of the four Ross men on slips of paper and, using the other magnets, arranged them in a circle around the photo: the skunk for Jon, the squirrel for Leeland, the deer for Fred, and the beaver for Steve. On a scrap of paper he scribbled *rope* and put it off to one side with the raccoon. He wrote *bones* on another and taped it underneath the rest.

Then he opened a beer and stepped back to consider the makeshift incident board. Cubiak didn't have much to go on: one tenuous clue, ancient remains that had no apparent connection to anything, the picture of a missing man, the name of a dead man, and three potential suspects.

What now? he wondered.

When Cubiak got back, he'd hoped to find Cate at home. Instead he found a book on the back porch with a note from Bathard that read, "Came across this in the library's local history room. Thought you'd be interested."

After he finished with the refrigerator magnets, Cubiak picked up the book. It was a history of America's golden age of summer camps.

The phenomenon began in the 1920s, when camps sprang up all across the country, a direct result of the prosperity that swept the nation following World War I. The camps for boys were heralded as an antidote to the affluence and the "overcivilization" that were turning young American men into weaklings, while those for girls were meant to prepare young women for the many new opportunities they would find in the postwar world.

Many of the facilities went bankrupt with the crash of 1929, but as the nation slowly recovered from the economic upheaval, the camp movement was revitalized and went strong until World War II. In the fifties, there was another resurgence that lasted nearly a decade. Sneider's Forest Home opened during that period. The book gave it two full pages. There were photos of boys shooting arrows into targets at the camp archery range and hiking through the camp's thick woods. Ebullient letters home told parents about thrilling moonlight swims, boat races, and javelin-throwing contests. "We're learning to be brave," a young summer camper exclaimed. The author devoted several laudatory paragraphs to Sneider's charity work but dismissed the needy boys with a few condescending sentences. The sheriff read the single throw-away paragraph a second time and tossed the book aside.

Cubiak had first visited Door County as a charity-case Boy Scout, a distinction, he realized, that gave him something in common with Jon Ross. Had Ross learned to be brave at Sneider's camp, or was that where he learned to be mean?

It was eleven when Cubiak phoned Rowe. "Sorry for the late call, but I want to go ahead with the dive. How soon can you be ready?"

"Tomorrow, if conditions improve. The lake was pretty rough today. But Friday for sure."

Despite the three beers the sheriff had nursed through the evening, he had difficulty falling asleep, and once he did he dreamt of Cate. She was one of the privileged girls at an exclusive Door County camp for young ladies where he worked in the kitchen. While Cate and the other girls dined in a spacious room lit by chandeliers, he sat on a stool in a gloomy narrow room surrounded by a high concrete wall and peeled buckets of potatoes. Only a dream but not that far removed from their realities.

MEN FROM BOYS

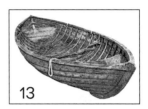

13

The high-pitched screech of a seagull in distress rattled Cubiak awake. He could ignore his several alarms when he remembered to set them but not the bird's urgent and prolonged squall. The bed was empty and the room cold. When he'd turned down the heat the night before, he'd forgotten to toss the quilt on top of the thin wool blanket that he and Cate had been using. Trying not to think about where she might be, Cubiak rubbed his hands warm and listened to the raucous bird. There are those who would take the shrieking as an omen, but he didn't believe in such things.

Eventually the bird quieted, and Cubiak made his way to the kitchen. From the window he checked the weather. Beneath a red sky, a ridge of black clouds blotted the horizon, and sharp, short waves churned the lake. The sheriff texted Rowe: *OK today?* The reply was immediate and what he expected. *Too rough.*

Tomorrow, then, Cubiak thought, as he opened the door for Butch. Seeing his breath crystallize in the cold air, the sheriff remembered that the weatherman had predicted plummeting nighttime temperatures. A record low, the forecaster had said. Had the kidnappers paid attention to the forecast? he wondered. If Sneider was being held outdoors or in an unheated room, they might be in a race against time.

While Butch whined at the door to be let in, Cubiak studied the refrigerator door. He hoped his array of possible clues would inspire some new insight, but he came away feeling at even more of a loss on how to connect the bits to each other.

In a nod to the cold weather, Cubiak cooked oatmeal, drank an extra cup of coffee, and dug through the hall closet for his winter jacket. He skipped his morning run and headed to the office. Maybe today he'd get there before the feds.

The sheriff was turning into his spot when another vehicle came up behind him. He hoped it was Rowe coming in early, but no such luck. Wrong car, wrong plates. The morning sun reflected off the tinted windows, making it impossible for him to see the driver, but this early he figured it was Moore. He seemed the type to be up at dawn. As Cubiak stepped from the jeep, the front door of the other car swung open, and a familiar pair of shiny black shoes hit the pavement. But they were heels, not wingtips.

"Morning, Sheriff," Agent Harrison said. She smiled at him, bright-eyed and uncharacteristically chipper. "Finished your run early?"

Cubiak grunted, miffed that the feds were aware of his routine. Suddenly he wished he had gone for a run that morning and not wimped out because of the cold. Harrison was bare legged and hatless. Her only shield against the weather was a fringed plaid shawl wrapped tightly around her ubiquitous suit coat. Cubiak unzipped his jacket.

"Big day, today. I can feel it in my bones," the FBI agent said as she got in step alongside the sheriff. "If I'm reading this situation right, and I think I am, the perps will contact Andrew Sneider today and tell him where to make the drop."

"Right on schedule."

The sheriff meant to be sarcastic but if Harrison caught his meaning she ignored it.

"Something like that. I'm guessing he'll hear from them by twelve, maybe three," she said. "They usually don't wait more than a day or two, and it's already Thursday. They're anxious to get hold of the money and be finished with the whole business."

Oblivious to the icy gusts that had dogged them from the lot, Harrison stopped outside the door. "For your ears only. We've got a couple of people in our sights. Not locals."

"The Madison link."

"All indications point in that direction. Quigley's in Green Bay now coordinating efforts with the district office."

"You think they're holding Sneider somewhere down there?"

"Probably not. They don't shit where they sleep—pardon my language. If anything, they're keeping him ensconced as far away from their home base as possible."

"So we wait for the signal from Agent Moore and then coordinate our approach." He saw her look away. "Or we just sit tight while your team closes in."

Harrison pressed a finger to Cubiak's shirtfront. "You got it."

The sheriff's pique ratcheted up and then Harrison turned away, forcing him to follow her into the lobby. "We've got trained officers and resources . . . ," he said. Cubiak was about to go on, arguing for greater involvement, when he noticed a man with a mangy dog at the reception desk. The man was waving his arms and demanding to see the sheriff, while Lisa was trying to lower a bowl of water to the floor. In her condition, this was not an easy maneuver.

"Jesus," the sheriff said, muttering under his breath.

Harrison smirked and uttered a quip about lost animals when the man turned and started hurrying toward them, dragging the dog along.

As Harrison clicked down the hall away from the lobby, Cubiak waited.

"Sheriff. Bob Franklin." The man held out his hand.

"This isn't the animal rescue society," Cubiak said curtly.

"I know, of course not. But this here's Verne Pickler's dog. I found her tied up by the canal. Hungry and thirsty. Wet, too. Looks to me like she's been there a couple of days."

"Who's Verne Pickler?"

Franklin rubbed his skull and tottered unsteadily.

Was the man drunk? Annoyed, the sheriff went on. "Maybe Verne forgot to come back for her. Why don't you go ask him? Better yet, I'll have my assistant call him. You got his number?" Cubiak glanced toward the desk but Lisa wasn't there. That was unlike her to disappear without a word. Was she okay?

"I did call him," Franklin replied, suddenly composed. "And I went over to his house, too, but he wasn't home. You don't understand, Sheriff. Verne's a real animal lover. He'd never leave Maize like that."

At the sound of her name, the dog began whining. Franklin took a biscuit from his pocket and let her eat it from his hand.

"All I can say is something must have happened to him. Maybe he was kidnapped like that Sneider fellow."

Cubiak had been watching for Lisa to reappear at her desk. Hearing Gerald Sneider mentioned, he turned his full attention to the visitor. "Why would you say that?"

"Because Verne used to work for Sneider. When this kidnapping business happened, he got kind of nervous and said maybe he'd better start looking over his shoulder, too. I thought he was kidding, but now . . . I don't know. Maybe he was serious."

"What do you mean, he worked for Sneider? What did he do?"

"I don't know. He never said."

"When did you last see Mr. Pickler?"

"A couple two three days ago."

"And after you found the dog, you went to his house?"

"Right, like I said, but Verne wasn't there. I knocked on both doors, front and back, but there was no answer."

"He didn't leave a spare key around that you knew of?"

"Verne don't lock his house, Sheriff. He's old-fashioned that way."

"But you didn't go in, even though you were worried that something might be wrong?"

Franklin colored. "I've never been inside Verne's place, and it didn't seem right. That's why I came here. I figure you can walk into a man's house uninvited."

Cubiak took a deep breath. "When exactly did you find the dog?"

"About six o'clock this morning. She was tied to a tree midway between the two overlooks along the canal."

"You walk that way every day?"

Franklin had bent down to pet Maize. "Nope, I can only walk on days when it's not too windy. I got tinnitus"—he pointed to his ear—"and wind makes it worse."

"When's the last time you were out that way?"

"Sunday. It was sunny early and I took a nice stroll before church."

"And you didn't see the dog?"

"No." Franklin shook his head vigorously. "Maize wasn't there."

Verne Pickler lived on a little-traveled road not far from the Sturgeon Bay coast guard station. The area was heavily wooded, and the house wasn't visible from the road. From the mailbox Cubiak followed a long, narrow lane through thick woods that led to a modest frame house. There was no yard to speak of, just enough cleared land amid the towering trees to hold the small brown ranch and matching garage. Judging from the thin layer of moss on the two rooftops, very little sun penetrated the encroaching forest.

Despite what Franklin said, Cubiak didn't feel right walking into a man's house uninvited, even when he knew he had good reason to, and the isolated nature of Pickler's place made him even more uneasy. Maybe Franklin was wrong about Pickler not being home. The man could be waiting inside, prepared to shoot anyone who trespassed. Or maybe he'd booby-trapped the place before he took off.

The sheriff looked in all the windows and checked the exterior before he pushed the back door in and stepped into a mudroom crammed with the usual assortment of jackets and boots. The inside door opened to a glossy white kitchen. All neat and tidy. Nothing out of place. Dishes washed. Sink clean. Stove spotless. A fresh plastic bag in the trash container. A single placemat laid out on the small oak table under the window. In one corner, a fifty-pound sack of dog food leaned against the counter, near bowls of water and kibble. All signs of a compulsively orderly mind, not that of someone who would leave a beloved dog tied to a tree two miles away. Unless Pickler had tidied the house in anticipation of an extended absence. Then why not make provisions for Maize?

The sheriff considered Pickler missing, on the basis of Franklin's discovery of the dog and Pickler's sister's statement, when he reached her by phone, that she hadn't heard from Vernie in several days, which she said had never happened previously. Well, almost never. There'd been a couple of times when they'd been out of touch for two or three days but that had been years ago and she hoped he wasn't falling back into old habits. Clearly agitated by Cubiak's call, she said she had intended to notify the sheriff's office herself if her brother hadn't telephoned by the afternoon. Cubiak found her explanation overwrought and had the suspicion she was less concerned about her brother's well-being than about having Franklin assume the lead role in her brother's alleged drama.

According to both Franklin and the sister, Pickler was a confirmed bachelor. No girlfriends that they knew of, though he'd "played the field" in his younger days. Now at nearly sixty-nine, he was a quiet man, given to looking out for himself and his dog, they both said. Nothing in the house raised any concerns. Pickler watched TV on a big flat screen, collected bird nests that he arranged on shelves in the living room, and filled all the remaining wall space with black-and-white photos of bridges, those that were local and those well known and far flung. In one of the two small bedrooms, he'd built wall-to-wall work counters and on them was constructing two elaborate matchstick models of bridges. The second room held a double bed covered with a plaid wool blanket that was laid over the mattress. A plain wooden cross hung over the bed, and a well-thumbed prayer book sat on the nightstand.

As Cubiak walked through the house, he glanced about, looking for some hint of the ordinary mess that people leave in their wake, but Pickler had moved through the damp house like a whisper of wind, leaving nothing unruffled. Even the hunting magazines stacked on the rough-hewn coffee table were aligned edge to edge. Cubiak checked the closets for a rifle or shotgun but found no weapons.

The garage was empty, but a fresh oil stain on the floor meant his car had been there recently. What did Pickler drive? Cubiak wondered. He'd get that information from Franklin and put out an APB.

The sheriff was nearly at the jeep when instinct turned him around and pointed him back toward the garage. Walking behind it, he found a nondescript wooden hut. The building, which looked like a garden shed or a Finnish sauna, seemed to be deliberately tucked away. And it was locked.

Why would Pickler leave his house open and lock the shed? Cubiak wondered.

The sheriff broke the lock and stepped inside. "Well, would you look at that," he said as his eyes adjusted to the dim interior and the contents came into focus.

Cubiak had seen many strange sights over the years, and this was one to add to the list. On the wall to his left, dozens of cattail whips hung in a neat line. The whips were made of leather and rope and varied in both length and number of tails—five, nine, and twelve, each one knotted at the end. The facing wall was filled with barbed and spiked chains of various lengths and thicknesses. It was a private torture chamber.

Seafarers, jailers, and religious fanatics were known to use whips and chains as tools of discipline and punishment. But they were also instruments favored by masochists. So how to explain Pickler's collection? Cubiak wondered. Did he use the instruments on others or on himself? Did he belong to a cult of self-abusers or did he act of his own accord? In either case, what drove a seemingly benign man like Verne Pickler—a professed lover of dogs and a builder of matchstick bridges—to resort to such abhorrent behavior?

A wooden cupboard hung on the wall opposite the door. It was about three feet high, roughly the size of the cabinet over the sink in Cubiak's utility room. The cupboard was installed at eye level and stained a dark mahogany that blended in with the surrounding wall. Cubiak crossed the room and opened the double doors. This was no ordinary cabinet; the interior was a shrine that held a large, color print of the Sacred Heart of Jesus.

Cubiak winced. This was the Christ image that had hung in the classrooms of his Catholic elementary school. For eight years, he'd been forced to look at and study under the benign gaze of this smiling Jesus whose parted cloak revealed a flaming heart set in the middle of his chest. The nuns said that the flames represented the transformative power of divine love, whatever that meant. The heart was surmounted by a cross, pierced by a lance wound, and encircled by a crown of thorns, all neatly orchestrated to remind the world of the horrible nature of the Savior's death. The image was meant to help the students understand the pain Jesus had endured for them, but mostly it gave young Davie nightmares.

Months after Lauren and Alexis died, when he was in the deepest throes of grief, Cubiak had stumbled into a local church in search of solace. But instead of peace, he found a large rendering of the image that had haunted his youth. With his own heart racked with pain, he'd finally understood the torment the portrait was meant to convey, and, in the darkened church, he'd fallen to his knees and wept.

Looking at the image in Pickler's shed, he felt cold and unmoved. Pickler's bedside cross and prayer book indicated a moderate devotion to religion, but the enshrined icon along with the instruments of self-flagellation were signs of an excessive and out of control infatuation with punishment in the name of religion. Did Pickler belong to a radical

Catholic group devoted to the Sacred Heart of Jesus, or was he one of a kind, a religious fanatic on a mission of his own?

Cubiak was about to close the cupboard when he noticed a wide slat nailed across the inside of one door. Several pieces of paper were stuck behind the thin lath, and when he tugged at a loose corner, he pulled out two slim booklets.

The title of the first pamphlet was printed in a large, bold font that was easy to read even in the dim light: "Men from Boys: A Manual."

The prose was stilted and old-fashioned but the message clear. Children were born uncivilized and possessing a pure animal nature. They required the guidance of a firm, mature mentor to ensure their safe passage into meaningful adulthood. Boys more so than girls were in need of special handling.

What followed was a strict, no-nonsense step-by-step guide on how to eradicate the rebellious and curious nature of young boys and to transform them into "mature, right-thinking men of strong moral character."

Under a section headed "Behavior That Is Not Allowed" was a long list of forbidden activities: back talk, questioning of orders and directives, idle free time, the reading of any forbidden books or magazines, inappropriate thoughts, fighting, subversive behavior, daydreaming.

"Behavior That Is Mandated" included daily cold showers, weekly haircuts, surprise inspection of quarters, obedience, proper address of yes, sir and no, sir, morning and evening prayer, Bible study.

An adult who'd discovered the right path had a moral obligation to provide direction and guidance, following the seven laws for adult interaction with youth.

1. Discourage free thinking.
2. Use corporal punishment to correct deviant behaviors.
3. Act as the authority in all matters.
4. Demand obedience at all times.
5. Exalt physical strength.

6. Prohibit sexual excitement and punish all unclean actions.
7. Discourage individual pride.

The second pamphlet, "The Spiritual Wasteland of Poverty," declared that God was just and rewarded the righteous. The poor were deprived of goods and material comfort because they lacked the mental and emotional ability to appreciate the wonders of God's creation.

According to the treatise, the average person sinned once every twenty-seven minutes, but among the poor, the rate jumped to a sin going down every thirteen minutes. Poverty's spiritual wasteland encompassed all manner of ills, including diminished mental capacity, moral stagnation, a natural propensity to take things that were not one's own, an inability to distinguish right from wrong, a natural tendency to lie and to embrace the baser instincts of humanity, as well as six of the seven recognized vices: sloth, envy, lust, gluttony, wrath, and greed. Which was missing? Cubiak wondered. Of course: pride! The author went on to caution that some of the poor, those firmly entrenched in their lower state, were capable of assuming an arrogance that defied comprehension.

But thankfully all was not lost, declared the author. The poor were not to be blamed for their sorry condition. Through rigorous effort they could be saved and delivered to the path of righteous behavior and thought. The younger the age at which appropriate correction was provided, the more likely the chance of success.

And herein lay the challenge to the blessed, those with the higher intelligence and material solidity that allowed them to be spared the more sordid nature of the poverty stricken. To them fell the task of elevating the poor from their ignoble natural state, using whatever means necessary.

In other words, boys were inherently evil and poor boys were the worst. Cubiak shook his head. It was not hard to imagine where this kind of sanctimonious demagoguery would lead. Who had written these diatribes and what was Verne Pickler doing with them? Cubiak walked out into the light and skimmed the pamphlets. On the back page of each, in a line of small print at the very bottom, he found the answer.

The author was Gerald Sneider.

LUNCH AT PECHTA'S

14

The beige sedan was creeping down the wide open road when Cubiak closed in on it and swung into the other lane to pass. As he overtook the car, the sheriff glanced at the occupants. There were four people inside: a silver-haired driver and three elderly passengers, the lot of them gawking out the windows at a hillside of red sugar maples.

In another two days, Door County would overflow with weekend tourists like this quartet, up for the late fall colors. The visitors would stay at the resorts, dine in the restaurants, and hopscotch through the autumn festivals scheduled in the waterfront towns and villages. The influx would be good for the merchants and artists who relied on the tourist trade to pump much-needed dollars into the economy, but it was also sure to slow traffic and could potentially affect how quickly his team or the feds could move around the peninsula. Heavy traffic might even help the kidnappers travel about unnoticed. Could it be, the sheriff wondered, that the people who were holding Sneider knew Door County and had factored tourist traffic into their scheme?

Since Rowe had postponed the dive to Friday, Cubiak had time for his weekly lunch with Bathard. And after what Marilyn Ross had said and what he'd seen at Verne Pickler's place, the sheriff was glad for the opportunity to confer with his friend. The retired coroner had a long history with Door County, and more than once his familiarity with the peninsula had proved helpful.

Most Thursdays, the two men had Pechta's pretty much to themselves. But that day Cubiak had to elbow his way through a mob of people waiting for tables.

"Good thing I got here early or we wouldn't be eating for another hour," Bathard said when the sheriff reached their booth.

"Who are all these people?" Cubiak said.

"Some are locals but most are outsiders. I imagine they're drawn by the lure of the lurid and the prospect of treasure. You didn't hear? This morning Andrew Sneider announced that he is offering a reward for information contributing to the safe return of his father, and I'm guessing many of these people are hoping to sniff out the trail and get to Gerald Sneider before the feds do."

"But what are they doing here?" Cubiak hadn't seen so many people in the Fish Creek tavern since Ben Macklin's unofficial wake four years earlier.

"It's lunch time and people need to eat. They might also be hoping to pick up tips and leads."

"What's next, a reality TV kidnap show?" Cubiak said as his phone chirped. "Sorry, I've got to check this." He thought Moore was sending him an update on the drop, but the message was from Lisa's husband: *It's a girl! Mother and child fine.* Cubiak showed Bathard the text.

"She didn't need all that excitement," the sheriff said after he relayed the story of the morning's run-in with Bob Franklin.

"Maybe she did. Babies can get rather comfortable in the womb. Sometimes a little excitement helps jump-start the process." Bathard looked at Cubiak. "You worry too much," he said.

Cubiak shrugged. "So, what do you know about Pickler?"

"Not much, other than that he runs a lawn and cottage maintenance business and there are signs up and down the peninsula with his name and number."

"I found out this morning that Pickler used to work for Sneider." The sheriff spoke just as Amelia arrived with their usual order of Thursday's specials.

"Are you talking about Verne Pickler? Now there's a name from the long lost past," she said, sliding two baskets of potato salad and roast beef sandwiches onto the table.

"You know him?"

"Do I know him? Of course, I know him. I know everybody." Amelia gave Cubiak a mock punch. Then she shuffled behind the bar to her collection of old snapshots and photos and lifted a framed photo from the wall.

"Take a look at this," she said and dropped the picture in front of them. It was a photo from the Forest Home. "Gerald Sneider, a bunch of spoiled rich kids, and Verne Pickler, that crusty old goat," she said, pointing to a gangly young man with tousled blond hair. Amelia folded her arms and offered her version of a beaming smile. "We were kind of sweet on each other there for a while."

"Did Pickler live at the camp?" the sheriff asked.

"You mean like those charity kids? No, sir-ee. My Vernie had himself a good job back then. He was camp director."

Cubiak sat back. "Which meant exactly what?"

Amelia frowned. "That he did whatever Sneider told him to do." She swiped at a crumb on the table.

"Did Pickler like working for him?"

"Yeah, sure, the job paid okay and so at first, he liked it plenty well. Times were pretty lean around here, and Verne wasn't from the moneyed side of the tracks, as you probably guessed, so any job was a blessing. But after a while, he started resenting having to work there. Sneider was a hard nut, a real stickler for the rules. From what Vernie said, Sneider rode him pretty hard. Had rigid standards about work and life. A religious nut, too. He even came in here a few times preaching at my old man, trying to convince him to either close the shutters on Sundays or just sell soda pop to the folks. You believe that? Christ, I can tell you that went over like a giant balloon with a big hole in it."

Amelia slipped in next to Cubiak. "Look at Sneider smiling like that. You'd think he was a hell of a guy, wouldn't you? Taking in all those poor boys? People couldn't say enough about his good deeds and generosity. Some still hold him in high esteem, mostly because of what he did to help the Packers. But Vernie said Sneider had another side to him that he kept well hidden. He said he'd seen Sneider do things no one would believe. I asked him what he meant, but he wouldn't tell me. He said he could hardly believe it himself, and then one day he said he was going to quit, that he'd had enough."

"And did he?"

"Never got the chance. The camp up and closed and that was it."

"Did Pickler say why Sneider closed the camp?"

"No, and anyway it didn't matter. The place burned down not long after. There was nothing left but a few rotting timbers. Back then, there were summer camps all over the peninsula. Rich city folks wanted their children to enjoy fresh country air and good old-fashioned cooking. Most of the camps were adventure camps for boys but there were some for girls, too.

"In fact, one of the largest and fanciest camps for young ladies was located on Chambers Island. More of a summer charm school than anything."

Amelia pushed to her feet. "Good manners, dancing, and such," she said and twirled around twice before she stopped and steadied herself against the table. "Anyway, one by one they started closing so no one paid much attention when Sneider shut his operation."

She picked up the framed photo. "You gentlemen should eat. And I need to get back to work. No rest for the wicked," she said with a harsh laugh.

"That woman is going to work herself to death yet," Bathard said, loud enough for Amelia to hear, and she laughed again, giving a backward wave to them both. The doctor waited until she pushed through the kitchen door. "Do you think the people who snatched Sneider grabbed Pickler as well?"

"I doubt it, especially if the kidnappers are linked to terrorists. There's no payoff in holding Pickler."

"He didn't simply vanish. There has to be an explanation."

"Maybe he was scared and ran away. At this point there's no reason to think that his disappearance is connected with Sneider. Unless Sneider's kidnapping has something to do with that defunct camp. If that's the case, it could be that Pickler has an inkling of who snatched Sneider—and why—and has gone into hiding because he thinks he might be a target as well. Remember, he was Sneider's factotum at the camp."

Cubiak pushed his plate away. "Or Pickler is the one who grabbed Sneider. Why, we don't know, but it could have something to do with the Forest Home. Except for the dog, the timing works."

"If Pickler's involved, he wouldn't be able to take the dog along and risk it barking and drawing attention to wherever they're hiding out. Or maybe he figured he wouldn't be around for a while and didn't have anyone to take care of the animal. Rather than leave the dog home alone, he tied it up near the path along the shipping canal. Plenty of people walk the trail, assuring Pickler that someone would see the dog and take care of it, at least temporarily."

"You're starting to think like a detective," Cubiak said.

"I think like a doctor faced with a situation that requires a reasonable explanation."

"Well, then, explain this," Cubiak said and described Pickler's shrine.

"A heart stabbed with thorns? No wonder you had nightmares," Bathard said. "What is it about religion that there seems to be so much focus on fire and brimstone and all the horrors that will descend upon humanity? I always thought the Christian God was supposed to be a God of love."

Amelia plopped two heavy steins on the table. "Sometimes he's a God of money." She gave them a knowing look as she wiped the beer that had sloshed out. "You don't think so, turn on the radio Sunday morning. Or even better, go to church." She tucked the bar rag behind the waistband of her apron and saluted. "See you gentlemen next week."

When they were alone again Cubiak laid the pamphlets on the table. "Then there are these," he said.

Bathard slid his reading glasses from his pocket. "I have the feeling I'm not going to like what I see here," he said as he picked up the pamphlets. As he skimmed through the material his face clouded. When he finished, he remained silent for several seconds.

"These represent an abomination of the highest order. Arrogance coupled with good intentions that move so far asunder they tip into perversity. A man bloated with self-righteousness who dares to pass judgement and impose his will on others, worse even, on innocent youth. It roils the blood to think of what can come of such twisted thinking. What the hell did that man do to those kids?"

"That's what I want to know. And how involved was Pickler?" Cubiak wiped his glasses against his sleeve. "After seeing his shed, I figured he was some kind of religious fanatic trying to purify himself for imagined sins, taming the flesh and all that." The sheriff paused. "Of course, it's also possible he was punishing himself for actual misdeeds, things he did even though he knew they were wrong. Things his boss Gerald Sneider ordered him to do."

UNDER THE CLOCK TOWER

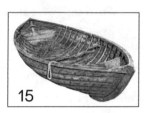

15

At the station, Cubiak found Agents Moore and Harrison huddled over a laptop in the incident room.

The feds were both suited up. Another press conference? New developments? the sheriff wondered. The agents seemed surprised to see him.

"I thought you were off dealing with a lost dog," Moore said.

Cubiak ignored the comment. "When's the drop?" he asked.

"We haven't . . . ," Harrison started to say but Moore interrupted. "Day's not over. Plenty of time to go," he said, and then he glanced at his watch as if looking for reassurance.

Cubiak was enjoying the moment. "So nothing yet," he said. He turned toward the window and closed the blinds against the bright afternoon sun. Cubiak suddenly was tired and wanted to sit, but the feds were still on their feet and he knew it was important to stay at eye level. He crossed his arms and leaned against the wall.

"Since we're in this together, let me share what I've got," he said.

Moore picked up a stack of computer printouts. "Go on."

Cubiak hesitated. The feds had added more reports, newspaper clips, and coded entries to the incident board, bolstering their theory that a fledgling terrorist organization was behind the kidnapping scheme. Moore had already rejected the suggestion that the bones found on the beach warranted any consideration despite their proximity to Sneider's camp for boys. He'd be as quick to dismiss Marilyn Ross's suspicion about nightmarish events at the Forest Home as the ramblings of a grieving widow. If Cubiak brought up the possible link between Leeland Ross, the rope used to tie up the bag of kittens he'd pulled from the bay, and the rope found in Sneider's home, Moore would say he was letting his imagination get the better of him.

The sheriff had to give them something concrete. "Remember the dog that was brought in this morning?" he said.

Moore skimmed the top sheet and gave it to Harrison. "That's what you're giving us, a report on a lost dog?"

Cubiak bristled. "The dog isn't lost. It belongs to a local man named Verne Pickler who for unknown reasons left it tied up along a popular walking path." The sheriff sensed Moore's growing impatience. "Indications are the dog was left on Sunday, which by itself isn't of any importance. What might be significant, however, is that Pickler once worked for Gerald Sneider."

Moore looked up from the sheaf of papers in his hand. "Go on," he said again. This time both agents were attentive.

Cubiak told them what he'd learned from Amelia Pechta about Pickler's job at the Forest Home. "Something happened that made him decide to quit," the sheriff said. Then he walked them through Pickler's house and shed.

"What you're telling us is that the man's a religious fanatic. There are plenty of them around."

"Look what else I found there," the sheriff said as he passed the pamphlets to Moore.

"Pretty disgusting stuff," Moore said, handing the material to Harrison. "But all this proves is that Gerald Sneider, the exemplary citizen, had some pretty extreme ideas and was a bigot from way back. There's nothing here to connect Pickler to his disappearance."

"What about the neighbor's suggestion that Pickler took off because he feared being a possible target himself?"

"Why? Because of alleged misdeeds that occurred at the camp decades ago? An incident or incidents that no one has ever actually described? This is like one of those modern-day urban legends that spreads across the Internet. Everyone believes something to be true even though no one can prove it. Does that stop anyone from repeating the story? No. It's taken as gospel when in fact it's nothing more than gossip."

Moore pinched the back of his neck. "You think I'm being too narrow on this, focusing on the terrorist connection, don't you? But you're doing the same, refusing to see any possible solution that doesn't involve the bones you found on the beach. Not far, as you've pointed out, from the former site of the Forest Home. But also not far from the site of half a dozen shipwrecks."

The agent looked at Cubiak and hardened his gaze. "And that's not all. I've done my homework, too. Door County has been inhabited by one group of people or another for a very long time. Those bones you found could be the remains from a young logger killed in a drunken brawl or a fire that burned an old bunkhouse. They could be the bones of Native Americans who died before the first French trappers showed up. Tell me this, Sheriff, in all the time Sneider's camp was operational, were there any complaints made to authorities, any reports of misdeeds or foul play?"

Cubiak stiffened. "Not that I'm aware of, but . . ."

Moore's phone rang. "There you go, then," he said as he tapped the screen and both he and Harrison turned their backs on the sheriff.

Cubiak wasn't sure which he found more irritating: his humiliation or the fact that Moore was right. They were both being stubborn. The problem was that the federal agent had accumulated a good amount of hard evidence to back up his theories. And all Cubiak had was hearsay. Black and white versus gray.

"Ultimately, it doesn't matter who's right. The important thing is to find Sneider," he said. He was talking to Rowe, who stood in front of the sheriff's desk, unsure how to respond.

Cubiak shoved a drawer shut with his knee. Who was he kidding? Of course it mattered. It was human nature to want to be right—at least some of the time.

"Wouldn't surprise me if the whole thing blew up in their faces," he said. Then, chagrined by his pettiness, he pointed to the stack of papers Rowe carried. "What's the story out there?"

"Front-page news," the deputy replied, setting them on the desk.

Cubiak skimmed the headlines. Five of the newspapers continued to give the Sneider story top coverage, but there was nothing about the missing man in the first few pages of the *New York Times*.

When the sheriff looked up, Rowe was still standing in front of his desk.

"We're on for tomorrow?" Cubiak asked.

"All set."

"Whatever comes down later today, we follow through on this."

"Right, Chief, as long as the weather holds."

Alone again, Cubiak combed through the *Times* searching for some mention of the Door County kidnapping. What he finally found was a brief paragraph in the Nation section, an item picked up from a news wire.

What the hell was going on with Steve Ross? the sheriff wondered. He checked the time. It was a few minutes to four, almost five on the East Coast. Maybe he could still get a call through.

It took Cubiak several minutes to negotiate the paper's automated answering system, and even after he reached an actual person he was bounced from one desk to another before he finally landed in the news department. The woman who took the call said she was the assistant editor. She had a heavy New York accent and seemed amused to be getting a call from a sheriff in the Midwest. He could almost hear her saying, "Wisconsin, really? Now where exactly is Wisconsin?"—though she was too polite to actually voice the question.

"Gerald Sneider, yes, I'm aware of the situation but we haven't assigned the story yet. We're waiting for further developments," she said.

"But you have a reporter, a Stephen Ross, who's up here working on it," Cubiak said.

"Excuse me, whom did you say?"

Cubiak repeated the name.

"There's no one by that name in the news department," the editor said, adding, "but a lot of people work for the paper. If you hold on a minute, I'll check the directory."

Cubiak heard the familiar click of her keyboard. A few moments later, the editor came back online.

"Sheriff Cubiak, you're correct there is a Stephen Ross on staff. But he's in the obit department," she said. "He writes death notices."

As Cubiak lowered the phone, he glanced up to find Gwen Harrison in the doorway. Her eyes were wide and her hands clenched. "Look, about Agent Moore," she said, but then she paused, uncertain how to continue.

"No need to apologize for your boss. We're all on edge," the sheriff said, wondering if that was all she'd come for.

Harrison walked forward and quieted her voice. "Eight o'clock tonight. Andrew just got word."

Cubiak felt her excitement ripple across the room. "Where?"

"Fourth and Main."

Cubiak was puzzled. "That's a very public location."

"With all the inherent disadvantages, I know, but it gives us more cover as well. The kidnappers have scaled back their demands to one million. Andrew's to come alone and leave the money in a duffel under the bench by the clock tower. The message was delivered by a kid on a bike who said he was hired off Craigslist, if you can believe that."

At this point, Cubiak thought, he'd believe anything. The previous demands, first for four hundred thousand and then for four million, had led him to wonder if there was some significance to the number *four* or if the money was simply to be split four ways. The current ransom demand seemed to deviate from the pattern, though it was for an amount evenly divisible by four.

"How do you know this is genuine? With all the publicity, the note could be from someone else trying to take advantage of the situation."

"Sneider's driver's license was in the envelope, and minutes after the note was dropped off, Andrew got a call from his father. It was very brief, barely a couple of seconds, just long enough for him to say a word or two. Andrew recognized his voice."

Harrison slipped into the chair facing the desk and crossed her legs. "Also, they want the payoff in Sneider's 'GB duffel,' which Andrew says is an old Packers bag his father's had for years. Who else would know about that?"

She rested both hands on the desk. "Agent Moore wants you to go up to the estate. You're to send the bag back with the deputy and then stay with Andrew and make sure he's on board. We'll take care of things at this end and let you know when we're ready for you to drive him down."

"Why'd they lower the ransom demand?" Cubiak said.

"They want the money in hundreds so it's probably about the logistics of taking possession."

"You'll pay up then?"

With a dancer's grace Harrison rose to her feet and stood before him erect and alert. "We'll make them think so."

Cubiak waited for an explanation but then realized that she was looking at the wall clock. It was four fifteen. "You were right about the call coming today. Congratulations," he said.

Harrison beamed. Watching her triumphant walk toward the door, the sheriff wondered what it was about strong women that he found so attractive.

When Cubiak was halfway to Ellison Bay he texted Cate that he'd be home late and not to wait up for him. Immediately he regretted sending the message. Would she even be at the house? Did she care? The last two days, she'd stayed at her own place and he didn't know why. Was it something he'd done, or was it because she was spending time with her ex-husband?

Maybe the feds were right about the kidnappers, Cubiak thought, pushing aside his personal concerns. Although the reduction in the ransom was puzzling, Harrison's explanation made sense. He tried to imagine a million dollars in hundred-dollar bills and hoped the duffel was large enough to hold it all. By now Cubiak's resentment against the feds had dwindled away. As the case moved forward, every step was crucial. The payoff had to go smoothly—Sneider's life might depend on it.

The wind had shifted, bringing in warmer air, and Cubiak drove with his window down, enjoying the occasional whiff of burning leaves. The peninsula had put away the things of summer and embraced the emblems of autumn. Pumpkins and dried stalks of corn festooned the homes and shops along the way. Midway through Sister Bay, he stopped to let a troop of miniature witches and pirates cross the street. They dashed in front of the jeep, twitching with excitement and toting festive bags and plastic buckets in the shapes of pumpkins and skulls. It was Halloween, he remembered.

"Trick or treat," Cubiak said aloud as the children hopped to safety on the curb.

A plastic skeleton in a shop window made him think of the bones on the beach. By this time tomorrow Rowe would have made his dive looking for the source and the FBI would have rescued Gerald Sneider, nabbed those responsible, and recovered the ransom money. The sheriff would have wrapped up his role and left the feds to the paperwork and the prosecution of the kidnappers. There'd be plenty of time for him to sort through the situation at Baileys Harbor.

The media camped outside the estate had grown to a small mob with rows of vehicles parked along the road in both directions. A few of the reporters had rolled out sleeping bags to mark their turf near the gate. One had even set up a green pup tent. When Cubiak turned in, they swarmed the jeep and begged for news, like kids asking for Halloween treats. The sheriff wished he'd brought a bag of candy for them.

In the main house, Andrew waited in the media room. A movie flashed across the large screen but when Cubiak asked what he was watching, Andrew looked blank. "I don't know. Something," he responded.

Andrew had cleaned himself up. He was showered and shaved and dressed in sporty charcoal corduroy pants and a muted yellow turtleneck. A black wool jacket hung on the back of a chair.

Sneider's canvas Green Bay Packers bag was on the coffee table. Andrew saw the sheriff looking at it. "One of my father's good luck charms. I found it in an upstairs closet," he said.

Cubiak rolled the duffel into a grocery bag and gave it to the deputy to take back to sheriff's headquarters.

"Aren't we going now?" Andrew asked.

"We've got time."

Cubiak asked to see the note that had been delivered to the house. Word for word it read just as Harrison had told him.

"The feds said you talked to your father," the sheriff said.

"Not really 'talked.' He was on just long enough to say my name. He sounded different, weak and scared, but I knew it was him," Andrew explained.

He clicked off the television.

"Where are they getting the money?" he asked. There was more idle curiosity than urgency to the question.

"I don't know," the sheriff replied.

"Agent Harrison said I wasn't to worry, that they would take care of everything."

Cubiak nodded.

"I wouldn't mind a drink."

"Not a good idea," the sheriff said. "Hungry?"

Andrew shrugged.

In the gourmet kitchen, Cubiak heated a can of tomato soup and fixed grilled cheese sandwiches. Comfort food, he realized, as he set the meal on two TV trays.

Andrew had turned the TV on again and switched the channel to a documentary on blue whales. "They're big as school buses. Did you know that?"

"Yeah."

"You ever see one?"

"No."

"Me neither. You fish?"

"Not much any more. I did a lot when I was a kid."

"Me, too. I used to catch bluegill off the dock."

Small talk filled the void.

Cubiak was cleaning up in the kitchen when Agent Moore called. They ran through the specifics and then the sheriff went to find Andrew.

"Time to go," he said.

Andrew slipped on his jacket but his nerves failed when he tried to work the zipper. "You'll be okay," Cubiak said.

To hide him from the reporters, the sheriff had Andrew lie on the back seat, and then he covered him with a blanket. The last thing they needed was the paparazzi chasing them down the peninsula. Once they were through Ellison Bay, Cubiak turned onto a side road and pulled over on the shoulder. "Coast is clear. You can move up front now," he told Andrew.

They drove in silence, Cubiak thinking of the many things that could go wrong that evening, Andrew with his head back and his eyes shut.

"You okay?" the sheriff said.

Andrew grunted, then replied, "I'm praying."

Good idea, Cubiak thought as he steered into the darkness.

Some time later, Andrew emerged from his stupor, and the closer they got to Sturgeon Bay, the more agitated he grew: fidgeting with his fingers, tapping the dashboard, shifting his weight in the seat. They were several miles from town when the red lights on the giant radio broadcast towers appeared against the evening sky. Andrew groaned and folded over into himself. Cubiak could smell the fear rolling off him. "Take it easy," the sheriff said, even as he tightened his grip on the wheel.

To avoid the media crowd gathered outside the station, Moore and Cubiak had agreed to meet at the sheriff's house. The agent was waiting when they pulled in.

"That's it, just him?" Andrew said, looking around wildly as if expecting to find the cavalry. He fumbled with the door and practically fell on top of Moore. "Where is everyone?" Andrew asked, ignoring the agent's outstretched hand.

"They're in town, already in position. We have time," Moore replied. The duffel was on the ground at his feet. It had plumped out nicely.

While Butch sniffed his shoes, Moore set the bag on the kitchen table. "Go ahead, open it."

Andrew undid the zipper and peered inside. "So that's what a million looks like." He raised the duffel several inches off the table. "It's heavy."

"Twenty-two pounds," Moore said.

Suddenly Andrew dropped the bag and threw up his hands. His face was wet with sweat. "I can't do it," he said.

Moore made a show of pulling out a chair and sitting down as if this were just a casual get-together of friends. "Why not?" he asked.

"I . . . I don't have my car. If they know what I drive, they'll expect to see it."

Moore smiled patiently. "It's Halloween. There are a lot of people out and about, and we've made sure the streets in both directions are parked up. If anyone's watching, they'll see you walking up the street and figure you had to park a couple blocks away. Ideally you reach the bench at eight, stop to listen to the chimes, put the bag underneath, and then continue on your way."

"What if I'm early? What then?"

Moore picked up the bag and walked to the other side of the kitchen. "Easy," he said as he turned and started back toward the chair. "If you get there before the hour, sit down with the duffel in your lap—like this—and wait." He spoke slowly, demonstrating each step. "The bell tower chimes at eight. Ding, ding, etcetera. When it's finished, bend over, slide the bag under the bench, and then walk away."

"That's it?"

"Right."

"What if someone tries to grab me?"

"No one's going to come after you. All they want is the money. Here, try it."

Moore gave the bag to Andrew and motioned him across the room. "Go on, show me," he said as if he were coaxing a child. First time through, Moore sounded the chimes as Andrew approached the chair. "Don't rush. It's okay if you're a little late, makes it more credible." The second time, he made him sit and wait.

"Okay?"

Some of the color had returned to Andrew's face. "Yeah. Okay," he said.

"The rest is up to us," Moore said and clapped Andrew's shoulder. "Don't worry, we've got it covered."

At half past seven, Cubiak pulled into the post office parking lot and stopped in the shadows behind the loading dock. "You know where we're at?" he asked. In the dim light Andrew nodded.

"You got three blocks to cover. Take your time. Look in the store windows. Play tourist or shopper, whatever. Go around the long way," he said, pointing toward the park. "I'll watch until you reach the corner and then I need to get in place."

Cubiak lifted a brown wig and cowboy hat from the back seat and put them on. "A wannabe Willie Nelson. My disguise," he explained.

Andrew almost laughed.

When it was time to begin, the sheriff retrieved the duffel and went around to open the passenger door.

"It's okay to be nervous," he said as he handed the bag to Andrew. "But don't worry, everything will be fine. We've got this covered." Cubiak realized that he was echoing Moore. But did the feds really have everything under control? the sheriff wondered. The kidnappers had probably spent days, maybe even weeks, laying out the scenario, and the FBI had had only hours to plan a response.

Andrew walked away like a man petrified with fear. With each stilted step, the cumbersome bag bounced awkwardly against his knee. He kept up like this for a full block. It wasn't until he rounded the corner onto Main that he started to relax. Cubiak waited until he lost sight of Andrew, and then he took off in the opposite direction, circling toward the bank on the street north of the clock tower. At five minutes before the hour, he entered the glass-walled lobby and assumed his position at the ATM. From there he had a clear view across the alley and through the small park to the corner where the clock tower and the bench were located.

Along Main Street strings of twinkling orange lights softened the darkness and gave the downtown a festive feeling. Thanks to an unexpected warm front that had pushed through in the afternoon, it was a balmy night, and people were out. One woman wore a witch's hat. Another who was dressed in black leggings and a sweater sported cat ears and a tail. Someone costumed as Darth Vader strode along behind them. Tourists or FBI? Or residents on their way to a party?

Stores and restaurants were still open, and people stopped to look at window displays or wandered in to shop or eat. Kids were downtown as well, trick-or-treating from one shop to another.

Andrew reached the bell tower four minutes early. He was on target, but for a moment he looked around as if lost or confused. "Sit down," Cubiak muttered under his breath.

Andrew glanced up at the clock and lowered himself to the edge of the bench. Only his back was visible to Cubiak but it seemed clear from the way his shoulders curved forward that he was holding the duffel on his lap as instructed.

At eight, the clock chimed. For several minutes, the soft tones filled the night air. Then they faded to nothing, and in the silence that followed, Andrew bent over as if to retrieve something he'd dropped.

He was taking too long. "Come on," Cubiak said, urging him to be done with it. Finally, Andrew sat up and slowly rose to his feet. In the light from the streetlamp, Cubiak made out the dark lump beneath the bench. The duffel was in place.

Nothing happened.

Andrew strode to the corner and froze.

"Don't look," Cubiak said.

As if he'd heard the sheriff, the Sneider heir crossed the intersection and passed a couple stopped outside an antique store. Soon he was just another shadowy figure walking along the street.

Cubiak checked his watch. Two minutes had elapsed and the bag remained under the bench.

Darth Vader strode purposefully past the tower, his cape billowing in a sudden breeze. Cubiak tensed, waiting for him to snatch the duffel.

Another five minutes dragged by. Half a dozen cars had stopped at the intersection, one long enough to drop off a young couple outfitted in hockey uniforms. Still the bag sat unclaimed.

Moore had given orders that they wait as long as needed, but Cubiak was getting restless. What if one of the young trick-or-treaters spied the bag and picked it up? What would the kidnappers do?

The sheriff started to text Moore. Suddenly without warning a flash mob of teenagers in costumes swarmed the corner. Running and riding bikes, they flew in from both sides of Main and the cross street. Waving banners and blowing horns, the crowd swelled to an outrageous number of youth. Almost instantly the intersection churned with chaos.

Cubiak bolted from the lobby and raced toward the throng. Rap music blasted and the kids danced and gyrated to the beat. Five boys jumped onto the bench and began yelling "Party! Party! Party!" Glass bottles hit the pavement and shattered.

When Cubiak reached the fringe of the frenetic crowd, a whistle blew and the kids scattered. Flying like the wind. As one girl raced past, the sheriff grabbed hold of her cape but the flimsy fabric ripped and he was left holding a long sequined scrap of nylon. He dropped to his knees and looked under the bench for the duffel. The bag was gone.

Moore ran up, redfaced and furious. "The duffel?" he asked.

Cubiak shook his head.

"Fuck!"

Cubiak waited for the outburst to continue. Instead Moore clenched his mouth tight and slowly settled down. When he spoke again, he was calm. "They think they've outsmarted us but there's a tracking device in the bag and my guys are following it now. In the meantime, we've collared three of the revelers. We'll get what we can from them," he said.

Cubiak was doubtful. The kids were probably ripped on adrenalin, he thought. They wouldn't know anything.

An hour later, the team reconvened at sheriff's headquarters. In a small conference room, Agent Harrison talked to Andrew, trying to calm him down. In the incident room, Moore monitored reports from the men tracing the bag.

"They're headed north, up the peninsula," Moore said.

Moments passed. He leapt to his feet and hurled his phone to the wall. "Goddamn. Those fuckers left the empty bag in a cornfield," he said. Moore slammed a clenched fist to the table. "They must have emptied it earlier and then split up." He kicked a chair halfway across the room. Then, as quickly as he had erupted, Moore calmed again.

"Go talk to those kids, see what you can get from them," he said.

Cubiak grabbed a bowl of Halloween candy from the lobby and walked into the room where the three teens were waiting. The boys regarded the sheriff with sullen indifference but beneath the thin bravado he sensed fear.

"You know who I am?" he asked.

They glanced at each other and nodded.

"You're not in trouble," Cubiak said. He shoved the dish of candy across the table toward them.

It took a minute but first one, then another, and then all three helped themselves to chocolate bars.

"If you tell me how this all worked, you can go home," Cubiak said, reaching for a piece of licorice. "Your parents don't have to know."

Did they believe him?

Cubiak pretended to receive a phone message and excused himself, leaving them time to confer. When he returned after five minutes, they were ready to talk.

The call to meet on the corner was sent over Twitter and Facebook. They were promised a party. Music and free food at eight o'clock. Bring a friend.

"Didn't you wonder who was behind it?" he asked.

All three shrugged.

"Who cared? It was something to do," one of them said.

When he was satisfied they'd told him all they knew, Cubiak sent the kids home.

Moore was still in the conference room when the sheriff reported back to him.

"That's about what I figured it would be," the agent said and went back to pounding on his laptop.

Cubiak waited at the window. It was late and the landscape was dark except for the sprinkle of stars above the tree line. "What now?" he said.

"Plan B." Moore didn't elaborate.

"How much was in the duffel?"

"*Not* a million dollars. We put about ten grand on the top to make it appear authentic. The rest was paper."

"You'll play around like that with a man's life?"

Moore exhaled loudly. "The kidnappers aren't going to harm Sneider. They want the ransom and know they won't get it unless they can prove he's still alive. They'll try again but this time they'll up the ante and . . ."

Before he could finish Andrew burst through the doorway and hurtled himself across the floor toward Moore.

"The money's gone?" Andrew was red faced and waving clenched fists in the air. "What the fuck does that mean. This was supposed to lead to my father, to get him back! Now what?"

Moore didn't flinch. "We have a . . ."

Andrew cut in. "A what? A contingency plan?" His voice dripped with scorn. "You know what, fuck you. Fuck all of you."

COLD WATER

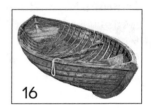

16

Cubiak bolted awake. After four hours of sleep, he was edgy but felt rested enough that he knew it was pointless to stay in bed. Following the fiasco with the ransom money, he'd hung around headquarters for more than half the night, caught in the undertow between Andrew's ongoing rant and Moore's studied silence. Even after one of the deputies drove Andrew back to Ellison Bay, Cubiak remained, ready to help as needed. When it was obvious there'd be no new developments that night, he left. But at home, he was too agitated to sleep. Trusting in beer to counter the effects of the caffeine he'd consumed through the evening, he sat up and drank with only Butch for company.

Cubiak's first thought was about Moore, who'd probably been up all night hatching a new plan to rescue Gerald Sneider. The sheriff almost felt sorry for the FBI agent. Sometimes things went awry. But, fuck it, he thought, echoing Andrew. The feds own this; let them plot things from here.

His next thought was about Cate. Where was she? What was happening to them? Before he could change his mind, Cubiak dialed her landline. He didn't expect her to answer and was startled by the soft hello that drifted over the wire after the third ring. At least she was at her place and not at some hotel with her ex-husband.

Cubiak wanted to ask her when she was coming back—if she was coming back. That's where he wanted to start. Instead, hearing her voice, he told her he might need her to take some pictures later that day for official business.

"You called because you want me to do a photo shoot?" she said. She sounded disappointed.

"Only if we find anything worth documenting." He knew he was being deliberately vague, something she didn't like.

"Where?"

"Near Baileys Harbor."

There was a noise in the background on her end. "Just a minute," she said into the phone and then something with her face away from the receiver that he couldn't catch. Was she talking to a neighbor? Had she called a plumber to repair the dripping pipe he'd promised to fix but hadn't? Or was it the former husband dallying over morning coffee?

"Where Butch found the bones," she said finally.

"Not exactly, but close by. I'm going out with Rowe this morning. I don't want to waste your time unless we find something. That is, if you're available."

"Of course I'm available. What are you looking for?"

You. I'm looking for you, he wanted to say, but pride stopped him. Cate had pulled away from him; she should be the one reaching out, not him.

"I don't really know. Whatever we find, if anything," he said, and then he hung up.

The sheriff's third thought concerned the weather and got him up from the bed and over to the window. The weather had flip-flopped again. Skies were cloudy, temperatures were down, and there was more wind than had been predicted. He called Rowe but the deputy insisted they were still on.

Before he left, Cubiak checked for messages. Nothing from Moore. Fine then. I'm on my own, he thought.

The *Speedy Sister* was tied up at the marina just past the steel bridge in downtown Sturgeon Bay. The twenty-five-foot cruiser was one of the last vessels still in the water. The boat looked sleek and sassy. Cubiak had never been on board, but he'd often heard his deputy talk about the vessel's powerful engine and the top speeds he and his friends hit on the open water. Youthful braggadocio, the sheriff hoped as he made his way down the pier.

Rowe was alone on the boat.

"Where's your friend?"

"He's sick and had to cancel."

The north wind bit through the several layers Cubiak had on. He pulled up his hood and looked down at the undulating water. "I thought you're not supposed to dive alone. Are you sure about this?" he said as he clambered aboard.

"I know that area. I'll be fine. And it's always calmer underneath. As long as you're okay up top, we're good to go."

Lesson number one that Cubiak had learned from Bathard: on the water, the captain was always in charge. "Your call," the sheriff said with a brisk salute to his young deputy.

Rowe swallowed a yawn, and Cubiak noticed the pouches under his eyes. "How much sleep did you get last night?" he said.

"Enough."

Rowe tossed a pair of gloves to the sheriff. "You're going to want these, too," he said, and then he turned the ignition switch. The motor coughed several times. When it caught they began making their way east through Sturgeon Bay toward Lake Michigan.

Water levels were at a record twenty-year high, and when they reached the bridge Cubiak ducked. Rowe laughed but then he lowered his head as well. The bridge was both the oldest and the lowest of the structures that spanned the bay. "Damn thing's always needing repairs,"

Rowe said. But he spoke with pride as they slid beneath the historic structure.

They passed under two more bridges before they entered the Ship Canal, a seven-mile channel that connected the bay to the lake. The waterway was made up of two segments; the first was a dredged portion of the bay and the second was a trench that had been dug through the land itself in the late 1800s. The trench was 1.3 miles long and 125 feet wide. Rowe steered down the middle. "You should see the tankers come through. There's no room for error for the big boys," he explained.

As the coast guard station came into view, Cubiak felt the boat fighting the current. Was it a mistake to be going out today? he wondered. He glanced at the deputy, looking for a sign of worry, but the young man at the wheel remained unperturbed.

"Fantastic, isn't it?" Rowe said as they motored past the boxy red lighthouse at the end of the north pier and entered the lake.

To Cubiak, the twenty-five-foot *Speedy Sister* was one very small vessel on a body of water that stretched some three hundred miles from end to end, a ratio that was more intimidating than fantastic.

Rowe pushed the throttle forward and pressed the bow into the waves, sending spray billowing up on either side. They seemed to be flying recklessly over the water. This had to be top speed, Cubiak thought, when incredibly they started going even faster. A few minutes later, the deputy stepped away from the wheel. "You want to take over? I need to check my gear," he said, shouting into the wind.

The sheriff had no choice but to trade places.

"Keep us about half a mile offshore and we'll be fine," Rowe said.

Still struggling to find his sea legs, the sheriff grabbed the wheel and held on as it thrummed in his grip.

Cubiak was too cold to talk and grateful to see that his deputy had come prepared with hot coffee. After they'd each taken several swallows, Rowe starting sorting through the pile of equipment in the cockpit.

They traveled the rest of the way in silence: past the county boat launch at Lily Bay, past the pearly sands of Whitefish Dunes State Park and Cave Point, past the sleepy village of Jacksonport, nearly empty of tourists this late in the season. By the time they reached Baileys Harbor, Cubiak had become accustomed to the speed and almost regretted having to slow down. He watched Rowe suit up.

"You going to be warm enough?" the sheriff asked.

"Like a baby in its crib." Rowe tugged at the sleeves of his dry suit. "Where exactly are we headed?"

"Over there." Cubiak pointed to the curve of land that formed the outer barrier of the town's wide-open bay. "We'll start on the lake side."

"The shipwrecks are pretty far out."

"Well, there may be something closer in. Worth a look."

"Whatever you say, Chief. It's just that it's not a likely spot." Rowe picked up an air tank. "But always happy to poke around."

Cubiak steered the boat in toward land. When they were about a quarter mile from shore, he dropped anchor and Rowe went over the side.

As much as the cockpit allowed, Cubiak paced. Everything involving scuba diving worried the sheriff: deep water, unknown hazards, potential equipment failure. So many things could go wrong. What if there was a leak in the air hose? Or Rowe found a wreck and got trapped inside? The longer Rowe was gone, the more Cubiak wished his deputy hadn't made the dive alone.

A cold gust came up. Cubiak started to cross his arms but the boat bobbled and he had to fling them wide to find his balance. He hoped it was true, as Rowe had said, that things were calmer beneath the surface.

Cubiak checked his watch. Ten minutes had passed since Rowe started the dive. The deputy claimed he was an accomplished diver, but was that true? the sheriff wondered. All he had to go on was the young man's eager reassurance that he knew what he was doing. Cubiak leaned over the side of the cruiser. What the hell had he been thinking?

He'd sent his deputy down and was responsible for him. Four years after his daughter's accidental death, Cubiak struggled with guilt over the circumstances. How could he bear it if something happened to Rowe, a young man he looked upon as a son?

Another five minutes slogged by before Rowe popped through the surface of the slate-colored water and pulled off his mask. He was some ten feet off the bow. "Nada," he called out and then started swimming toward the boat.

Cubiak insisted Rowe rest and have more coffee before going down again.

The second dive was made off the point and lasted nearly twenty minutes. Again, Rowe came up empty. Cubiak started to wonder if he hadn't overreacted to the discovery of the bones on the beach. Given the geography and history of the peninsula, maybe old bones washed ashore more often than he realized.

The sheriff checked his phone again, but there were no messages from Moore. Maybe the agent was right about the kidnapping being part of a larger pattern of domestic terrorism. The FBI had wasted no time regrouping from the previous day's fiasco. Federal agents were probably already on the culprits' trail. There'd be a flurry of excitement when they nabbed the suspects. Then, after all the stories had been filed and the journalists raced away on the trail of other breaking news, life on the peninsula would return to normal.

"Sir!" The shout came from behind the boat. "Chief!"

The sheriff turned.

Rowe had swum from the lake into the bay. He was treading water with one hand and holding something aloft with the other. When he saw that he had Cubiak's attention he headed back. Rowe was a strong swimmer. Even with the current pushing against him, he covered the distance quickly and was barely out of breath when he reached the boat.

Cubiak leaned over to help him.

"Take this first," Rowe said. He handed the sheriff a long, slender segment of bone. The piece was smooth and icy cold. Cubiak felt a quiet dread as he laid it on one of the boat cushions.

"You were right," Rowe said. He'd climbed aboard unaided and was shrugging off the harness and air tank. "There was nothing in the lake, but on the bay side, the bottom is covered with rocks. I found that wedged between two good-size boulders. And that's not all," he continued as he toweled off his face.

"I went all up and down from the point to the curve, too. For the most part, the water's pretty shallow, but in a couple spots where it's deeper, there are some good-size rocky ledges jutting out. The overhang closest to the bay entrance has something wedged under it. I couldn't really make it out but whatever is down there, it's made of wood."

"Maybe it's part of a barge," Cubiak said. On several occasions, Bathard had told him about the wooden barges that had been used for hauling lumber a century earlier. Many of them had run aground on rocks and sandbars, and while most of the wrecks had been salvaged, many were left to slowly disintegrate underwater.

"I don't think so. It looked small, more like a rowboat. I marked the spot. There. See it?"

Rowe pointed toward the inlet. The waves had picked up and formed a rolling surf that rose and broke against the rocky shore. At first, Cubiak saw only water, but then, in the shallow trough that formed between two long waves, he spotted a red plastic flag. As the water moved beneath it, the marker lifted up and then dropped down, a singular and sinister splash of color in the dark water.

"You're right, you know. Something's down there," Rowe said.

Cubiak remained still. Not for the first time in his life, and certainly not for the first time as sheriff of Door County, he wished he was wrong.

"My uncle runs a small salvage and hauling business. He's got an old barge that he uses. It's nothing fancy but I'm pretty sure it can handle the job."

Rowe shook off water like a wet dog. He was animated, excited by the discovery. "We can't just let it stay there."

Cubiak hadn't expected anything like this but he realized his deputy was right.

"You want me to call him?" Rowe asked.

"Tell him we need him today."

It was nearly noon when Cubiak dropped off Rowe at home for a hot shower. The deputy looked done in.

"Try and get some rest, too, if you can," Cubiak said.

The sheriff regretted pushing Rowe, but he had no choice. Leaving his deputy, he drove to Emma Pardy's office. He waited while she finished a call to her daughter's school and then gave her the bone Rowe had recovered that morning. To the sheriff it was the latest specimen of what he was now viewing as evidence. But evidence of what, he wasn't sure.

"I can't do anything without a DNA analysis," she said.

"I know that, but I think we're going to be finding more. Maybe enough to allow for an educated guess."

"When?"

"Hopefully this afternoon. Tomorrow for certain. I'm not really sure, but soon." He glanced out the window, where storm clouds were gathering in the west. "It depends on the weather."

"As it often does around here," Pardy added.

Cubiak was on the bridge, heading to the east side of Sturgeon Bay, when Rowe phoned. "I just talked to my uncle, George Waslow. He said he can be there by two, if that works for you," he said.

"Good, thanks," Cubiak said. He called Cate. While the phone rang, he wondered what he'd do if she'd changed her mind.

"I'm set to go," she said when she finally answered.

"We'll be on the water so you'd better bundle up," he said.

The sheriff had another stop to make. Cruising up and down the town's main streets, he searched for the red car with the New York plates. On his second pass, he came across it outside the Rusty Scupper. Steve Ross was inside. He was unshaven and sullen and wearing an old flannel shirt that made him look more like a lumberjack than a New York reporter. Steve was hunched over the bar, the signature popcorn basket at one elbow and a tumbler with a slosh of amber liquid on the bottom at the other. He was drinking early and taking it neat. Not a good sign.

"Lunch?" Cubiak asked, indicating the half-empty popcorn basket.

The former Door County resident grunted and then caught Cubiak's reflection in the mirror and sat up. "Sheriff."

A trio of loudmouths filled the space next to them and Cubiak moved closer, not wanting to share the conversation with the rest of the clientele. "There's something I'd like you to see, if you're free this afternoon."

"What?"

"I don't know yet."

Ross tossed down the rest of the drink. "Then why do you think I'd be interested?"

"Let's say I have a gut feeling. Something like instinct. You'd probably call it a nose for news."

Ross frowned. "Why me? The town is crawling with reporters."

"True enough, but you're the hometown boy. Only seems fair to give you a leg up on the competition."

Ross bent over his empty glass as if considering the offer. "Do I have a choice?"

Cubiak's quick smile was the only answer he gave.

Ross snorted and grabbed a fistful of popcorn as he slid off the stool. He took a moment to find his balance, then fished a ten from his wallet, tossed the money on the bar, and walked toward the door with Cubiak on his heels.

The sheriff was still cold from his morning on the water, but he made the drive to Baileys Harbor with the windows down, hoping the fresh air would help sober up his passenger. When Cubiak pulled up to the marina at the edge of town, Steve Ross looked around in alarm.

"What are we doing here?" he asked.

"Fishing," Cubiak replied as he cupped Steve's elbow and steered him toward the dock.

Cate and Rowe were waiting alongside the *Speedy Sister*. "You all know each other?" Cubiak asked, and then made introductions.

With the diving gear and Cate's tripods and camera bags on board, they were forced to squeeze into the cockpit, all uncomfortably cozy.

"Where we going?" Steve Ross asked, shivering in his thin jacket. He tried to sound nonchalant but his voice broke.

Cubiak pointed across the bay to the salvage barge that lay in the water like a big brick. "There. Everyone ready?" he said.

Ross stared gloomily ahead. Cate nodded, her face unreadable. If she had questions, they were hidden behind a mask of professionalism. Rowe turned the engine key. Ignoring the No Wake signs posted around the harbor, he roared away from the dock, driving fast the way he liked.

As they bounced over the waves, Ross lost his balance and lurched, first to one side and then to the other. No matter what he did to try and find his equilibrium he was always one movement behind.

"Spent a lot of time on the water, did you?" Cubiak said.

Ross gave him a sharp look, the kind that said water sports were for rich snobs and not the likes of him. It was the same attitude Cubiak would have assumed at one time, but since he'd started sailing with Bathard he'd gained a new respect for the water and for those who worked and played on it.

Balance wasn't an issue for Cate. Oblivious to the roll and bounce of the boat, she stood as if on solid ground and calmly attached a massive telephoto lens to her camera. Cubiak had seen a photo of a young Cate on the deck of her grandfather's two-masted schooner. She'd been born with sea legs.

Waslow waited on the bay. He had the mooring lines ready, and when the *Speedy Sister* came alongside he tossed the lines aboard and quickly secured the boat to the barge. Then he helped transfer people and gear from Rowe's sleek motorboat to his bulky salvage vessel. No doubt, the old man's boat was an odd sight in the idyllic bay. Cubiak wondered who was watching from shore and what they were thinking of the strange congregation he had assembled on the water.

The clouds had pushed down, dimming the light and releasing a cold mist that slowly seeped through hats and jackets, chilling them as they stood on the *Helen of Troy*. His uncle had named the vessel after his wife, who was from East Troy, Rowe had explained. The deputy was right about the barge being nothing much to look at. *Helen of Troy* was a floating workhorse. The deck was twice the length of the cruiser, with a small pilot house at the fore and an assortment of lines and metal bars piled along the back. On the port side, a dual-cabled electric winch was bolted to the deck. Waslow had been hauling rocks for a sea wall, and the cargo had left him and everything on the boat covered with fine white dust.

With the equipment, five people were a crowd on the barge. Milling about, they tried to stay out of each other's way. Cate busied herself with her cameras; Steve paced a circle in one corner while he tried to shake a signal into his phone; Rowe remained uncharacteristically quiet as he suited up. An anxious Cubiak watched the darkening sky.

Only Waslow, who stood at the helm of the clunky craft, was at ease. Glancing back at his passengers, he wore his curiosity openly. Rowe and the diving equipment, well, that went with the territory. But a photographer? And that local boy, Ross, whose father had just died. The sheriff, even. Why were they on board? Cubiak could read the questions in the captain's eyes but said nothing. Along with the rest of them, the old captain would find out soon enough.

The sheriff directed Waslow toward the red flag. When they were ten feet from the marker, the seaman cut the engine and let the barge ride the rolling waves in silence.

"Okay here?" he called to no one in particular.

Cubiak looked to Rowe, who gave the nod for Waslow to drop anchor.

The deputy took another minute to check his gear. When he was ready, the three of them—sheriff, diver, and captain—conferred in hushed tones. This was the first Waslow was hearing of the trapped boat, and he listened quietly as the sheriff explained the boat's discovery and position. Of the three, the salvage captain was the expert in the recovery process and would know how to proceed.

On his first descent, Waslow said, Rowe should try and dislodge the boulders that kept the boat trapped under the ledge. If he couldn't push them away, they'd hook up a cable from the barge and use the winch. After the rocks were moved, Rowe would dive again and hook the barge's two cables to the boat, fore and aft or as close as he could get to those two areas. The winches would do the heavy work, of first tightening the cables and then dragging the boat out from under the ledge. Once the boat was clear, they'd depend on Rowe to evaluate its condition, and they could decide what to do from there. On his third dive, Rowe would either drill the boat full of holes that would drain the water as it was lifted, or he'd attach flotation bladders that would help raise it to the surface.

"All ready to go then?" Cubiak said.

Under the lowering sky, Waslow and Rowe nodded, and then with a minimum of fuss, the deputy went over the side.

As Rowe swam toward the marker, the others quietly formed a line down the side of the barge and watched: Waslow near the bow, then Cubiak, Cate, and finally a reluctant Ross.

No one said a word. Beneath their feet, rising waves slapped against the hull. Overhead, a curious gull circled and screeched. Rowe dropped from sight and no one moved. Moments passed and still they remained staring at the water.

A sharp ugly bleat from Ross's phone broke the spell. Turning quickly, the young man stabbed a hand into his pocket, but almost instantly Cubiak was on him. Before Ross could step away, the sheriff reached past him and knocked his cell to the deck.

Ross dove for the phone but Cubiak got to it first. "It's your cousin," he said, holding the screen for Ross to see.

"So what?" Ross tried to look unconcerned, but his eyes had narrowed and his skin gone pale.

"We're incommunicado out here," Cubiak said.

Ross started to protest, then gave an exaggerated shrug. "Whatever."

The sheriff maneuvered the young man to the stern. "That's hardly the response I'd expect from an eager reporter. In fact, I'd have thought you'd be in contact with your editor and not your cousin. But then again, you're not really on assignment, are you?" Cubiak said, his voice low and hard.

Ross's features tightened.

"You must think you can use this story to leap from writing obits to getting on the news desk."

"Something like that," Ross replied and held out his hand.

"Not yet," Cubiak said, pocketing the phone.

Ross glared. "You can't do that."

"Try me," Cubiak said.

A shout from the water made the sheriff step away.

Rowe had surfaced. Moments later he was alongside the barge. The deputy gave a thumbs-up sign. "The boulders are out of the way," he said.

Waslow turned on the motor that controlled the winch and lowered the first hook into the water. As Rowe grabbed the hook and began swimming it back, the barge captain slowly released the cable, giving the deputy as much line as he needed. Once again, Rowe disappeared beneath the surface.

Fog started coming in.

"I can't shoot much in this," Cate said.

"Get what you can," Cubiak said. He watched the marker. Still no sign of Rowe. What was taking so long? Should he postpone the operation?

By the time Rowe returned for the second hook, the fog had thickened. But the deputy brushed aside Cubiak's concerns about the weather. "It doesn't bother me down there. We're okay," he assured.

Again they waited: Waslow at the winch, the engine idling. Cubiak following the cables into the water. Cate with the camera around her neck. And Steve Ross distancing himself as much as possible.

A shout. It was Rowe calling from the fog. "Now. Go," he called out.

Waslow reengaged the motor and the gears began to rotate. With a low grinding screech, the teeth of one metal wheel interlocked with those of another and almost imperceptibly, the cables grew taut. When they were fully extended, the barge lurched and Waslow idled the engine, careful to keep the steel lines rigid. The mist momentarily parted, and Cubiak saw Rowe dive and then surface again. Treading water, he circled one hand slowly over his head, a signal to the captain to start the delicate process of dragging the sunken boat closer to the barge.

The sheriff had removed himself from the line of command and left all communication between Waslow and Rowe. Directives and questions, more hand signals going back and forth between the man on the barge and the man in the water. Slow. Fast. Wait. More.

Cubiak squeezed Cate's hand. Her fingers were cold.

"It's not going to be pleasant, is it?" she said, turning so her question went only to him.

"No." Then, under the angry cry of a seagull, he added, "I'm sorry."

She gave a quick, resigned smile. "It's okay. It's what I do."

Suddenly Rowe reappeared. He was nearly at the barge. He pushed the mask back off his face and signaled Waslow to stop.

The deputy looked bewildered. He backstroked away from the barge, pulled the mask back on, and dove again. Moments later, he bobbed back up. Treading water, he pointed at a dark shadow barely beneath the surface. Then he went down again.

Cubiak fell to his knees and grabbed onto the barge's low side wall. Rowe was close enough that the sheriff could see him circling around just beneath the surface.

Suddenly Rowe shot through and tore off his mask. He was ashen.

"Oh, God," he said, his cry plaintive.

Cubiak leaned forward and stared into the bay. The water was clear but in the dim light all he could see was a low dark shape, a nothing shape really, something more like a telephone pole or a long piece of blackened driftwood than a rowboat. What had Rowe seen that had startled him so?

The sheriff was aware of Cate kneeling beside him with her camera pointed at the water, the shutter clicking.

Behind him, Waslow reengaged the winches. Slowly he reeled in the cables, dragging the salvage boat closer. Rowe remained in the water, shaken but able to monitor and guide the recovery process. When the sunken boat was within a few feet of the barge, he signaled Waslow to start bringing it up.

Cubiak tensed. The small vessel had been underwater for years, decades even. Its planks weakened, the caulk that held them in place had eroded. Waslow was working as carefully as possible, but it was Rowe who seemed to have taken charge. Diving repeatedly, he propelled himself from the bow to the stern of the recovered vessel, bracing the boat with his hands, doing everything he could to guide it safely upward.

At another signal from Rowe, Waslow cut the winch engine. The motor pulsed and then went silent. In the afternoon stillness, the bay was eerily quiet.

For the first time the rowboat was clearly visible.

Alongside the salvage vessel, the little wooden boat appeared especially small and fragile, more like a toy than the real thing. There were no oars and, oddly, no benches, just the shallow hull with its planks blackened with age. In contrast to the dark wood, the bones heaped across the bottom looked startlingly white.

There were more bones than the sheriff could count, and they were more or less arranged in four separate mounds. They were human bones, a fact confirmed by the four skulls that lay among them. Not large. Child size.

Tufts of seaweed clung to the boat, and in the gently undulating water the kelp billowed like gossamer wings ready to carry the victims away from this watery grave.

Cubiak crossed himself. He wanted to turn away but did not. He was certain that they'd found the source of the remains that had been discovered on the beach. The bones had not drifted to shore from a distant shipwreck in the lake. They had floated up from the bottom of the rowboat and been carried the short distance across the bay to the shore.

The sheriff thought of his daughter and how he had cradled her in his arms as she lay dying, never knowing if she was aware of or had gained any comfort from his touch. Whoever these children were, they had died a miserable, terrifying death, the water chilling their flesh and sucking the air from their lungs, with no one but each other to hear their final frightened cries for help.

Had they been passengers on a sinking ship who'd been put in the rowboat and set off from the doomed vessel with the wild hope that they would reach safety? Were they local boys or summer friends who had foolishly rowed out together on a whim, full of their own bravado and confident that no harm would come their way? Or had something far worse prompted this tragedy?

Cate touched his arm. "What do you think happened? Why didn't they jump out and swim to shore?" she asked.

"Maybe they were scared, or they couldn't swim. Or maybe . . ." Cubiak got one of his bad feelings. He looked away. After a moment, he turned back to Cate. "I don't know what happened, but instinct says they'd do everything they could to survive. It's almost as if they were trapped and couldn't get out," he said.

Suddenly Cubiak remembered that Rowe was still in the water.

The sheriff called him on board and grabbed his elbow when he was halfway up the ladder.

"You okay?"

The deputy nodded but Cubiak felt him trembling and wrapped an arm around his shoulder. "I'm sorry, but it had to be done."

Rowe blinked hard and then looked away.

Cubiak glanced at the others. Waslow remained propped against the winch engine. Cate had started shooting again but her movements were stiff and slow. Ross sat hunched on the deck, staring at nothing.

The image would remain with them for a very long time.

A DIFFICULT TASK

17

With a heavy heart, Cubiak considered the task before them. They could retrieve the bones and lower the rowboat back into the water to be recovered later. That would save time and effort but expedience seemed wrong. The victims had died in the boat that had sheltered their poor bodies for years, perhaps decades. The sheriff decided that the least they could do was to try to keep the boat intact and bring both it and the fragile cargo safely on board the barge. But even that solution was fraught with problems. If the rowboat split apart as it was being lifted from the water, the bones would scatter over the bottom of the bay, and, although there was little chance of identifying the victims, there'd be even less then.

"The wood's got to be rotten as hell," he said.

Waslow shook his head. "You'd think so but no, not at all. Water keeps the wood moist. It's when the wood hits the air that it starts to rot. If this little thing's stayed wet, it's strong as the day it was made. Course we don't know how well the planks will hold together. Caulk might be weakened or washed away, so we'll need to lighten up the load as much as possible as we bring it up."

The way to do it, he explained, was to punch holes in the hull, allowing the water to flow out as the boat was lifted up.

"You sure that's going to work?" Cubiak asked.

Waslow didn't bother with an answer. Instead he turned to Rowe. "Think you can manage it?" he said, handing him a drill.

"This runs underwater?"

"Wouldn't have any use for it if it didn't," the captain replied.

Once again Rowe went over the side. While the deputy worked with the drill, Waslow inspected the cables. Cate shot duplicates and triplicates of the barge, the bay, and the distant shore. Cubiak shifted boxes and coils of line to make space on the deck. Then he rearranged them again and half-heartedly checked for messages from Moore and Harrison. Still nothing. What if the feds suddenly needed him? Cubiak resisted the urge to turn off his phone.

Even as they kept themselves occupied, they continued to maintain a silent vigil over the rowboat. One at a time, they returned to the edge of the barge and stood watch over the nightmarish vision of the cursed little boat with its sad cargo.

The spectacle affected them all differently. Cubiak silently prayed for the victims, though he'd long ago abandoned his faith. Cate for a moment would forget what she was doing and let her camera fall silent. Waslow took his turn when he thought the others weren't looking. "Poor beggars," Cubiak heard him mutter.

Of the four on the barge, Steve Ross was the one who kept his distance from the doomed vessel. Only Ross did not give the rowboat a second look. Instead, he remained planted on the low bench where Cubiak had steered him earlier, his feet pulled up onto the seat, sitting head down hugging his knees, curled into a human cocoon.

The more Cubiak thought about Ross's behavior, the stranger it seemed. It was odd that he didn't have a notebook and pen or recorder with him, the sheriff thought. And strange that he wasn't interested in every detail about the boat and the bones. Wasn't curiosity a hallmark of a good reporter? Ross said he was working on an in-depth story about the kidnapped Sneider, but here was another big story unfolding before him and he hadn't asked Rowe a single question about how he'd located the boat, hadn't asked any of them for their reaction. Wasn't that what a reporter did?

Cubiak sat down next to him. "Pretty sad stuff," the sheriff said.

Ross did not respond.

"You're awfully quiet about all this. Any ideas?"

Ross grabbed hold of his shoes and shrank further into himself.

"When you were growing up, did you ever hear stories about lost rowboats or missing kids?"

"Uh-uh." It was the only sound the ersatz journalist had made in an hour.

"There are always rumors."

Ross tried to spin away from the sheriff and nearly lost his balance. He put a foot on the deck to steady himself, and then suddenly he was standing, shouting at Cubiak. "I want off this boat. You can't keep me here."

"No one's going anywhere until I say so."

"You have no right."

"You're a witness to the afternoon's events."

The color drained from Ross's pale face. "I didn't see a damn thing. Your deputy found them," he said.

Cate's camera clicked and Ross whirled toward the sound. "Stop taking my picture!" Then he turned back to Cubiak. "What about that? I know how to run a boat. Let me take that," he said, waving at the *Speedy Sister.*

"Can't do that. We're going to need it." Cubiak rose and moved in on Ross. "What I want to know," he continued, speaking so only the young man could hear, "is why you're in such a hurry to get off the barge? Why so eager to run from a big story?"

Ross dropped back to the bench. "None of your damn business."

"Oh, but that's where you're wrong," Cubiak said.

The sheriff was suddenly exhausted. The discovery of the bones was far more than what he'd expected. He'd have to call Pardy and Bathard and the coast guard. Local officials would need a report. And then there was the media to deal with; all those reporters who were waiting for the Gerald Sneider saga to play out would jump all over this story.

Cubiak looked at Ross. "I'll deal with you later," he said.

Not long after, Rowe surfaced and swam to the front of the barge. He handed the drill up to Waslow. The holes were finished; it was time to put the rest of the plan into motion.

Rowe looked more exhausted than Cubiak felt. "You need a break," the sheriff said.

His deputy demurred. "Let's get this done," he replied.

Cubiak looked at Waslow.

"We got it this far," the captain said.

Cubiak knew they were right. The wind had come up, and if the weather turned it could be days before they got back. If they lowered the rowboat to the bottom of the bay, it would be left unprotected in open water, susceptible to the currents.

"Go ahead," Cubiak said.

Waslow gave Rowe five minutes to dive and get into position before he started the winch engine. With the motor on its lowest speed, he wound the cables, and inch by inch the rowboat rose through the water.

The gunwales broke through the surface, spreading ripples of waves across the water.

The upper rail emerged. Then the first row of planks.

The winch stuttered to a halt. The rowboat shuddered and the precious bones shifted and resettled.

Would the boat hold?

Waslow hunched over and fiddled with the engine, coaxing the motor back to life. The second row of planks rose up from the bay.

The boat was still full of water. It's too heavy, Cubiak thought. He waited for one of the hooks to tear through the wood, upending the boat and sending the bones cascading to the floor of the bay.

Cubiak was about to tell Waslow to stop when the vessel lifted past the first series of holes that Rowe had drilled. Water streamed through the punctures, as if from a sieve. The higher the boat rose into the air, the more water drained away.

As the bones emerged into the air, Cubiak wished there'd been sunshine to kiss them dry but there was only fog and wind.

Higher and higher, the boat rose. With a whoosh, the bottom planks broke through and the boat was completely above the water. For several minutes Waslow let it hang in place, allowing more water to drain out. Finally he reengaged the winch and continued to lift the vessel until it cleared the side of the barge.

Cubiak still worried. How long would the hooks hold? he wondered.

Waslow was already two steps ahead of him. As Cubiak watched, the old captain pulled a tall lever that sent a long metal plate sliding out over the water away from the barge. When he had it in position, Waslow lowered the rowboat to the platform.

Cubiak pulled Rowe on board.

"Good work, son," he said.

From the barge, the deputy had his first clear look at the boat and its contents. Cubiak gave Rowe a moment alone and then stepped alongside and poured the last of the hot coffee for him.

Cate joined them and even Ross took a few steps closer.

Waslow pushed to the head of the line.

The old man's demeanor had changed. His brisk efficiency had vanished. Standing with them, he appeared tentative, even fearful. His brow was furrowed, his mouth grim. After a moment, he spoke. "We'll have to bring it on board, you know. Can't get it to shore like this," he said to no one in particular.

He's worried that he'll jinx the barge, Cubiak thought. At sea, the dead were dropped overboard and consigned to the depths. And here they were doing the opposite, lifting the dead out of the water and setting them down on the vessel.

"These are the bones of innocent children. There are no ghosts," the sheriff said, but he wasn't sure if Waslow or anyone else believed him.

Once they had the rowboat securely in place, Rowe and Waslow piloted the barge to the marina harbor. Cubiak, Cate, and Ross rode back in the *Speedy Sister*. On the way, Cubiak pulled Cate aside.

"Are you okay?" he said. It was the same question he had asked Rowe earlier.

"Yes."

"I'm sorry. I didn't mean to ignore you."

"It's okay. It was better that you didn't fuss over me. Made it more like a job. I didn't have to think or feel, just shoot."

They glanced back across the bay to where the red flag had become a tiny dot of color on the dark water, near the spot where the rowboat had been found.

"We're not done yet," Cubiak said.

"I know, but now the rest is up to you, isn't it?"

Despite the cold wind that had come up, a small crowd was gathered at the Baileys Harbor marina. As soon as they tied up, Ross leapt from the cruiser and took off. Cubiak watched him push through the onlookers and head across the road into the local bar, probably looking for a phone. For now, Cubiak didn't try and stop him. He had enough to do to move the onlookers away from the docks and to help secure and cover the rowboat after the harbor cranes lifted it onto the flatbed truck he'd called for earlier.

Rowe would take the jeep and give Waslow a lift home. Cate had her own car. The sheriff would ride back with the truck.

"Anyone asks anything, it's *no comment*," he said.

Before they left, the sheriff phoned Pardy and Bathard.

"You'll need a staging area. Someplace large, like an empty factory or warehouse," the coroner said.

Cubiak remembered what the shipyard workers at the Rusty Scupper had said about one of the hangars going dark. "Lakeside just finished a big job. I think there might be space for us." The sheriff reached the company CEO at home and explained what he needed: an empty building, a cradle for a small boat, and a large raised platform. "I'm sorry I can't tell you anything more at the moment except that it's important and I need it all tonight."

There was a long pause before the CEO agreed to the unusual request and promised the sheriff that everything would be ready.

INSIDE HANGAR THREE

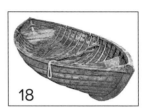

18

The flatbed truck trundled over the steel bridge bearing the cargo of human bones on its back. Heavy fog blanketed the base of the bridge obscuring the lower portion of the truck and blurring the glow from the antique lamps that lined the narrow passageway. In the eerie setting, the shroud-covered rowboat floated into the heart of Sturgeon Bay like an iceberg riding a moonlit cloud.

Cubiak remembered what Cate had said about the long processions of carts piled with bones that had been escorted through Paris at night by robed priests who chanted prayers and burned incense. There would be no such public display of reverence and respect for the remains he was escorting that night. For now at least the rowboat and its sad freight had to be kept secret.

The fog and rain had cleared the streets. To any locals who ventured out and noticed the truck, this would be just another load of material heading to one of the shipyards.

Exiting the bridge, the truck made a wide left turn and followed a silent street for the last quarter mile of the journey to the charcoal-colored building known as Lakeside Industries Hangar Number Three. The nondescript metal structure was one of several that lined the waterway just blocks from the downtown businesses that catered to tourists. It was an odd juxtaposition of the two industries that formed the bedrock of the local economy.

The overhead doors of the four-story hangar opened and the truck rolled into a well-lit cavernous space. Most of the usual array of equipment—metal scaffolds, forklifts, generators, and an assortment of welding tools—had been moved to the rear wall. Closer in were the wooden cradle and the platform that the sheriff had requested.

Emily Pardy, Evelyn Bathard, and the two deputies Cubiak had called in on special assignment waited near the entrance. They wore protective coveralls and gloves. Respirator masks hung around their necks. When the truck stopped, the four moved forward and stood in the shadow of the shroud-covered boat.

Cubiak dropped from the cab, just as Rowe hurred in and joined them. "I'm afraid it's going to be a long night," the sheriff said.

Before the bones could be touched, the boat had to be transferred off the truck and into the cradle. The cursed vessel had been tugged and dragged and raised from the lakebed. How much more abuse could it sustain? Cubiak wondered.

When the sheriff met the crane operator that Lakeside had sent, the sheriff worried that he was too inexperienced for the delicate task. But in one smooth motion, the young man grasped the boat in the crane's orange jaws and swung it over the cradle. Then, as if he were nestling a tiny infant into its carriage, he lowered the vessel into place.

For the first time in years, perhaps for the first time since it had been built and launched into the bay outside Baileys Harbor, the doomed little boat rested on solid ground.

Under the hangar's bright light, the canvas that covered the boat glowed a murky white, like the color of the bones hidden beneath. Cubiak and Rowe untied the tarp and slowly peeled it off. Inside the sleek, modern hangar, the sight of the simple wooden vessel filled with human bones was as riveting and distressing as it had been on the bay.

No one spoke.

Then the building exhaust fans kicked on. Cate's camera clicked.

Cubiak explained the process they were to follow. Rowe was to document the position of every bone before it was removed. As he finished with each of the pieces, the other two deputies would carry the remains to the platform where Doctors Pardy and Bathard would lay them on the tarp. Cate would photograph the process step by step.

"It appears there are four skeletons in the boat, and while some of the remains may have shifted due to currents or while the boat was being transported, it seems reasonable that each group of bones represents a different individual. We'll run tests later, of course, but in the meantime I need you to be systematic about the work," the sheriff said.

While they were focused on the contents, he would work on cleaning the boat. "If there's a name or marker, we'll know where it came from, and that might be helpful later in identifying the victims," he said.

To make it easier for the others to work on the interior, Cubiak started by pulling the seaweed from the side of the boat nearest the platform. The plants were wet and cold and unpleasant to the touch. In places, thick algae coated the wood. As best he could he scraped it off.

The sheriff was kneeling behind the boat when Rowe came around.

"Sir, you need to see this."

The deputy pointed to the first set of bones. By now most of the skeletal pieces had been removed, but about a dozen remained in place and with them were two narrow stips of blackened leather that were tied in loops. There was a bit of rag as well, and both ends had been knotted together.

"What do you think this means?" Cubiak said.

The deputy looked stricken. "That at least one of the victims was bound and gagged."

Cubiak nodded. "One, yes, but probably they all were."

The sheriff moved closer. "What's this?" he said, reaching for what appeared to be a thick ribbon of seaweed on the bottom of the boat.

Beneath the slimy surface he felt the rough texture of rope. Careful not to disturb the remains, he checked the line. There was more than enough to reach from the bow to the stern. And at one end was an eye hook. Cubiak ran his hand along the upper planks until he found a small hole at the front of the vessel. There would be another at the back, of that he was sure, and maybe one or two along the sides. He closed his eyes and imagined the rope strung through the hardware and then twisted around the young victms.

Cubiak called Cate over with her camera. "They were tied to the boat; that's why they didn't get out. They couldn't."

Then, to Rowe, he added, "Bag all this as evidence."

With renewed vengeance, Cubiak went back to scraping off the moss. After a few minutes, he aimed a flashlight at the wood. The boat had been painted green. The sheriff saw a faint blue letter *m*. He cleared away another inch of scum and the letter *o* emerged.

Cubiak could hardly breathe. He scraped off more detritus. *H* and then *s* appeared. Not all the lettering had withstood the ravages of time, but despite the bits that were missing, recognizable words began taking shape. By the time the sheriff cleared off the rest of the frame, he knew what he'd uncovered. The rowboat filled with bones was from the Forest Home for Orphaned and Needy Boys.

Wishing he had a cigarette, Cubiak stood outside the hangar and waited for Moore. The sheriff had never asked where the agent was staying but it couldn't have been far because it took only five minutes for the familiar black SUV to arrive.

"What the fuck is this all about?" Moore asked, his voice husky and thick with exhaustion, as if he'd been half asleep or nodding off in front of the TV. Still, he'd managed to put on a pair of neat khakis and a black cotton sweater so that even without a suit, he emitted an air of spit and polish.

Cubiak ran a hand through his hair. He was a crumpled mess. "Something you need to see. In here," he said and shoved the door open.

Moore blinked against the bright interior and crossed the threshold. His aggressive posture suggested that he was about to say something harsh, but whatever it was evaporated before the sight of the eerie tableau inside the hangar.

Bathard and Pardy had finished assembling the first human skeleton. In the huge space, the figure looked alarmingly diminutive. Under the glare of the lights, the white bones shone with an eerie luminescence. Red tags marked the three discovered on the beach.

For several moments, Moore was uncharacteristically silent.

"You kept looking, didn't you? And you found all this?" he said finally.

"Yes."

"In there?" He pointed to the rowboat from which the sheriff's deputies were carefully lifting two more bones from a second small heap of remains.

"It looks like four bodies. The victims appear to have been tied to the boat and bound up with these." Cubiak held up one of the leather loops.

Moore inhaled sharply.

As they talked, the two men approached the platform where Bathard was setting the right scapula of the second skeleton in place.

"Jesus. They were just kids, weren't they?" Moore said.

"Most likely. We'll know more after a detailed analysis. I assume we can count on your resources to help with that."

"Absolutely. With something of this magnitude, we'll do everything we can to assist."

A moment later, Moore tightened his already square shoulders, a signal to Cubiak that the FBI agent was done with being sentimental and was about to resume his no-nonsense mantle of authority. "Very tragic, of course. But why call me? Unless . . ." Moore stopped and cupped a hand to his chin. "Oh, sweet mother of God. I don't believe it."

Wordlessly, Cubiak led the agent way past the platform and around the back of the boat. At the stern, he trained a flashlight on the transom, illuminating the lettering that had survived decades underwater. The words were faded and Moore had to bend down to read them.

"Forest Home is the name of the camp Gerald Sneider operated," Cubiak explained.

Moore straightened. "The camp for orphaned and needy boys," he said. He was suddenly alert. "This changes everything. We'll have to get on this right away. But of course you already realize that."

It was meant as a compliment and they both knew it.

Somehow Rowe had rustled up an urn of coffee and a platter of cookies for the crew. The cookies were left untouched but the coffee went quickly. Against the hum of the overhead blowers, Cubiak and Moore drank their share of coffee black while they waited for Cate to print the photos the sheriff had requested.

"A woman named Marilyn Ross may know the story behind this, or at least a good part of it," Cubiak told the agent. "I thought of bringing her here but I'm not sure she could take the shock of all this." They turned and looked at the tarp where the second skeleton was being assembled.

"The photos should be enough," he said.

"Mind if I tag along?"

Cubiak was startled by the agent's request. "If you want, sure, but it's probably better for me to talk with her alone."

Moore drained his coffee and tossed the cup into the trash. "Of course. You're local. I represent something foreign and scary."

The sheriff called the widowed woman. Apologizing for the lateness of the hour, he explained that he needed to stop by. Something had come up.

A few minutes later, Cubiak and Moore were on their way.

The fog had cleared, and they made the drive under a sky that brimmed with stars. "That's the Milky Way, isn't it?" Moore said, looking up. "Don't see that in the city anymore. But you're probably used to it."

"Not really."

"Aren't you from here?"

In the dark, Cubiak smiled to himself. Who'd ever have thought he'd be taken for a local? "I've only been living here for four years."

The agent seemed surprised. "And before?"

Might just as well lay it all out, Cubiak thought. "Chicago. CPD. Homicide," he replied.

"Ah." Moore made the single syllable translate into something like, Well, that explains a lot.

When they reached the Ross home, Cubiak went in alone as planned.

Marilyn had a pot of tea waiting for the sheriff. They sat at the kitchen table again, a sign that he was being welcomed as a friend and neighbor. Cubiak knew they were both playing a game but for several minutes he went along with the pretense. Then he put down his cup and as gently as possible he explained why he'd come to see her.

He started with the bone Butch had found on the beach outside Baileys Harbor. When he repeated what Emma Pardy had said, that it was a human bone, she went rigid.

"There's more," Cubiak said and walked her through the events of the past few days: The retrieval of two additional bones in the same location. Rowe's underwater investigation. The discovery of a sunken rowboat.

A clock in the living room chimed the hour. In the overheated house, Marilyn pulled her sweater tight and shivered.

"What was in the boat?" she asked in barely a whisper.

Cubiak showed her one of the photos.

It was the picture Cate had taken when the rowboat hung suspended alongside the salvage barge. The wooden vessel was still submerged and all that was discernible was the outline of the gunwale and the four blurred light-colored spots against the dark background. Cubiak pointed to the white blotches.

"These are all bones," he said.

Marilyn stared at the image. Her lower lip quivered.

"I think you know what this is about," Cubiak said.

The late Fred Ross's wife touched the edge of the picture. "What else do you have?" she asked in a faint voice.

Cubiak set out two more photos. The first was of the boat in the hangar, before the remains had been removed. The second was a picture of the first complete skeleton.

Marilyn pulled an embroidered handkerchief from the wrist of her sleeve and pressed it to her eyes.

Cubiak waited for her to stop crying. "You had nothing to do with any of this," he said quietly. Then he added, "It's what tortured your husband, isn't it?"

Her head bobbed. She sniffled and twisted the handkerchief in her gnarled hands. "Fred couldn't let it go. He told me about it when we were first married, and to be honest I don't think I believed him. I didn't want it to be true. They were all just kids."

She looked at Cubiak beseechingly, as if he had the power to undo the past and make things right again.

"I'm sorry," he said.

Marilyn nodded. Things were what they were. "The older Fred got, the more obsessed he became. On his death bed, he kept talking about the four boys." She hesitated and then went on. "He and Jon tied them up in the boat! No one was supposed to get hurt. It was another of Sneider's lessons. That horrible, awful man."

She began to cry again. Cubiak sat with her for several minutes, and then he slipped the photos back into the envelope.

"I need you to tell me what you know about that night," Cubiak said.

Marilyn watched him refill her cup. She blew on the tea and took a sip; it was barely a taste but it seemed to revive her.

"They were afraid of water—the four boys—and being tied up in the boat and made to sit out all night in the dark was supposed to cure them. Sneider had done it before with other boys; it wasn't the first time. But a storm came up that night. And in the morning, the boys were gone.

"Sneider claimed they'd run away. He told the others that he'd gone out during the storm and rescued them. He said they'd learned their lesson and as a reward he took them to his house for a hot supper. In the morning they were gone. 'Ungrateful scum ran off,' he said.

"A couple of months later a postcard came in the mail. It was from one of the four boys saying they were okay and living in Iowa somewhere. That was his proof the boys had survived. But Fred didn't believe it."

"Why not?"

"I don't know, he just said it was all wrong."

Marilyn sat up, her face flushed with indignation. "My husband died full of guilt and regret. 'I was too timid. I was too afraid,' he told me over and over until I was sick of hearing it. He was just a kid, Sheriff, and kids have wild imaginations. It got to the point where I started to think he and the others had made it all up. And now this . . ." As suddenly as it had come on, her anger drained. Slumping back into her chair, she pointed to the place on the table where Cubiak had laid the photos. "His last wish was for his brother, Jon, to do what he'd been unable to do all those years earlier."

"Confront Sneider and make him confess?"

The old woman crossed herself. "Yes," she said in a whisper.

"Did he?"

She clutched her hands. They were freckled from sun and age and crisscrossed with ridges of thin blue veins. "Jon never does anything he's asked to do," she replied. But she kept her head bowed, and the trembling in her sagging shoulders told Cubiak that this was one time Marilyn Ross feared she was mistaken.

Cubiak stopped at the edge of the yard and glanced back at the house. When he'd walked out of the kitchen, Mrs. Ross had been sitting at the table under the dim overhead light, the rest of her modest home in the dark. Now every window blazed as if lit from inside with a flaming torch. From the time he'd walked out the front door, she had gone from one room to another and flicked on the wall switches. The sheriff didn't think she was one to indulge in such luxury, but perhaps her anxiety about being alone in a dark house on a deserted stretch of road many hours from dawn trumped the need for frugality.

"Well?" Moore said as Cubiak slid into the driver's seat and turned the key.

The sheriff cut a sharp U-turn in the drive. "It's pretty much what I thought," he said.

Moore waited until they spun out onto the road. "And?" he said.

"One more stop. If I'm right, this is it."

"You know where Sneider is?"

Cubiak grunted.

They were passing through woods thick with deer. Watching for the bright flash of eyes reflecting their headlights, the sheriff hunched over the wheel and pressed the accelerator to the floor as he aimed the jeep down the middle of the dark road. If he was right, Gerald Sneider's time was limited and what mattered was getting to Jon Ross before it was too late.

Moore had his phone out. "I'm calling for backup," he said.

"Not yet."

The jeep hit a series of ruts, and the agent grabbed the door handle. "I hope to hell you know what the fuck you're doing," he said as they turned off the road and into a bumpy drive.

THE RESCUE

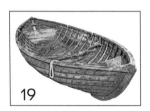

19

The outline of Jon Ross's dilapidated homestead was clearly visible in the cold starlight. On one side of the driveway, the ramshackle house and garage stood together; on the other side, at some distance, was the machine shed and the weathered barn with its tall silo. The area between the two buildings was vacant. The corncrib, granary, and chicken coop that had filled the space had long since been dismantled and their bricks and boards repurposed.

The yard was dark. The familiar blue pickup was parked under a sprawling oak. Next to it was a red car. Cubiak was surprised to find the vehicles in plain sight. No dog was barking, though. It was probably muzzled to keep it from drawing attention to the place. In the thick silence, the only sound was the almost imperceptible burble of the creek that ran unseen in the deep woods bordering the back of the yard.

Earlier, Cubiak had placed his gun in the glove box. Reaching for it now, he caught the flicker of recognition in Moore's eyes.

"This time you come with," the sheriff said.

At the top of the porch steps, Cubiak banged on the door. Jon Ross threw it open almost instantly. Framed by a strip of yellow light, he stepped into the doorway and pressed his large hands against the doorjamb. He seemed to have grown taller and bulkier in the few days since Cubiak had last seen him.

"Expecting someone?" the sheriff said.

"Who's that?" Ross ignored the question and tossed his head with its helmet of unruly hair at Moore.

The agent held up his badge. "FBI."

Ross sneered but beneath the contempt Cubiak caught a hint of alarm.

"Your son's home," the sheriff said.

"Maybe."

"You have company, too." He indicated the red car.

"Yeah, my nephew's here, visiting his cousin. Nothing wrong with that, is there?"

"Where are they?"

Ross ran his tongue around the inside of his cheek. "Around."

"What are they doing?"

"Hell if I know."

"I believe you do." Cubiak stepped closer and held up a photo of the rowboat that Cate had taken at Hangar Number Three before any of the bones were removed.

Ross tried not to react but in the dim light, Cubiak saw him blink hard and caught the twitch in the corner of his mouth.

"Go on, take it. I got plenty more," the sheriff said, pressing the photo into his chest.

Ross turned away.

"Look at it," Cubiak said.

"I seen it," Ross said as he picked at the chipped framework of the doorway.

The sheriff knew the man's temper. Ross would just as readily grab a shotgun from behind the door and blast them as try and punch his way past.

As he waited, Cubiak was aware of Moore moving up behind him. The sheriff didn't dare glance around to see if the agent had his weapon out but hoped that, at the least, he had it ready.

Finally, Ross turned back. Keeping his face in check, he looked at the picture again. "This supposed to mean something to me?" he said. His tone remained gruff but some of the meanness had drained away.

"I think it means a lot. I think it's linked to the time you spent at the Forest Home and that it's the proof you're trying to scare out of Gerald Sneider."

"What the fuck you talking about? I got nothing to do with Sneider." Ross tried to laugh and knocked the photo from Cubiak's hand. "You're not gonna pin that one on me. It's terrorists that got him. Tell him, tell this dick wipe of a sheriff that it's terrorists he should be looking for," he said, nearly shouting at Moore.

Cubiak picked up the photograph.

"There are four sets of bones in that boat, and there were four boys put in it the night the boat sank. You and your brother tied them up. You had to. You were just kids yourselves, and Gerald Sneider made you do it. It was supposed to be another one of his lessons, nothing more. The boys would spend the night on the water and learn not to be afraid. It was how he did things."

Ross's face was wet with sweat. "Who told you this?" he asked.

"The boys never came back, did they?" Cubiak said. "There was a storm that night—lightning, thunder, and high winds. The waves came up the way they do on the water. You and your brother and the other kids were scared. You were sure your friends had drowned but Sneider said no. He claimed to have rescued them. He said he'd taken them to his house for a hot meal but that the next morning, when he got up, they were gone. Sneider told everyone they'd run off."

Ross reached for the picture. He was quiet a long moment. "The bastard called them ingrates. Said they'd probably hopped one of the quarry boats headed to Chicago."

"You believed him?"

"Not really, but it sounded like a dream come true—which one of us kids wouldn't have gave anything to be in Chicago rather than at that stinking camp. So yeah, we believed his story even though we were pretty sure it was a lie." Ross pulled a hand down over his jaw. "A lie we couldn't prove."

"You spent a lifetime trying to forget that night but Fred couldn't. He was tormented to the end. He knew—you both did—that the boys had died. Something tipped you off. What was it?"

Ross's face clouded. He worked his mouth hard. "It was the postcard. A couple months went by and then this postcard comes, addressed to me and Fred. It was from one of those four boys. Chester. That was his name. 'We made it. Good luck,' it said, something like that. All written like in a boy's hand. It wasn't sent from Chicago like we'd been told but from Iowa. Probably to make us think the boys had moved on." Ross gave a sour squawk. "Sneider was always one for the dramatic. Only thing was, you see, Chester couldn't write. He'd never learned. He didn't even know the alphabet."

Ross handed the photo back to Cubiak. "It was me that taught him to print his name, and he was damn proud of that. Even if someone else had penned the message for him, he'd've insisted on printing his own name just to show me that he'd remembered how."

"You think Sneider was responsible for sending the card?"

Ross scoffed. "Who else? It was just the kind of lousy trick he'd pull."

"What about Verne Pickler?"

Ross's eyes opened wide. "Verne Prick, you mean?" He almost laughed and then grew somber again. "Yeah, him, too. He's the fucker that towed the boat out to the rocks. The rest of us stood on the shore and watched him. Prick was Sneider's man. He had a hand in everything that went on at the place."

"And now he's gone missing, too," Cubiak said. "The man whose dog was found tied up along the ship canal," he added for Moore's sake.

All the while he'd been talking with Ross, the sheriff had been keenly aware of Moore listening to the exchange. To his credit, the FBI agent hadn't interrupted once, but Cubiak trusted him to have pieced together the main parts of the story.

"You've got them both here, don't you?" the sheriff said.

Ross narrowed his gaze and peered over Cubiak into the darkness. He was a man whose life had been shaped by harshness and who had bullied his way through one decade after another with increasing meanness—angry about everything, sure that he'd never gotten a fair shake. And maybe he was right. Maybe he had been cursed by birth and circumstance. Wrung dry of human compassion, he'd turned into stone and surrounded himself with all the sourness he could gather into one place. Yet. Yet, he'd risked everything to fulfill his dying brother's last wish, to try to right a wrong that had been long lost to history.

Cubiak realized that Ross's desire for justice, twisted as it was, originated in a deeply buried shred of decency. Given the man's long-standing resentment of authority, the sheriff decided that his only chance of reaching him was to show him the respect he thought he deserved.

"I could lie and tell you my deputy is on his way with a warrant but I won't do that," Cubiak said, hoping this was enough to gain Ross's trust.

At first, Ross didn't react. Perhaps he hadn't heard. But after a moment he looked at Cubiak full on and blinked. "I appreciate that, Sheriff."

In the half-dozen encounters Cubiak had had with the local renegade, it was the first civil word he'd heard from him.

Time was slipping away. Cubiak knew they'd been talking for just a few minutes although it felt much longer. He'd take one last stab at convincing Ross to cooperate. "We need to get to them now. Before it's too late," he added.

Ross hesitated. Then he stepped onto the porch. "This way," he said as pushed past the two men. "Follow me."

Despite his bulk, Jon Ross was quick on his feet. Bounding down the steps, he set a surprisingly fast pace as he ran for the corner of the house. He's heading for the root cellar, Cubiak thought as he raced to catch up. But once Ross reached the back of the house, he kept going into the yard and toward the creek.

The yard sloped at a sharp angle and was heaped with junk and discarded furniture. In the dark, Ross zigzagged through the obstacle course as Cubiak and Moore struggled to keep up. Moore tripped over a discarded tire and sprawled to the ground. The sheriff's foot caught on a tree root, and he went down hard on one knee. As he scrambled back up, he scanned the tree line along the creek bed for a glimpse of Ross. The man had vanished. Cubiak swore at the night air. He'd been a fool to trust Ross. Sneider was being held somewhere on the farm, and Ross had only pretended to cooperate so he could get past the two lawmen and run to warn the others.

He could still be ahead, doing a low crawl toward the water. Cubiak started forward. He advanced several feet and then stopped and spun around in time to see a dark figure dash across the driveway. Ross had backtracked and was moving away from them toward the barn. Cubiak broke into a run and caught up with him at the side door.

"Full of surprises, aren't you?" Cubiak grabbed Ross and pressed his arm up behind his back.

Moore materialized out of the gloom, and the sheriff tightened his grip on Ross. "Not a word," he said as he unlatched the oversized door and shoved him inside.

The barn was a black hole of silence and dust. Mildew thickened the stale air. It was cold, too, a cold that bit into the lungs and squeezed them with a fierce, shackling force.

Cubiak brushed a cobweb from his forehead and hesitated, straining for the slightest sound or movement. Had Ross deliberately led them astray again?

Slowly shapes emerged from the shadows: A small calf pen in the far corner. On the floor, an overturned metal dish from which a barn cat might have lapped warm milk.

In the unnatural stillness, they moved to the wide aisle that bisected the barn. It had probably been decades since the last cows had lumbered down the concrete walkway. Exhaling their warm breath, their massive heads bobbing gently, and their bags swaying heavy with milk, they would turn to one side or the other and slip their necks through the stanchions that would clang shut and hold them in position for milking. It was another family farm overrun by big money or driven to extinction by its owner's incompetence. All that remained now was the memory of a better time, a legacy etched in the faint aroma of the pieces of hay left in the feeding troughs and the bits of straw that had dropped from the last retreating hooves as the cows were led to the auction block or shipped to the slaughterhouse.

Suddenly, they heard a noise—a sharp, quick scratch of tiny claws scrabbling unseen. From the far end of the barn, there was a faint swish like a sudden wind coming up. Ross stiffened, and Cubiak prodded him forward. They moved slowly, step for step, the sheriff with his mouth close to Ross's ear, warning him to remain still. Cubiak was ahead of Moore but he sensed the agent close behind and was relieved by his presence.

When they reached the middle of the barn, Cubiak stopped again. Ahead, along the wall, a stray beam of starlight lit a glass block window, and in the pale smudge that filtered through the gloom, he spied a humped shadow on the far wall.

Cubiak shoved Ross to his knees and hissed at Moore to watch him. The sheriff drew his gun and crept forward. The shadow swayed. It was the size of a calf or a large dog. As Cubiak drew nearer, the shadow assumed the shape of a man. Finally he was close enough to see clearly. The man was skinny and old and kneeling on all fours in a layer of his own filth. His head had been placed between the metal bars of a stanchion and tied in place with a rope. His wrists and ankles were bound with baling twine, his mouth covered with duct tape, and his eyes blindfolded with a white rag. A plastic grocery bag hung directly overhead, and from a hole in the bottom cold water dripped on his head and then ran down his cheeks. The bag was nearly empty but it must have been full at one point, judging from the large pool that spread across the floor.

Cubiak had seen enough photos of Gerald Sneider to know this wasn't him.

"Verne Pickler?" he said.

The captive trembled and pressed into the wall as if trying to disappear or make himself invisible.

Cubiak squatted down beside him. "I'm the sheriff," he said and rested his hands on the bound man's shoulders to calm him.

Pickler sobbed. The fight left him and he collapsed.

Cubiak undid the blindfold. Then he wrapped an arm around the man's chest to keep him from falling down and loosened the restraints. When the fetters were off, Cubiak opened the stanchion. Then he lifted the scrap of a man to his feet and held him up so they stood face to face.

"Verne Pickler?" he said in a whisper.

Eyes wide, the man nodded and pawed at the tape that sealed his mouth shut.

Cubiak stayed his hand. He knew Pickler couldn't help but scream when the tape came off and he couldn't chance that. The sheriff pointed to the tape, shook his head, and put a finger to his mouth, hoping he was understood. Pickler nodded again.

"Where's Sneider?" the sheriff said.

Pickler looked around, confused, and then raised his hands in a gesture of helplessness.

Of course, he'd been snatched after Sneider had been taken and was probably blindfolded long before he reached the barn. He wouldn't have seen anything worthwhile.

"It's okay, everything will be fine," Cubiak assured him. He led Pickler to the side of the barn and eased him down on a bale of straw. "Stay here. Don't move," he said. Then he slipped back to the center aisle where he'd left Moore.

The agent had kept Ross's arm pinned up alongside his back.

"One down. Now tell me where Sneider is," Cubiak said, taking over for Moore.

Ross sneered. But Cubiak kept bending his arm until he relented.

"You lead and I'll follow," the sheriff said as he released his hold and pushed Ross forward.

Ross staggered and fell. Still on all fours, he tried to scramble away. Then suddenly he was up. He ran ahead several feet and then jumped off the center aisle and dodged between two stanchions.

Cubiak was right behind. Searching the barn wall, he saw a recessed doorway off to the side and realized that that was where Ross was heading.

They reached the opening together. Cubiak lunged and grabbed Ross's shoulder.

"Now!" Ross yelled, as the sheriff slammed him into the wall.

Cubiak hurtled into the entrance and slid across the floor of the passage into a small room that was even colder than the barn. He gagged on the sour stench of rotten corn. An arm's length away, the startled figure of Steve Ross huddled against the base of the silo.

"I tried to stop them," he said.

Cubiak looked around. The concrete blocks that formed the structure were spalling from age and neglect. The row of small access doors that ran up the side of the structure were encased inside a long metal chute. From the ground only three doors were visible, and they were sealed shut.

"How do I get inside?" the sheriff said.

Steve pointed to a series of metal rungs that ran up alongside the doors.

The sheriff knew this was the end of the line. Sneider had to be in the silo.

Cubiak stepped onto the first metal rung and hoisted himself up into the darkness. Climbing as fast as the cold and the slick footrests allowed, he scrabbled up the narrow confine.

Cubiak had climbed past several closed doors when one foot slipped, then the other. He dropped and jerked, and for a moment he dangled in the dark. Just as he was about to lose his grip, he regained his footing.

Stifling his fear of heights, Cubiak forced himself upward. Suddenly, higher up still, a glimmer of light flitted out from the silo. Cubiak paused and stilled his breath. He had no idea how far he'd ascended. Twenty feet? Thirty? Did it matter?

He climbed toward the light and when he reached the opening, he peered in.

Leeland Ross was inside the silo, his back to the door. Standing on a wooden platform, a half circle of plank flooring that had been cleverly attached to the wall, he faced a tall wooden contraption. The apparatus was bolted to the floor and secured by wires that ran to the steel bands lining the inside of the silo wall. Two beams jutted from the top of the frame, and attached to each was a complex system of ropes and pulleys. It took Cubiak a moment to realize that the setup was a jerry-rigged block and tackle. Two sets of ropes ran over and around the pulleys and then dropped straight down into the silo. With absolute certainty, Cubiak knew they led to Gerald Sneider.

Leeland was lowering the ropes into the great abyss.

"Stop," Cubiak said.

The shout startled Leeland. He spun toward the door. As the sheriff dove through the narrow opening, Leeland grabbed an axe and began hacking at the ropes.

Cubiak tackled him and knocked the axe free.

The sheriff pressed the beefy young man to the floor and tried to hold him down but Leeland broke away. Both men scrambled up on all fours, breathing hard. The axe lay between them. The sheriff glanced at it and then looked up at Leeland, figuring his odds. Leeland was big like his father but younger and stronger and maybe even meaner than his old man.

"You don't have to do this," Cubiak said.

At the same time, the two lunged for the axe.

Leeland got to it first but then, unable to stop, he slid over the edge of the floor.

There was a loud splash.

The silo was full of water.

"You fucker," Cubiak said. He grabbed the frayed ropes and strained to pull them up but the weight at the other end was too heavy. Looking down, he followed the ropes toward the black water. They were attached to a metal cage that was almost completely submerged in the deep pool.

Inside the cage's dome-shaped webbing, he saw the top of a man's head and the shadowy profile of his face.

Nearby, Leeland thrashed wildly. "I can't swim," he said as he flayed helplessly.

Cubiak jumped in. After his ordeal with the kittens, he thought he was ready for the impact. But the water in the silo was colder than that in the bay and the shock left him momentarily dazed. He sunk until his feet hit bottom. Then he kicked his way back up and struggled to keep from sinking again. He would not die like this. He couldn't. He tried to think straight. If necessary, he might be able to pull himself out, but could he save the others? Which one to rescue first? Leeland Ross, a man who'd proven himself to be a blight on the community and whose absence many would consider a blessing? Or Gerald Sneider? He had to be the man in the cage. Depending on how long he'd been submerged, he might not even be alive. If he was alive, Cubiak would be a hero— at least to some—until the news of the four boys in the boat became known. And if it was true that Sneider was responsible for the boys' deaths, then Cubiak would be a hypocrite because didn't Sneider, by all accounts, deserve to die in cold water?

The cage was closer. Cubiak spun toward it. Sneider was inside. He was gagged, and the sheriff imagined him tied up the same way the boys in the boat had been bound: Hands behind his back. Ankles shackled together. A rope around his neck to hold him upright, ensuring that he'd remain fully aware that he had no way of escape.

The water lapped at Sneider's jowls. His eyes were wild. He blinked and jerked his torso. A strand of rope snapped.

"Don't move," Cubiak said. Even if he could hold his breath for long, he wasn't tall or strong enough to stand beneath the cage and push it out of the water and onto the makeshift floor. Treading water, he ran a hand over the frame, searching for a door or latch. The cage was welded shut.

If he got Leeland out, maybe the two of them could pull the cage up. But would the younger Ross help save the man he'd been trying to drown?

Cubiak had been wrong about Leeland's father; would he be wrong about the son as well? The sheriff knew he had to take the chance.

Leeland had managed to kick his way to the far side of the cage. He was hanging on and working his way toward the sheriff one hand over the other.

Cubiak reached out to him. "We need . . . ," he said as Leeland gripped his arm and hurled forward toward him. With a renewed fury, Leeland latched onto Cubiak's shoulders and shoved him under. The sheriff kicked and punched, fighting to break free, but Leeland would not relent.

Cubiak felt himself weaken. The heavy drag of his wet boots and clothes were pulling him farther down. I am going to die, he thought.

Then suddenly, the punishing weight disappeared and he was being lifted up. Lungs on fire, he broke through the surface, coughing and gulping at the damp air.

"You okay, Chief?"

Cubiak nearly wept. Rowe was in the water with him. His deputy had come to save him. How did you get here? How'd you know? the sheriff wanted to ask, even as he realized that at some point Moore had called for help.

A second pair of hands reached down and grabbed Cubiak by the wrists. The sheriff looked up to find the FBI agent lying face down and hanging over the edge of the platform. As best he could, Cubiak held on to Moore. Between the two of them, Rowe and Moore half lifted and half-dragged Cubiak from the icy pool. Then they pulled Leeland out as well.

The young man remained bellicose, and Rowe handcuffed him to the pulley mount.

As Cubiak staggered to his feet, the bleating shriek of sirens erupted in the distance. More backup was on the way.

But Sneider was still submerged, trapped in the cage. The ropes holding the cage had frayed further.

"The water's twelve, maybe fifteen, feet deep. We can't let the cage fall," Cubiak explained. He looked at Rowe. The deputy was six foot five and had a long reach. Just maybe he could stand on the bottom and support the cage from beneath. If only he had his diving equipment, the sheriff thought.

Rowe had shrugged off whatever freezing cold he felt and was already halfway out the silo door.

"My gear's still in the car," he said.

They were thinking alike.

"Get it," the sheriff said.

As the deputy dropped down the chute, an army of sirens roared into the yard.

"Reinforcements," Moore said.

Within minutes they heard footsteps pounding through the deserted barn.

"Up here," Moore called down the chute.

Cubiak sent Leeland down with the first deputy who came up, and then he sent down the second deputy with orders to bring long, thick ropes or cables, anything strong enough to replace the fraying line.

Moments later, Rowe returned. There was no time to bother suiting up, so he stripped down to his skivvies and strapped on his scuba tanks.

"How much air do you have in there?" Cubiak asked.

"Ten minutes. Maybe more," Rowe said, checking the gauge.

With a thumbs-up sign, the deputy jumped into the pool and disappeared.

Up top, the other deputy returned with coils of heavy rope. Cubiak and Moore rethreaded the pulleys as best they could and then started to pull.

The Rosses had used a double pulley system, but given the combined weight of the cage and the man trapped inside and the distance they had to lift, the job was hard. Despite his cold, wet clothes, Cubiak began to sweat from the effort. He took deep, measured breaths and ignored the burning in his muscles. The cage rose slowly, and bit by bit, the naked, shriveled figure of Gerald Sneider was revealed. He was bound up just as the sheriff had imagined, a replica of the boys in the boat.

Once the cage cleared the water, Rowe clambered onto the platform and the three of them lowered it to the floor.

The man inside looked comatose. Was he still alive?

"Gerald Sneider?" the sheriff said.

The captive remained motionless.

"Gerald?"

The man's eyes fluttered. He stared as if he were blind.

"Mr. Sneider?"

He blinked.

How the mighty have fallen, Cubiak thought. He had no sympathy for the pathetic specter of the rescued man, but he didn't want his condition to deteriorate further. They needed to work fast to keep him alive.

"It'll be another minute," the sheriff said. Then to Rowe, he explained, "We can't get this damn thing through the door. Fuckers must have built it in sections and then dragged the pieces up and welded it together here. They may have been working on it when I came out to talk with Jon earlier this week. I remember seeing sparks through the door of the machine shed. That's where the tools are. We need them."

Rowe leaned out of the silo and was shouting directives to the men below when Cubiak added, "Not a blowtorch. Tell them to bring a hacksaw. And blankets."

"Stay with us," Cubiak said as they waited for the equipment.

In all, the sheriff and his deputy wrecked three blades opening the cage. But they got Sneider out in time. His breathing was shallow and his pulse weak, but he was alive. Rowe undid the gag as Cubiak cut the cords that bound the captive's wrists, ankles, and neck. When they were finished they traded places with Emma Pardy and an EMT who'd been waiting on the ladder.

"I called Evelyn, too. He's outside," Pardy said.

"Good. Thanks." The sheriff looked at Sneider. "Save him," he said.

Dr. Pardy brushed past. "I will." She spoke with conviction but no sympathy, and Cubiak knew that she, like him, was thinking of the four boys in the rowboat.

Cubiak had no memory of the climb back down the chute. He had no idea how he and Rowe, as cold as they were, had managed to hold on to the ladder.

The scene on the ground was one of controlled chaos. Someone had found the master switch and lit up the barn. One of the deputies, probably alerted by Moore, had blankets and dry clothes for Cubiak and Rowe.

After he changed, Cubiak returned to the barn. He watched Bathard tend to Pickler, and then he listened as Agent Harrison read their rights to the three Ross men—Jon, Leeland, and Stephen. Moore had the trio handcuffed and lined up against the wall: father and son standing tall and firm in their defiance, the nephew crumpling and blinking back tears.

Door County's fleet of three ambulances pulled in from the road where'd they been waiting. Bathard put Pickler in one. Moore walked alongside the gurney that carried Sneider to the second vehicle. Cubiak thought the agent would ride back with the rescued kidnap victim but he sent Harrison instead. Then, ignoring their protests, Moore escorted Cubiak and Rowe to the third ambulance.

"You were both in the water a long time. Too long by my count," he said.

A contingent of the media had followed the flashing lights to the farm. By the time Sneider was out of the silo, the crowd of reporters and cameras had swelled, but Cubiak's staff kept the swarm from entering the yard, leaving only Cate to document the event. Taking advantage of the abundance of artificial light in the yard and the barn, she easily photographed the grounds. Moore was reluctant to let her enter the silo but finally relented and allowed her five minutes to climb the ladder and shoot the scene through the open door. She took seven and made it down in time to ride back in the gray-and-blue vehicle that carried Cubiak and Rowe to the hospital.

PRAYING FOR ANGELS

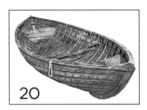

20

For the second time that week, Cubiak and Moore stood in the lobby of the Door County Justice Center and faced a mob of reporters and cameras. An hour earlier the two men had met privately to iron out the details of what would be revealed that morning and what held back until later.

The sheriff squinted into the bright lights. He wore his familiar rumpled jacket and tie and was once again in sharp contrast to Agent Moore, who'd shown up in a tailored three-piece suit, maybe one he kept ready for such an event. As they took up their positions behind a bank of microphones, Cubiak glanced down. His shoes gave new meaning to the word *dull*. Moore's gleamed, as usual. A forgivable foible, thought the sheriff.

Moore tapped a mic and waited for the room to quiet. "We've called this press conference to announce the safe recovery of Mr. Gerald Sneider."

Most of the reporters had been at the Ross farm the previous night. Though the announcement was not news to them, the room still erupted in a buzz.

Moore went on undeterred. "I am also announcing the recovery of Verne Pickler, who was abducted and held against his will, and the arrest of two Door County residents and one former resident in the kidnapping and attempted murder of Mr. Sneider and the unlawful detention of Mr. Pickler. Charges are pending against the three suspects and will be filed on Monday.

The questions popped immediately.

When had Gerald Sneider been found? Where had he been held? What was the motive for the kidnapping? Who was Verne Pickler? How was he connected to Gerald Sneider? What else could Moore tell them about the suspects?

Moore provided few specifics.

"Are the suspects being charged as domestic terrorists?"

Moore hesitated, and a flush of color came up from his collar. "No, they are not."

"Did federal agents locate Mr. Sneider?"

Moore gave a small smile. "Both Gerald Sneider and Verne Pickler were recovered as a direct result of action taken by Door County Sheriff Dave Cubiak."

The news brought another murmur from the crowd, and Cubiak was aware of cameras turning in his direction.

"Where is Sneider now?"

"In the Sturgeon Bay hospital." Under guard. That detail Moore didn't mention.

"And the suspects?"

"For now, they are being detained in the jail across the lobby." Moore pointed over the assembly.

Heads swiveled around and then came back. Hands were still up.

"No more questions," Moore said and nodded to Cubiak. Let's go.

In the jail, Cubiak listened as Moore and Harrison interrogated the three suspects, all of whom had waived the right to have an attorney present.

The feds started with Leeland.

"Whose idea was it to kidnap Sneider?" Harrison asked.

The suspect said nothing.

"Why did you kidnap him?" Moore asked.

Silence.

The session went on for some forty minutes, and during that time Leeland refused to answer any questions.

His only response came when Moore told him that his lack of cooperation wasn't helping his situation. Hearing that, Leeland laughed.

Stephen was second up. The Door County native made up for his cousin's reticence. Steve placed the blame for the crime on his uncle, Jon, and painted himself as an unwilling participant. The young man claimed that grief over his father's recent death had contributed to his irrational decision to go along with the scheme. He also insisted that he'd been led to believe his uncle and cousin were just trying to scare an apology from Sneider for events that had occurred at the Forest Home many years back.

Of the three men, only Jon Ross was belligerently proud of the operation.

"Yeah, it was all my idea," he said. "It was me that convinced Steve to lure Sneider from the game. The bastard would rot in hell before he'd have anything to do with me or my boy. 'Course he wouldn't know Leeland, except by reputation, and he'd claim to not remember who I was, but I think that'd be a lie. So I convinced Steve to pretend he was doing an interview for that bigshot newspaper of his. I knew Sneider couldn't resist the chance to get his name in lights again. Mr. Philantropiss, I call him."

It was all so easy, a piece of cake, he told them. "Steve told Sneider that his editor wanted some pictures of the Packer memorabilia, and so they drove up together, Steve recording all the bullshit Sneider was dishing out. When they got to Oostburg, Steve stopped like planned and I took over. Leeland was waiting for us at the house in Ellison Bay, and once Sneider turned off the alarm we waltzed in and left the note. It was Leeland's idea to tie the Super Bowl ring to the rope. Can't believe the fucker has three championship rings."

Agent Harrison asked about the spiders.

"Yeah, that was my idea, too. I knew all about how he was afraid of them 'cause of how he used to try and be brave in front of us kids, putting one fucking little spider on his hand like it was some big fucking deal. 'OK, Gerald,' I says to myself. 'Let's see how you do with a whole shitload of the little buggers.' Turns out he didn't do so good, did he?"

At the break Cubiak told the feds to ask about the kittens.

"The kittens were part of this?" Moore asked in a way that made it clear he recalled the circumstances of their initial meeting.

"With that guy, anything is possible. And I'd just like to know."

When Moore posed the question, Jon Ross erupted with a good laugh. "Yeah, that's right. I almost forgot about the damn kittens." They always drowned the ones they'd didn't need, he told the agents, as if he were letting them in on a private joke. When the feds didn't react, he went on.

"Leeland insisted he had to have an alibi for the afternoon Sneider disappeared. We figured there'd be plenty of people watching the game at the Tipsy Too and that it was a good place to be seen. On his way there, Leeland was supposed to toss the litter in the bay. And what fucking good luck that the sheriff was sitting on the ledge fishing. Leeland saw the jeep and thought it'd be fun to throw the bag in right in front of him. Can't believe the fucker went in after them, but that was good, you see, 'cause then later when he spotted Leeland's truck in the parking lot and put two and two together, he actually came in and confronted him. The sheriff said he knew it was Leeland what tried to drown the cats. Now what better alibi can you have than your own fucking sheriff seeing you sucking down a beer when the crime of the century is being committed?"

"It's hardly the crime of the century," Harrison said, but the elder Ross merely scoffed.

"What'd you do with the ransom money?" Moore asked.

"We never got it. Damn kids picked it up. I know you were there. You saw what happened."

"And you know what, I'll give you that it was a pretty clever ploy to try and distract us that way. But we know you grabbed the bag. So where's the money?"

"I told you, we ain't got it."

At that point, Cubiak joined the party.

"It's pretty interesting about the money," he said, picking up where Moore had left off. "Not just the business about the drop but the fact that the ransom demands were not multiples of three, which you'd expect since there were three of you. Instead, you demanded amounts that could be evenly divided by four."

Cubiak laid down a photo of the four completed skeletons that Cate had taken that morning.

"Four victims. You wanted Sneider to have to pay for their lives, didn't you?"

Ross's nostrils flared. "Something like that."

"Which also explains the spiders and the cage. Money wasn't all. You wanted Sneider to pay with fear, and maybe even his life."

"We weren't gonna kill him!"

"You'll have to convince a jury of that." Cubiak looked thoughtful. "I'll tell you what I don't get, Jon, is the business with the snakes."

"Andrew didn't say nothing?" Ross sneered. "I'll be damned. I can't believe he forgot. Maybe he was just too embarrassed. The snakes were to remind him of the summer he was one of the rich-kid campers. Andrew hated snakes. One day we decided we'd do to him what his father did to us and made him sit on his bed with a snake around his ankles and another in his lap. Like we figured, he pissed his pants and worse. Before we could get him to the shower, his mother showed up on one of her surprise visits and that's the last we seen of him at the camp."

"Were you punished?"

"Oh, yeah. But that was one time it was worth it. Andrew was just like his father, always acting like he was better than us, and it felt good to cut him down to size."

"I see." Cubiak made a show of cleaning his glasses and then adjusting them on his face. He looked at the suspect. "Did you ever get to know any of the summer kids?"

"Naw. They stuck with each other."

"What about the boys who lived there?"

"Not much."

"What about the boys in the boat? I need to know everything you can tell me about them."

"There's nothing to tell."

"The kid you called Chester, did he have a last name?"

"None I ever heard."

"You know where he was from?"

"He talked about his folks losing their farm but hell, that happened to a lot of us. That's why some of us were there."

"And the others. Did you know their names?"

"Just one, Tommie. The other two were new boys, barely there a couple of days. I don't remember who they were."

"Ages?"

Ross shook his head. "We were all just kids."

"Anything else? Injuries, for example."

Ross snickered. "There were always enough bruises to go around. Prick made sure of that. I got a nasty scar from boiling water." He rolled up his sleeve to display a streak of gnarled skin that ran from his wrist to his elbow.

"What about broken bones?"

"Naw, not as I can recall. No, wait, come to think of it, Chester broke his arm the summer before. He was always complaining about how itchy it was inside the cast."

"Which arm did he break?"

"Hell if I remember. Why you asking me all this?"

"Because I want to find out who they were."

Ross straightened in his chair. "You can do that?"

"It's a long shot, but we can try."

"What happens if you do?"

Cubiak hesitated. He thought the term *closure* was overused but felt there were still occasions when the concept if not the word fit and this seemed to be one of them. "Then the people who knew those kids and who have been left wondering for years what happened to them will have answers."

At the hospital Verne Pickler was arguing with the attending doctor, who wanted to keep him another night for observation.

"Tell the doc, I got a dog to take care of," Pickler urged Cubiak, who'd just entered the room.

"I'm not concerned about your dog," the physician said.

"Well, I am," Pickler said.

Eventually he prevailed, and the sheriff drove him home.

Pickler seemed annoyed when Cubiak followed him into the house. "I already told the FBI everything that happened," he said after he'd fed Maize and was settled in his easy chair with the dog at his side.

"I read your statement. But I'm more interested in things that happened when you worked at Sneider's camp."

"Ah." Pickler looked down and scratched Maize's head. "That was a long time ago."

Cubiak held out a photo of the bones in the boat. "These are not the kinds of things you forget."

Pickler started and stared at the picture but said nothing. Cubiak let the silence settle around them.

Finally Pickler wet his lips. "I figured it would come to this one day," he said.

Speaking slowly, as if pulling the memories from a dark corner of the past, the former camp director at Gerald Sneider's Forest Home for Orphaned and Needy Boys told the sheriff what happened on the night the four boys drowned. His account corroborated Jon Ross's version of events.

"And no one tried to save them?"

Pickler brushed something from his eye. "That's not true. Once the storm got real bad, I wanted to go out there and bring them in but Sneider wouldn't let me. He said he needed me, but the boys, well, it didn't matter what happened to them. They were just throwaways. Their families didn't care about them so why should I risk my life trying to save them?"

"And for all these years, you've said nothing."

Pickler offered a wan smile. "Who'd believe me, Sheriff? The next morning I went and looked for the boat but it was gone, and I figured the currents pulled it into the lake. I had no proof about what Sneider had done. It was just my word against him, and I was nobody."

"The boys at the camp would have backed you up," Cubiak said.

"It wouldn't have mattered none. They were nobodies, too. Like me."

The sheriff knew that what Pickler said was true. "Instead, you punished yourself," he said kindly.

Pickler flinched and lowered his head. "I didn't know what else to do."

When he finished with Pickler, Cubiak drove back to the hospital. Visiting hours were over, but the nurse at the desk recognized him and waved him through.

"Room three-twelve," she said.

Lisa was sitting up against a battery of pillows, an unopened book in her hands. She looked tired but smiled when she saw Cubiak.

"I come not bearing gifts," Cubiak said with a nod toward the plants and flower bouquets that lined the windowsill and covered the small dresser. "Only good wishes. Are you okay?"

"Yes. And I'm glad you came. I've heard . . ."

Cubiak took her hand. "You don't need to bother with any of that, not now. There'll be plenty of time later to catch up. I understand it's a girl."

"Elizabeth Anne. For our moms. We're calling her Libby. You can see her on your way out. The nursery is right down the hall."

All babies look alike, Cubiak told himself when he left Lisa's room. He could wait to see Libby. But before he realized, he was standing outside the nursery window. Libby was asleep in the first bed. Her delicate tulip lips were pressed in an almost smile and her forehead softly crinkled beneath the tiny striped cap on her head. With her infant body swaddled in a white cotton blanket, she lay before him and the world so innocent and helpless, so like Alexis, he thought.

There were three other beds behind the nursery window, four new babies in all. Life in all its mysteriousness and sweetness renewing itself.

Who knew what the future would bring these children. Surely they deserved a better fate than that meted out to the hapless boys in the doomed rowboat or to so many other children who suffered at the hands of uncaring adults. Life could be wonderful and just as easily immensely cruel. Were guardian angels real? the sheriff wondered. Looking at the infants, Cubiak said a prayer that the protectors of these children would do their jobs well.

Then he pressed a hand to the glass, by way of offering his own blessing.

THE SPECIAL ROOM

21

Dawn broke dull and gray over the peninsula. The low, languid clouds rationed the light allowed to seep through the blinds in Cubiak's bedroom. Uncertain of the time, he lay under the covers and listened to the rhythmic shush of the waves rushing over the table rocks on the untamed beach. The sound was hypnotic and, although he'd slept longer than usual, he struggled to keep his eyes open. From the kitchen, there were other sounds, normal Sunday morning sounds: Butch bumping her metal bowl against the baseboard, demanding attention. Cate pouring water into the coffee maker.

The night before, she'd come home with him from the Ross farm, where Cubiak had helped the FBI gather evidence and she had documented more of the crime scene. There'd been no trace of the money, either there or at Fred Ross's house, where Steve had been staying with his mother. Had Jon Ross told the truth? Probably not. The sheriff figured Ross had the money well hidden and was hoping to use it as a bargaining chip down the road.

By the time Cubiak and Cate got back, it was late and they were both wired. They stayed up sharing a bottle of wine and talking, but only about the kidnapping. In the dim morning light, Cubiak remembered how she had curled into him and they'd both fallen asleep, too tired for anything more.

"Cate." He called her name but there was no answer.

He thought of going into the kitchen and taking her hand and asking her to come back to bed but he didn't. Their relationship had always been complicated, and within the past week it had become even more tangled. Now there were new questions to be answered as well as old issues to be sorted out. He knew that Cate would want to talk first.

But even that important conversation had to wait.

Cubiak wasn't done with Gerald Sneider yet. He still had work to do and it had to be seen to that morning. As the saying went, there'd be hell to pay when he'd finished. Of that, Cubiak was sure. He sighed and closed his eyes. He'd turn forty-six in another month and he was tired.

After a quick run with the dog, Cubiak headed to Sturgeon Bay. The hospital was on a quiet residential street near the edge of the small city. In the subdued light, the sheriff passed down roadways that were empty except for Sunday churchgoers. As he pulled into the hospital parking lot, a line of vehicles, led by the seemingly ubiquitous TV vans, rolled toward the exit. Perfect timing. The exodus signaled the end of the director's press conference, during which she had updated the media on the condition of her headliner patient, Gerald Sneider.

Earlier that morning Cubiak had called for a status report, so he knew what she planned to say to the roomful of reporters.

"Mr. Sneider is making a remarkable recovery, far exceeding my expectations," the director had told the sheriff. She was a noted internist who'd served on the staffs of prestigious teaching hospitals in Milwaukee and Boston before coming back to her native Door County. "You know, my father knew Mr. Sneider and thought very highly of him. Growing up, I remember listening to so many stories about the man that, for me, it's an honor to have him as a patient."

"I see," Cubiak said blandly. How else could he respond? The director would have reason to reconsider her opinion soon enough.

The third-floor nurses' station was overrun with flowers. It was "overflow" from their guest of honor, one of the nurses told him, peering from between two bundles of white calla lilies. "Room three-oh-one," she said as she stood and cheerfully pointed to the room at the end the hall.

A department deputy lingered outside the door, but at the sight of Cubiak, he snapped to attention and saluted. "Morning, sir. Congratulations, sir."

The sheriff couldn't help but smile though he shook his head sternly. Rowe's bad habits were taking hold throughout the ranks.

Not bothering to knock, Cubiak entered. The hospital director hadn't exaggerated when she described Sneider's recovery as remarkable. The patient in room 301 was not the shriveled, nearly comatose man Cubiak had pulled from the silo and saved from drowning less than thirty-six hours earlier.

Freshly showered and shaved, his mop of silver hair neatly parted on the side, the aging tycoon reclined against a bank of pillows that had been artfully arranged against the raised hospital bed. No skimpy hospital gown or ordinary fare for "the guest of honor." Sneider sported a blue silk dressing gown over matching pajamas. A pair of leather slippers rested on the floor alongside the bed. In the corner, an air filtering machine hummed quietly, sucking in dust motes and errant germs. The window ledge and the floor beneath it brimmed with flowers that perfumed the room.

Andrew sat amid the blooms, framed by two large sprays of blood red roses. An ironic touch, thought Cubiak.

He had the feeling he'd interrupted an important conversation. The senior Sneider had been looking at his son expectantly and words seemed to hang in the air, but all that was brushed aside when Cubiak appeared.

"Ah, Sheriff! The man of the hour. Do come in," Sneider said, his voice strong and firm.

Cubiak had never heard Sneider speak. After Thursday's phone call, Andrew said his father sounded weak and scared but this was the robust voice of confidence.

Andrew had been right when he said his orphaned father had inherited all the best genes from his unknown parents. In the hospital's artificial light, his gaunt cheeks and the thin blue vein that ran across his forehead stood out, but otherwise he seemed hearty and in good cheer as he held up his hand and beckoned Cubiak closer. "You are a welcome sight for sore eyes. I owe you my life, saving me from that pack of miscreants. If you had been an hour later, even thirty minutes more . . ." The former kidnap victim trailed off, shuddering.

The sheriff stepped over the threshold and pulled the door in, careful to leave it ajar. "I did my job," he said.

Sneider gave a barking laugh. "Your job! Listen to him, Andy. He did his job, indeed. We need a world full of men who feel that way. No, sir, Sheriff. You did far more than your job."

As the former kidnap victim talked, his son rose and moved to his side as if trying to add his gratitude to the thanks the old man was proffering. "Yes, indeed, you have proven yourself a man to be reckoned with," Sneider said. He paused again, and then like a prince judging a man's worth, he added, "A man to be rewarded."

Cubiak said nothing. Coming up through the ranks in Chicago, he'd had plenty of dealings with men like Sneider, men who felt they were too important to be ignored and who threw their money around, thinking they could buy whatever they wanted. The system pandered to people like Sneider, but that didn't mean he had to.

"What can we offer you, Sheriff?" Sneider asked. "Fresh brewed coffee. Cigars . . ." He pointed to a box of Cubans on the nightstand. "Anything at all . . ."

"This is not a social call. I'm here on business," Cubiak said.

Sneider's blue eyes flashed but just as quickly he regained his bonhomie. Brushing his son's hand from his shoulder, he sat up in his bed throne.

"Always happy to cooperate, Sheriff, though surely you realize that the FBI has already taken my formal statement."

"I've already read it. It's suitable for their purposes," Cubiak said as he moved to the foot of the bed.

Sneider frowned. "What other purpose is there than to punish those reprobates? You're from the big city, Sheriff. You should know all about scum like that, people whose very existence is a disgrace to the human race." He looked at Cubiak. "They were prepared to kill me. Have no doubt of that."

Or to punish you, Cubiak thought, even as he nodded for Sneider's benefit. "A terrible thing to happen here where you're so well known and have done so much good. But since all this did go down in my jurisdiction, I'm sure you won't mind answering a few questions and going over some of the details again."

Sneider softened. "Not at all, Sheriff, but I expect a little quid pro quo."

"Meaning?"

"Come now, don't be overly modest. Outsmarting the feds is no small feat. I want to know how you figured it out."

"We can get to that later. For now, let's start with you and your side of things. Like how the Ross bunch got you to meet with them."

"The Ross bunch did no such thing. Do you think I'd cross the street to accommodate them? Obviously I didn't know the three of them were in cahoots or I wouldn't have fallen for their scheme. Jon and that son of his are a couple of no-good parasites. They should be wiped off the face of the earth, far as I'm concerned." Sneider settled back against his pillows. "At the same time, I'm not above admitting that it was my pride that got me into this mess. It was Steve, Jon's nephew, that contacted me."

Sneider waggled a finger at the coffee pot and Andrew reemerged from the floral jungle to pour a fresh cup.

"Sheriff?" Andrew said, but Cubiak shook his head and the son slunk back to his seat as his father continued his story.

"Steve was in town for his father's funeral—another man who didn't amount to much of anything. But Steve seemed different. He was educated and ambitious, two qualities I appreciate in a young man. He sent me a note saying he was living out east and working as a journalist. For the *New York Times*, no less, and that he'd talked to his editor about doing a piece on me. He included his business card with the note. His message struck a chord with me. Here was someone trying to make something of himself, like I'd done. I like that in a man, Sheriff, and of course the thought of my rags-to-riches story in such a prestigious paper was hard to resist. If anything, I felt obligated to have it be told. After all, it's the epitome of the American Dream, and I felt it could serve as an inspiration for others."

"You didn't find it odd that he arranged to meet you in Chicago?"

"Not really. He contacted me that morning and said he was driving down with a friend for an opening at the Art Institute. The friend was staying in the city, and since he knew I would be at the game, he suggested we meet and drive back up together."

"And you couldn't wait until the game was over?"

"No. He said he had a deadline."

"Where'd you meet?"

"I picked him up on Columbus at the east entrance to the museum."

"And you gave him the keys to your car?"

Sneider made a deprecating gesture. "I'd had a few to drink, so it seemed the responsible thing to do. We started off talking about Door County and how it had changed since he'd moved away. Once we reached the toll road, he turned on his recorder and said he wanted me to talk about my life, what things were like when I was a kid and then how I went from having nothing to being a man of substantial means. I went into some detail about my early years growing up and my start in the lumber business and then later how I got involved with the Packers. He didn't say much, just let me ramble on. It wasn't until I mentioned the camp that he started asking questions. I'm sure you've heard about my camp, the Forest Home for Orphaned and Needy Boys, where I tried to help all those kids who'd been left pretty much on their own."

"What time did you cross the state line?"

Sneider seemed annoyed by the interruption. "Oh, I don't remember," he replied impatiently.

He took a sip of water and went on. "I suppose I was so caught up in relating my story that I didn't notice when the tone of the conversation started to change. Steve had been very personable initially but then gradually he became strident and started asking very pointed and harsh questions. That's when I realized he'd heard a lot of lies about me and the program—probably from his father and uncle. They lived at the camp for a number of years, you know. You never saw such ungrateful kids. They were never shy about taking advantage of my charity, those two. Steve's line of discussion was starting to get annoying and I told him as much. We passed a sign for Oostburg and he said he needed to take a piss. He turned off the highway and drove to a park-and-drive lot, where he stopped and got out of the car. I figured I may as well relieve myself as well and had just unbuckled my seat belt when Steve opened the door and yanked a hood down over my head."

Sneider stopped. "Honestly, Sheriff, I've already told all this to that FBI agent. Do I have to go through it again?"

"Yes, please . . ."

Sneider sighed. "All right, if you insist. At the same time that Steve pulled the hood over me, another man came up from behind and tied my hands. And that's when I realized I'd been set up. These two were kidnapping me, and I didn't know who they were. The second man was big and rough and smelled like stale beer. And the one who claimed to be Steve Ross? Until that day, I'd never met the man—it could have been anyone pretending to be him. The two of them dragged me out of my car and shoved me into the back seat of a different car. From there on, the second man, the one I hadn't seen yet, drove. He kept taunting me about being rich and saying that they were tired of being poor and how they were going to remedy the situation by making my son pay for my release. He called it a new age business negotiation and said there'd be no harm done."

"You believed him?"

"What choice did I have?"

"Is that why you gave him the alarm code to the house?"

"I turned it off myself."

"And you told them the combination to the safe."

"I did. There was some money in there and I wanted them to have it, hoping it might appease them some. I still didn't know for sure who they were but didn't think they really meant to hurt me, not at the beginning, so I cooperated, thinking the quicker things got underway, the sooner it would be over."

Sneider took another drink of water. "It wasn't until later that night that they took the hood off and I saw that no good bastard Jon Ross and his son, Leeland, just standing there in front of me, laughing."

"The other man, the one who said he was Steve, was he with them?"

"Yeah, he was there, too."

"How'd you know it was Jon Ross? Did you recognize him?"

"Not at first, but he talked about the camp and from the things he said, I knew it was him."

"Is that when you began to realize that the whole kidnapping scheme might be about more than the money?"

The room fell silent. Sneider folded his arms across his chest and scowled but his son jumped to his feet.

"What do you mean? They didn't ask for anything except money," Andrew said, moving to his father's side.

There was silence again until finally Sneider spoke up. "No good deed goes unpunished, is that it? Certainly they wanted the money, miserable failures that they were, living like—well, I can only imagine.

But maybe even more, they wanted to humiliate me. Jon Ross is a spiteful bastard. That business with the spiders should be proof enough of his twisted thinking. He resented having to live at the camp. He was a natural-born troublemaker who didn't like following the rules. I should have thrown him out, along with his brother, but I didn't. I kept trying to show him a better path."

"A better path." Cubiak let the phrase hang in the heavily scented air, and then he looked at Andrew. "Your father believed that the poor boys at the camp were mentally, emotionally, and spiritually warped and in need of salvation. He felt that it was his responsibility to whip the charity cases into shape," the sheriff explained, handing the heir a copy of one of the pamphlets from Pickler's shed.

Sneider bolted upright. "Where'd you get that?" he said, snatching the booklet from Andrew. "I was strict, that's all. I was always strict, with everyone. My own son included. Wasn't I?"

Andrew nodded.

Cubiak began reading from a copy he'd made of the second brochure. "'Use corporal punishment to correct deviant behaviors. Act as the authority in all matters. Demand obedience at all times.' Just a few of your father's recommendations," the sheriff said as he gave Andrew the material.

Sneider slammed his fist against the bed table. "Yes, I had a firm hand and took a firm approach. And I'm damn proud of what I did. I had no choice. Those boys were wild, undisciplined, all heading to the devil. That Jon Ross was among the worst, a born liar. He resisted everything I did. He didn't understand that I was only trying to help him. All those years later, he stood in front of me and had the nerve to say that what I'd done was wrong and that he meant to settle the score."

"What did he mean 'what you did was wrong?' What did you do?" Andrew said. The pamphlet quivered in his hand.

"Nothing! Everything he said was lies. All of it was lies."

"What kind of lies?" The panic of recent sex abuse headlines fluttered across Andrew's face.

Sneider went beet red. "Not that. I wasn't like that. Other lies."

Andrew turned to the sheriff. "I don't understand."

"You told me yourself about your father's unique way of dealing with fear. He used his methods at the camp and was unstinting in his belief that he was right. But one night things went terribly wrong."

Cubiak took a manila envelope from inside his jacket and undid the clasp. As father and son watched, he pulled out one of Cate's photos and laid it on the bed in front of them. "This was taken from a salvage boat moored outside the marina in Baileys Harbor, looking east toward the spit of land that curves out from the beach north of town, where the Forest Home was located."

Sneider glanced at the picture and then fixed his gaze on the far wall. "Could be. I really can't tell for sure. Plenty of shorelines here look pretty much the same," he said, waving dismissively.

Cubiak placed a second photo on the blanket. It was a picture of the bone-filled rowboat being raised from the water. Sneider continued to stare past the sheriff.

"What is it? What's that in the boat?" Andrew said.

"Shut up," Sneider said, swatting at his son.

"Those are human bones. Earlier this week, three bones were found washed up on the beach outside of Baileys Harbor. I thought they were from an old shipwreck, but these weren't adult bones and something about the situation didn't sit right so I asked one of my men to take his diving equipment and investigate. This is what he found."

Sneider still refused to look, so Cubiak held the photo in front of him. Sneider pinched his mouth as his jaw clenched and the color drained from his face.

"Who would do such a thing?" Cubiak said to Andrew as he laid the picture back down and then next to it the black-and-white of the boat with the name of the camp clearly legible.

"Oh, God." Andrew collapsed against the wall.

"It's a close-up of the boat, but you know what it says without looking, don't you?" Cubiak said, addressing Sneider.

The philanthropist's face tightened.

"Did you even know their names?" Cubiak said as he held up the last photo. The picture was taken at the shipyard after Pardy and Bathard had completed their work with the bones. It showed the four skeletons laid out on the platform with the rowboat in the background.

Cubiak placed the picture alongside the others and turned to Andrew. "These photographs document the recovery of the remains of the four young boys your father ordered bound and gagged and tied to a boat that was anchored off shore and left for the night. The experience was meant to teach the boys to overcome their fear of the water but a storm came up. There was no way the boys could free themselves and escape. These were young kids and they were left to drown."

"No, that can't be," Andrew said, shriveling under the impact. "These aren't real. They've been photoshopped. . . . Dad, tell him. Father, please . . ."

Sneider ignored his son. "Who put you up to this?" he asked Cubiak. "That scum Jon Ross? It was him, wasn't it?"

Again, Cubiak addressed Andrew. "Jon and Fred were eleven, twins and just kids themselves, when this happened. Your father forced them to rope the boys in and to tie leather strips around their hands and ankles. The two brothers went through life trying to escape the memory of that night. Jon drank to forget and nearly succeeded, but his brother was tortured by guilt to the end, and it was his dying wish that your father be made to pay for what he'd done. He made Jon promise."

Sneider erupted. "Sniveling bastard. He and his worthless brother both," he said, batting the photos off the bed. "Yes, I put the boys in the boat. I did that any number of times to different kids—not to hurt them, but to help them. Do you understand? Why do you think those miserable kids ended up at the camp? Because they had weak parents who had failed them. I was trying to help them get strong, like me. I had to teach them to confront their fears so they wouldn't grow up weak like their parents." By now he was shouting. "Don't you get it? I was their only hope."

Sneider looked around for Andrew, but his dazed son remained several steps back. "It's true that I sent the boys out that night, but I didn't leave them there. I tried to save them. You must believe me," he said. Desperate to explain himself, he reached for his son.

Andrew hesitated.

"Please," his father said, slowly luring him closer.

When Andrew was within reach, Sneider grabbed his arm. "It's the God's honest truth. I swear I tried to save them," he said again, clinging to his son as he proclaimed his innocence.

"I have testimony that says otherwise," Cubiak said quietly.

Sneider bellowed. "From whom? Jon Ross? You believe what that fucker told you? You're going to take his word against mine? Don't be a fool."

"Ross was just a kid that night and all he knew about what happened was what you told the boys afterward. He believed you; they all did. But you overplayed your hand with the postcard allegedly from one of the drowned boys claiming they'd survived and run away. According to Jon, the boy had never learned to write."

"Rubbish! Still his word against mine. The word of a mean, spiteful brat."

"There's more. Another eyewitness, an adult who was there the whole time and knows what really happened that night."

Sneider's eyes narrowed to slits.

"Who?" Andrew let the word out in a whisper.

Cubiak kept his eyes on Sneider. "According to the witness, you did nothing to try and save them. You didn't even send for help. The camp wasn't far from the resort that replaced the old coast guard station. There were plenty of boats there and people who could have helped rescue those kids. But you didn't want anyone to see what you'd done to them, did you? You valued your reputation more than their lives."

"Oh, Dad, how could you?"

Sneider's nostrils flared and the vein in his forehead pulsed. He pushed his son away. "Shut up," he said for the second time, and then he turned to Cubiak. "You better damn well know who you're dealing with and what the fuck you're doing because this is slander and if you start spreading these stories, I'll destroy you."

Cubiak shrugged off the threat. "I'm just doing my job."

Sneider breathed loudly. "I've got nothing more to say. No comment. Now get the hell out of here." He puffed himself up with importance and glared at the sheriff.

The arrogance of power, Cubiak thought, allowing himself a quick smile. "I'm not finished with you yet," he said as he stepped around to the side of the bed.

"What?" Sneider looked ready to spit.

Cubiak kicked the soft leather slippers out of reach and then took his time picking up the photos from the floor. As he slid the pictures back in the envelope he glanced from son to father, letting his gaze settle on the man whose silk pajamas had lost their elegant sheen.

Moments like this, he knew why he had become a city cop all those years ago, and why after abandoning the job, he'd later put on the badge of a county sheriff. To serve and protect the innocent, like the helpless boys in the rowboat.

In the charged atmosphere, Cubiak spoke calmly. "Gerald Sneider, I am arresting you on the charge of murder. Four counts in the first degree."

Sneider turned to stone.

"You have a right to remain silent but anything you say . . ." Cubiak went on as he informed the Door County hero of his rights. The sheriff's pronouncement was largely lost in Andrew's cries of despair and the sounds of shattering glass that erupted as he hurled vases of roses and lilies against the floor and walls of his father's very special room.

ON THE *PARLANDO*

22

Cubiak trailed a tour bus full of senior citizens through Sturgeon Bay on his way to Hangar Number Three. The previous day, the FBI had taken charge of the human remains the sheriff had recovered from Baileys Harbor. And that morning a special team of technicians had arrived to handle the task of tagging and packing the bones for shipment to the agency's forensic laboratory in Madison. Cubiak didn't have to go there again. His work was finished. There was nothing, and yet everything, for him to do. Pay his respects. Say a final goodbye.

Agents Moore and Harrison were standing inside the door, as if they'd expected him.

"It's done?" Moore said.

"Yes."

"Good."

For the first time that week, the three were a match, each of them in jeans and a black turtleneck.

Moore produced a bottle of brandy from his briefcase. "It's not quite according to Hoyle," he said as he filled the shot glasses Harrison had pulled from the leather tote bag slung over her shoulder.

"To justice," Cubiak said, raising his drink to theirs.

The sheriff and the two federal agents downed the shots, and like a whisper, the moment passed. The bottle and glasses disappeared, and they turned toward the platform.

The skeletons remained intact. Nearby the recovery team had organized the shipping containers and the materials the technicians would use to identify and wrap each bone.

"They'll be starting soon," Harrison said.

They'd waited for him, Cubiak realized. After thanking them, he approached the platform for one last look. Bathard had talked about Milton's concept of good and evil, but all Cubiak could think of were Dante's nine circles of hell. Those who acted violently against others were consigned to the outer ring of the seventh circle, where they were immersed in a river of boiling blood and fire for eternity. A fitting punishment for Gerald Sneider, Cubiak thought.

The sheriff bowed his head and prayed to all the gods of the universe. Before them he vowed that he would do everything he could to see that the boys would not be forgotten and that the justice he had saluted a few minutes earlier would be done in their name. Whoever they were, they were legion, and like all the world's suffering children they deserved better than what they got.

In the end, Cubiak uttered one word: *Peace*. Then he turned and walked away.

After he stopped in town for two coffees, Cubiak drove to the justice center for a meeting with Justin St. James. He found the young reporter pacing the lobby and led him to his office.

"You're familiar with Gerald Sneider's legacy on the peninsula, his philanthropic work, the camp for orphaned and needy boys," the sheriff said, dispensing with the usual introductory small talk favored by locals.

"Sure, who isn't, especially after this week. I knew some of the story before, of course, but now." St. James popped the lid on his coffee and dumped in two packets of sugar. "Gerald Sneider's a very famous man."

"Who's about to become infamous."

The journalist looked up. "What's going on? What's happened?" He put a small recorder on the table. "May I?"

"Sure." When the green light appeared, Cubiak went on. "This morning I arrested Sneider on four counts of murder."

St. James let out a low whistle. "I don't understand," he said. The reporter was pale with excitement.

"You will."

Cubiak started by laying down a picture of the bone Butch had discovered on the Baileys Harbor beach. From there he took St. James through the events of the previous week. He told him about the young Ross boys and Verne Pickler and about the boat filled with bones that had been recovered from the bay.

St. James blanched. "I grew up around there. I used to swim in that water," he said.

Finally, the sheriff told the journalist what he'd learned about the role that Sneider had played in the tragedy.

"You're getting all this?"

St. James shook his recorder. His hands trembled and he seemed to have trouble speaking. "I think so. But I just can't believe it. Four boys left to drown?"

Cubiak wasn't surprised by the young man's reaction. This was not the kind of news St. James was accustomed to reporting.

The sheriff laid out the series of photos that documented the story.

"Oh my God," St. James said. He studied the pictures, too overwhelmed to say anything further.

For several minutes, the room was quiet. Then Cubiak spoke.

"Later today the FBI will take the remains to a lab in Madison for DNA analysis. Most of the kids were orphans, but it's possible that there are relatives around who heard family stories of nephews or cousins who lived at the camp. If there are DNA matches, then there's a chance at least some of the victims can be identified."

St. James nodded but it took him a moment to pick up the train of discussion. "How come no one asked about these kids before?"

"Maybe somebody did, but who was there to tell them anything? There weren't any official records. The kids were gone; maybe they'd run away, like Sneider claimed. Then again, a lot of families had it tough back then and weren't looking for an extra mouth to feed. They figured that if the kid grew up and went off on his own, everyone involved was better off."

"You want me to write about all this?" St. James said.

"That's right, and I'm giving you the exclusive."

"But the others . . . there are reporters here with more experience . . ."

"This happened in your backyard. It's your story."

"It'll get picked up . . ."

Yes, thought Cubiak. The national media will pick up the story. TV stations and newspapers in towns and cities across the country will retell the sad saga, which would help widen the search for people who could put names and faces to the dead boys.

"That's the whole point," the sheriff said.

St. James picked up the photo that showed the camp's name on the side of the rowboat.

"Do you think the murder charge will hold after all this time?" he asked.

For a reporter about to break the biggest story of his career, perhaps the biggest story he would ever byline, St. James remained calm and focused. Cubiak liked that.

"Officially, yes, and it should. There's no statute of limitations on murder in Wisconsin, but off the record, no. Sneider will hire a squad of silver-tongued lawyers that will probably get the charge reduced to involuntary manslaughter. They might even get it thrown out entirely. If the case goes to trial, it'll come down to whom the jury believes: Gerald Sneider or Verne Pickler.

"But whatever happens, the deaths of those four boys will not go unnoted, and Gerald Sneider will be held accountable, at least in the eyes of the public, for what he did. I hope he serves time but even if he doesn't, he'll end up a prisoner in his own house, unable to show himself anywhere. Your story will tarnish his name and destroy his reputation. Gerald Sneider will no longer be known as a philanthropist and the savior of the Packers. He'll be known as a sadistic tyrant who sentenced four boys to a cruel death. Sneider's glass castle will crumble at his feet and he'll be powerless to rebuild it."

The sheriff looked at St. James. "Eventually, the truth comes to light. People like to think they can outmaneuver or outrun the past, but life generally doesn't work that way. The past doesn't stay behind lost in time. Sooner or later, it catches up."

Cubiak was a mile from home when the clouds started to lift. As he drove into the yard, a patch of blue sky widened over the lake and a swath of bright autumn light spilled onto the water. It was probably one of the last really nice days they'd have that fall.

Cate was at the kitchen table filling in the crossword when Cubiak popped open the back door. "If we hurry we can take the *Parlando* out and get in a couple of hours. Bathard's pulling the boat next week so it's our final chance this year," he said.

To avoid the tourist traffic, they came up the back way to the Egg Harbor marina. There was a concert in the park that overlooked the harbor, and strains of a familiar folk song drifted down to the docks. They'd stopped for groceries on the way up, and while Cate stowed their food and gear below Cubiak motored away from the dock. When they cleared the harbor, he cut the engine and they raised the mainsail.

The wind was light but strong enough to fill the sail. Minutes later, they reached the open waters of Green Bay. Cubiak pointed them south, and they sailed along the palisades that lined the shore.

The first time Cubiak went out on the boat with Bathard, he'd moved about clumsily and come close to getting sick. Within minutes of leaving land, he'd been overwhelmed. Everything he'd worked so hard to learn about sailing had blurred together and left him helpless, a true novice.

But Bathard was patient, and gradually Cubiak came to feel more comfortable and competent on the water. After two summers of tutoring, Bathard had finally let him take the boat out himself.

On his first time sailing solo, all the old fears came back. The twenty-six-foot boat was quick as a flea and seemed to respond to the slightest twitch. When Cubiak finally docked, he was exhausted. But hooked. And things got steadily better from there.

"You're quite good at this," Cate said as the *Parlando* sliced through the water.

"I've had a good teacher," Cubiak said.

"Indeed." Cate smiled and pulled up her hood. Hugging her knees, she leaned back on the bench and lifted her face to the sun. "It's nice out here," she said.

They continued like this for another half hour, Cubiak alert at the tiller and Cate immersed in her own thoughts. When they came within sight of Sherwood Point, she went below for the cooler. On deck, she poured two beers, filled a bowl with crackers, and then sliced salami and cheese on a square cutting board.

"A Wisconsin lunch," she said.

As they ate, a two-masted schooner approached from the west. The vessel moved with a magical grace, its giant sails a blinding white in the afternoon sunlight as it flew past. It was headed into Sturgeon Bay, in the direction of the shipyards.

"Do you think they're finished yet?" Cate asked.

They both knew what she meant. Cubiak checked his watch. It was nearly four. "Close to it," he said.

It was their only reference to the day's grim task at the Lakeside hangar.

The wind stayed with the *Parlando* a little while longer and then, as often happened that late in the afternoon, it died, leaving the boat adrift on the undulating water. Time had slipped by, and the giant orange ball of a sun was lower in the sky. The air felt cold.

"Should we take down the sail?" Cate asked.

There were strong currents in the bay and Cubiak kept a careful watch on the shore to see how far they were drifting. "Not yet," he said.

Without warning, a sudden gust came up and tipped the boat. Cate lurched against the mast as Cubiak turned the boat into the wind.

"Let loose the sheet," he said.

As she grabbed the line and released it from the cleat, the boom swung and they came around sharply. The canvas rippled and then sprang taut as Cubiak recaptured the wind.

"That'll keep you on your toes," Cate said as she picked the lunch things off the floor.

By the time she headed below, the wind died again and the sail went limp.

The click of doors opening and closing—the sounds of tidying up—came from the cabin, and then Cate reappeared, cocooned in a bulky red sweater. Tucking her feet beneath her, she curled up on the windward bench. A moment later she opened the conversation that Cubiak had been expecting.

"You're still angry with me, aren't you?" she said.

He hedged. "Why should I be mad at you?"

"You know why."

And of course he did.

"You're upset about Garth."

Was it that obvious? Cubiak wondered. "Yes," he finally admitted.

"You thought I was getting back with him when you saw us together at the Rusty Scupper."

"You looked pretty cozy."

Cate looked up and then laughed. "Cozy? It was so damn loud in there I had to practically sit in his lap to make myself heard." She grew serious again. "Okay, I admit I wasn't completely honest earlier. You asked if we'd talked about Ruby and I said we hadn't, but that's not true because we had and it was so hard trying to explain what had happened to her even while I was wondering if he had any right to know."

"And that's it? That's all?"

An errant wave smacked the side of the boat and Cate started. "I never thought I'd see him again, and having him show up like that was, well, it was so unexpected I didn't really know how to react. He didn't come because of me. He came for the story . . . but still."

Cate stared at the floorboards. Despairing of what she'd say next, Cubiak felt his chest tighten.

When Cate looked at him again, her eyes were soft. "The past has hooks that stay buried deep," she said quietly.

Pained, Cubiak turned away. Her words echoed his own self-righteous pronouncement to Justin St. James about the past never being left behind. He'd meant it in terms of others but knew it was true for Cate and for himself as well.

Cate started talking again. "I have so many reasons to despise him, but sitting there together brought back memories of the good times between us, and in a weak moment, I was overwhelmed with longing for the dreams we'd had and everything we'd lost. He said he'd changed. That he'd been immature and foolish when we were married. He begged me to give him another chance, and for a moment, I almost said yes. But even as I was thinking that maybe we could go back and make it work this time, I knew that it wouldn't. I'd already given him so many chances and he'd messed up each time. He wasn't going to change. It was just an illusion." She paused. "I think we all have them."

Cubiak forced himself to look at her. That last comment was for him.

"In the end, we have to learn to recognize the difference between what is possible and what is not," she said.

Cubiak had spent four years clinging to the memories of a life that was gone forever. He understood that this comment also was for him.

Cate squeezed his hand. "Nothing happened between Garth and me. It's you I want to be with."

It was what Cubiak had longed to hear, yet he found himself unable to respond. The possibility of losing Cate had reminded him of how harsh life could be. There were no guarantees. To trust meant being vulnerable to the pain that lurked in the shadows.

"I know," he said finally.

It was quiet on the water, the kind of quiet Cubiak remembered from childhood when he sat in the confessional and stared into the darkness, waiting for his turn. There were no secrets before God, the nuns had always said. If he loved Cate there should be no secrets between them. They weren't in the clear yet. This was the moment he had dreaded ever since she had moved back to the peninsula and into his life again.

Cubiak gripped the wheel. "There's something I need to tell you. It's about Ruby."

"My aunt Ruby." Cate hugged her knees close. "My mother's sister."

"Yes . . ." Cubiak was about to go on when Cate continued.

"They looked like twins, remember. You said as much that day at The Wood when you saw the picture of them in my grandfather's study."

Cubiak remembered the photo. He would never forget the image of the two women. Ruby and Rosalinde, tall and slim, aristocratic in bearing, posed like bookends alongside their oligarch of a father.

"I never thought anything of it, how much they resembled each other. When I was a little girl, people said I looked like my grandmother, but when I reached my teens, I became the very likeness of my mother. Even I could see that. But if I looked like my mother that meant I looked like Ruby, too."

Cubiak said nothing.

"In retrospect, it all makes sense. My mother was always frail and sickly and unable to care for me or to put up with the flurry of having a rambunctious child in the house. Every year, I was shipped up here to spend the summer with Ruby and Dutch. And I loved it. No tiptoeing around or being shushed and told to sit still. Truth is, I hardly missed my parents; I liked living with Dutch and Ruby, liked the freedom they gave me and all the things they taught me. It was the best, like being at my own private camp all summer long."

Cate smiled uncertainly. "I probably should have put things together sooner, but I didn't start to think about it until I lost the second baby and my doctor said that my inability to carry a fetus to term could be genetic. After my third miscarriage, she said it was unlikely I could ever have a child and that I needed to stop trying to get pregnant because I was endangering my health. All pretty much what my mother had gone through, it turns out."

Cate looked at the water and then back at Cubiak. "Which leads to two possibilities. Either I was my mother's miracle baby, or I was Ruby's daughter by birth. You want to hazard a guess? Or maybe you don't have to guess. Maybe you know."

Cubiak remained silent.

"If Rosalinde was my birth mother, then things are pretty straightforward and I know who my father is. But if Ruby was my biological mother, then I assume the father is unknown. Certainly it wasn't Uncle Dutch. Doesn't line up does it, my age and his long hospitalization after the war. Maybe Dutch didn't even know anything about it. Which means I was Ruby's secret, wasn't I?"

Cate locked Cubiak in her gaze. "Only, please, tell me that bastard Beck isn't my father."

J. Dugan Beck was a man whom Cubiak had come to know and despise during his first year on the peninsula. He looked down at his hand, the knuckles white from gripping the wheel, and then back at Cate. "No, it isn't Beck," he said.

"Unknown?"

"Unknown."

"And Ruby?"

"Yes."

Cate pressed her forehead into her knees. "Who else knows?" she said finally, looking up again.

"Bathard. He figured it out on his own."

A smile flitted across Cate's face. "He would, wouldn't he? And you, how'd you find out?"

"Ruby told me that last day on the dock, but she begged me not to say anything. She asked me to promise her that I wouldn't tell you."

"Did you?"

Cubiak shook his head. "I never got the chance. Before I could respond, you showed up."

Abruptly Cate stood, and Cubiak feared she would go below, leaving him alone with the miserable truth. Instead she moved toward the stern and sat next to him.

"I'm glad you kept Ruby's secret as long as you did, but I'm also glad you decided to finally tell me," she said and kissed his cheek.

"No secrets," Cubiak said.

He pulled her close and they clung to each other. They could stay like this forever, he thought. But dusk had fallen and he knew that finally it was time to head in.

He caressed her shoulder. "Let's go back," he said.

They busied themselves lowering and securing the sail and preparing the boat for the return trip. When they were finished, they nestled together behind the wheel.

Under the flickering glimmer of the first stars, they motored across the bay. The *Parlando* rode high in the water. The running lights marked the bow and stern of the boat, and a bright white beacon blazed from the top of the mast, showing them the way home.

ACKNOWLEDGMENTS

It really takes a village to write a book. There are numerous people who encourage, listen, read, critique, and gently nudge the process along.

Thanks are owed to many, and special thanks to those who took on one or more of the supportive roles that kept me going.

To my wonderful and talented daughters: Julia, for her map-making, technical support, and insightful editorial comments; and Carla, for providing needed food for thought with her discerning observations and suggestions.

To B. E. Pinkham, Esther Spodek, and Jeanne Mellett, the members of my writers group, for shepherding the project from beginning to end.

To Barbara Bolsen and Norm Rowland, for their excellent and very important reading of the first draft.

To Max Edinburgh, who again performed the herculean task of reading the completed manuscript out loud as I took notes and worried my way through.

Thanks also to the Chicago Office of the Federal Bureau of Investigation for answering my questions and explaining the finer points of how the agency functions. Any errors made and liberties taken are solely my responsibility.

Once again, I have enjoyed the privilege of working with the University of Wisconsin Press. My deepest appreciation to Director Dennis Lloyd and his exemplary staff, including Raphael Kadushin, Sheila Leary, Sheila McMahon, Adam Mehring, Andrea Christofferson, Terry Emmrich, Scott Lenz, and Carla Marolt, as well as to interns Megan Mendonca and Amber Rose. And thanks as well to copyeditor Diana

Cook for another thorough vetting of my work and to graphic designer Sara DeHaan for another riveting book cover.

Finally, I extend my gratitude to the many dedicated booksellers across the country who have welcomed the Dave Cubiak Door County Mysteries into their stores. And to the many readers who have reached out to say how much they enjoyed the first two books and have asked eagerly for the third, this one's for you.